UROPIA

UROPIA

Robert Rivers

ISBN 978-0-9558528-0-0

<u>This book is for Ted and Lillian,</u>
<u>who made all things possible</u>

Acknowledgements

My thanks are due to Bill B for invaluable advice on what might be possible and what is certainly not possible in the field of electronics, to Anita for her perseverance in creating the cover picture, and to my family for their tolerance and support.

UROPIA

CHAPTER ONE

Kathleen paused, her hand on the latch of the dilapidated timber gate which formed a notional demarcation between the inevitable muck of the farm and the dwelling house. Early dawn might have thought to linger but it was about to be summarily dismissed; following no more than a token glow of forewarning the impatient sun practically leapt over the horizon to pour its warmth and light over the hungry land.

The ancient beech trees along the eastern side of the field were heavy with foliage, almost impenetrable to the sun's first exploratory rays but where a gap did allow the light to pass through, the gleam became so intense that it diffused into a golden haze over the surrounding leaves. Sturdy trunks, bare of branches to above a man's height, cast long shadows over the brightening ground and, nearer at hand, the chimneys of the old red brick farmhouse, standing high enough to catch the sunlight over the trees, were sharply delineated against the stark blue clarity of the morning sky.

Although Kathleen had seen countless sunrises while doing the early morning chores she could rarely resist the temptation to stop for a moment in appreciation. She watched as a last few tendrils of mist hung ethereally above the dew-soaked hollows before being dissipated by the urgent warmth, and noted the synchronous ripple across the fields of ripe barley in response to a fleeting zephyr. The almost physical caress of the sun's rays on her body was more than adequate recompense for having to work at such an early hour, indeed it made the requirement almost a privilege rather than a burden.

She had been born and brought up on this farm, in this very house, one of the few which had escaped demolition during the blitz of compulsory modernisation some thirty years ago. The urban-based Produnits, where the bulk of the population were employed, provided accommodation in warren-like dormitory blocks adjacent to the production stations and even in rural areas most of the original dwellings had been replaced by 'compact' factory produced units. Although of undoubted thermal efficiency they were of unlovely appearance; christened 'squat-boxes' by some irreverent commentator, the name had become implanted in the language much to the chagrin of those serious and public-spirited officials responsible for the concept.

Kathleen had come as a late surprise to her parents, a hard working couple who had struggled through a never-ending stream of regulations to keep their farm viable so that it could be passed on, as it had been for so many generations. 'Beech Farm' it had been called then and she still thought of it by that name though the official designation was now AgUnit D/356 of Region N/Four of the Uropian Federation. She had tried to make herself forget the old name for fear that she would inadvertently use it in front of an official or indeed some busybody neighbour. Such a slip might suggest that she had hankerings for the past, didn't perhaps fully endorse the new order of things, and that would be certain to result in a black mark in her persaFile. Luckily, there was little likelihood of this happening; there were few opportunities for social chit-chat, and also most of the farm managers were newcomers to the district, newcomers whose knowledge of the locality extended no further than what was in the official publications.

Ever since the Directive which abolished private ownership of land and placed it under state control, farm managers had been appointed from a list of those who had acquired the appropriate qualifications. There was a yearly 'Target' for each Unit and if it wasn't met there was usually a change of manager, the failures being 'relocated' to supervised employment in one of the industrial conglomerates.

Kathleen couldn't bear to consider such a dreadful existence. Though hard and unremitting toil was necessary to ensure that the yearly Production Target was achieved, she was happy to do it, knowing she might as well be dead if she could no longer breathe the fresh air and feel the soft ground under her feet; walk by the hedges and hear the early morning birdsong and the almost sub-liminal hum of insects; savour the intoxicating scents of wildflowers in the hot stillness of a summer afternoon. Of course it wasn't so pleasant having to work outside in the cold and rain during winter but, when early darkness brought the day's labour to a close there were compensations. Stoked with whatever fallen timber had been gathered, the old open fireplace offered warmth and welcome relaxation in front of its dancing flames without any detrimental demands on their Energy Allowance.

She was a true child of the land, accustomed to animals and fields, farm machinery and farm dirt almost as soon as she could walk. Attendance at school had been to her a tiresome necessity; she would spend every moment she could about the fields and hedges which she regarded as her private domain, happy to help her parents with any labour of which she was capable. Now she was thirty-five, but, maybe because of a combination of gene structure and healthy living, her skin still held the bloom of youth while ample exercise kept her body taut and trim. Able to operate any of the equipment on the farm and with the instinct of true countryfolk that let her know when the time was just right for sowing, just right for harvesting, she had no intention of doing anything else for the rest of her life.

There had been no warning prior to the arrival of the Directive. Her father had passed it across to her mother with a grunt of derision, but after they had discussed the contents it was clear that there was no escape from the implications. Quite simply the order stated that private individuals no longer had any right to land ownership; from now on, all land would be held by the State on behalf of the entire populace and as food production was too important to be left to those with 'old fashioned views', managers would, in future, be appointed by the authorities. A concession allowed existing operations to continue as long as the managers complied with the new regulations and met the annual 'Production Targets'. There would be no prospect of Kathleen inheriting the property, or even staying on it once her parents had reached the end of their 'productive' years.

"This Section says we have to register the present manager," Kathleen pointed out. "Could you put it in my name now so that officially I am running the farm."

"This size of unit requires joint managers," her father replied. "Regulation 25(c) Part (iii). You could take on a farmhand with an AgriCol Certificate and put them down as joint manager but they then would be regarded as more qualified and could replace you whenever they felt like it."

"But you and Mum would be eligible wouldn't you?"

"There seems to be a grudging acceptance of existing partners for a transitional period," her father agreed.

"Put me and Albert down as the current managers then," Kathleen responded with a shrug. "He seems happy enough working here so that should solve the problem."

"That would be nice dear." Her mother, who had taken a liking to Albert, was perhaps hoping to see her daughter 'settled' in the old-fashioned way; her father was, however, rather less enthusiastic.

"Are you sure about that?" he asked her now, with a worried look. "There are things in life more important than this farm."

"You're wrong Dad," Kathleen replied. "There is nothing more important to me than staying on this farm. You know what the alternatives are; you can't call that life!"

So for the purpose of Regulations – but only for that purpose - Albert became joint manager of the Unit. He had been around for a year or so, helping with the heavy work as her parent's increasing age had made things difficult, but he was only a labourer and Kathleen had no expectation that he would ever amount to anything more. And although the new arrangement should provide security for a while, she had only suggested it in the absence of any alternative; Albert might have been a capable enough farmhand but, when he thought he was unobserved, she had been aware of him looking at her in a manner which caused her a certain amount of discomfort. From time to time she prayed that, as her parents never tired of hoping, something would happen that would restore the world they remembered.

When they were sure that no strangers were around, her parents sometimes talked about the old days, trying to explain to their daughter the freedoms they had regarded as their right, but it was difficult for her to comprehend. Born in 2005, Kathleen was too young to have anything more than a hazy memory of the 'holidays abroad' they mentioned, apart perhaps from a few images of warm sand and water, of red-roofed white villas tiered up a scrubby hillside. There had been no holidays for years now, except of course for the various grades engaged in administration; if 'productive' workers fulfilled their quota they might have enough for a frugal existence and that was all.

Her parents spoke of 'barter' and 'cash sales' which had helped to swell their earnings but the level of penalties for such transactions was now so high that you would be foolish indeed to take the risk. Anyway, there wasn't really anything to sell; the 'D' prefix in the farm's title meant grain producing and the mixed livestock they had kept in the past were now strictly disallowed.

Though in her teens at the time, she had never understood much about the 'troubles' though her parents had tried to explain what had happened. There had apparently been strikes and rioting in the towns after the President of the Uropian Federation had refused to accept the result of the North West Regional elections; the winning Independence party, being perceived as 'anti Federation', would not be acceptable to the Federal Governing Commission and was barred from taking office. The situation had apparently become quite serious; soldiers from Urfor had been stationed at strategic points, their armoured Transports had patrolled the roads; things had only quietened down when the leader of the Independence party had appeared on the VidCom to announce that his members would not take their Assembly seats 'in the interests of peace and democracy', and urged everyone to support the Interim Administration which had been appointed by the Federation President. Shortly afterwards a Directive had ruled that 'anti Federalism' would be regarded as a bar to standing for public office and, indeed, was so deviant that it would automatically lead to compulsory medical treatment.

After the 'troubles' were over, strict border controls had been enforced to stop the haemorrhage of population as those who were opposed to the new regime voted with their feet and left the country. Another Directive declared that, as only the State could guarantee a suitable environment for the raising and education of young persons, they would henceforth be removed from parental influence no later than the age of three. Huge training establishments were then set up, dedicated to the task of turning all these youngsters into unquestioningly loyal Federation citizens.

Although the production of these future citizens was encouraged by the awarding of additional credits, there was no compulsion and every woman had freedom to choose whether or not to comply. The decision was simple to implement for; on reaching puberty, every female was given a small implant which could be activated yearly by a private persaCom code. Although Kathleen might, at one time, have considered presenting her mother with a couple of grandchildren to fuss over, such ideas were long vanished. Her parents had gone to the retirement homes nearly ten years ago and anyway, she would not dream of producing children only to hand them over to the State.

She gave herself a mental shake; standing admiring the scenery and mulling over the past wasn't going to get any work done. Hurrying into the kitchen, she automatically checked that there was power available before half-filling a small pan with water and setting it on the glowplate. Her early morning excursion had passed by a hedgerow where a few half-wild hens foraged a living in blissful ignorance of their official prohibition; the three eggs she had collected would provide a welcome addition to breakfast for, although she was sure that the Healthy Citizen cereal she now tipped into three bowls did indeed contain everything for a balanced diet there was no doubt that a boiled or poached egg made for a more satisfied stomach.

As usual, there was no sign of Albert yet. Never full of

enthusiasm, in the aftermath of certain 'events' his indolence had developed gradually into outright laziness as he had come to realise that his position was secure. Over these years they had co-existed in a state of mutual detestation, locked together solely by the fear of moving from bad to worse. Her life would be a bit easier if he wasn't so fond of his bed she thought bitterly, banging on the ceiling with a broom handle.

The outside door opened quietly and Barney slithered into the kitchen. Gangly and awkward in appearance, he could move so unobtrusively when he wished that you could almost fail to notice his presence.

"Missa." He greeted her as he took a seat at the table.

"Barney." Kathleen responded, pushing a bowl of cereal and a carton of SoyMilk towards him. "Have you been out in the barley this morning?"

Barney nodded briefly as he poured blue-grey liquid over his cereal.

"Do you reckon it's ready for harvesting?" she asked him.

He nodded again, more vigorously this time, and made a running motion with his hands.

"What's that Barney," she encouraged.

His mouth worked for a while; after one or two grunts he managed. "Rain. Come."

"Are you sure?" Kathleen was surprised. "It feels okay to me and the Com forecast gives it like this for at least another week."

Barney shook his head stubbornly.

"How soon?" she demanded. Barney might not have been infallible about the weather, no-one could be, but he was far more reliable than the official bulletins.

"Two days?" she asked in response to his shrug. "Three?" He nodded vigorously in response.

"It's a good thing that the Inspector's coming today then," she commented. "Remember to keep out of the way while he's here."

Barney's reply was a disapproving grunt. Having to wait for official approval before harvesting could commence was beyond his understanding and beneath his contempt. After finishing his breakfast in silence, he wiped the back of his hand over his mouth and sidled quietly out of the door.

Kathleen didn't know where Barney had come from, how long he had been working on the farm or even how old he was, for her parents had never been forthcoming about his presence. He featured in her earliest memories, and the fact of being regarded as 'more than a bit simple' had been no obstacle to him becoming her childhood companion. It was he who had taught her to use natural cover so as to creep up on a bird's nest without disturbing the sitting hen; which wild leaves could be chewed for sweetness during those summer afternoons when supper seemed to be a long time away; how to avoid the thorns while reaching for the biggest and ripest blackberries. As she grew older, he showed her how to rub the raw earth between her palms and press it against the back of her hand or even her cheek, to assess the moisture content that was so essential at planting time; how to rub off the husk and chew the barley grains to check their quality and ripeness.

Barney seemed to know in advance what the year would be like for he was of the earth itself and of the animals which he loved with all his simple heart. To a stranger he would appear to be incapable of existence outside an institution for he had few words, gestures and grunts serving for necessary communication.

When she was a child he had called Kathleen 'missy'; as she grew older he obviously felt this to be incorrect but 'missa' had been the only result of his attempt at more complicated sounds. She had tried to get him to sleep in the farmhouse but he refused to leave the little haven he had fashioned in the loft above the barn. During the warm nights of summer he had been known to sleep in the fields, waking with the dawn to watch the early antics of small creatures which hid from human presence during the day. He didn't exist officially, which was why she had reminded him of the Inspector's visit. Had they found him, the Authorities would have taken him away for treatment; he probably would have ended up in one of the gangs of

Impys who cleaned city streets and did other extremely menial work.

Albert came clattering into the kitchen, bleary-eyed and tousled. 'He must have stayed up, watching the night-vids again' Kathleen thought drily as he gobbled down his breakfast.

"Remember the Crop Inspector's due today to grant us Harvest Approval," she told him.

"I'd forgotten that." He muttered a curse under his breath. "I've arranged to go to the depot to pick up some supplies this morning. I've booked the transport and you know what they're like if you try to cancel. You'll surely cope with the Inspector yourself?"

"You know I don't like dealing with that woman," she complained. "She's so full of her own importance and yet so ignorant it's difficult to be civil to her but we can't risk anything going wrong. I know that the crop is ready, Barney knows it's ready, but without Approval we can't get the Harvest Machinery Order. Leave it another week and the quality will be down at least one grade and that might drop us below Target."

"Jim from 355 told me 'silly Cicely' has been promoted and that there is a new Inspector for our area. Rumour is that this fellow got into a bit of trouble in his last post and has to be kept out of the way for a while. If that's right you shouldn't have any trouble with him." Albert sounded confident.

Kathleen felt a momentary flash of annoyance at his casual attitude, wondering briefly why he had to go to the Depot himself. Most supplies, including foodstuffs were ordered via the VidCom and delivered by the ITS.

He really wouldn't mind being thrown out of the farm and into a Produnit she thought, suppressing a flash of anger. She had to concede that he was right about the transport though. If you cancelled a booking it was still likely to be marked up against your allowance, and woe betide you if that was exceeded.

She remembered her parents speaking about going places in the car, visiting friends, going for a drive somewhere just because they felt like it. That was before the Federation had declared that ordinary citizens couldn't really be allowed to use valuable resources by travelling without proper controls and the new Integrated Transport System (ITS) was brought into operation with the stated aim of reducing congestion and pollution.

In theory it should have satisfied everyone's requirements. A selection of different sizes of vehicle was available; a Transi for two persons and a Tranca that could carry up to six was followed by a Tranbus for large numbers; there was also a range of differing sizes of Tranvans for carrying goods and everyone was given a monthly distance allowance which varied according to your 'value to the community'. All you had to do was to dial in your requirements on the VidCom or your persaCom and you would be given a time to be at your access point. A central computer processed all the requirements and allotted vehicles in the most efficient manner. Priority numbers ensured that essential journeys took precedence.

In practice though, you could be waiting at an access point watching your persaCom read-out change again and again as your allotted time was postponed because of higher priority calls to the network. The system had almost collapsed until all Federation officials had been given individual vehicles; this had relieved the pressure on ITS but had done nothing towards improving congestion and pollution; over half of the traffic - and of the workforce - was engaged in Administration. The personal distance allowance had gradually diminished too since the introduction of the scheme; environmental concerns were usually given as the reason.

After Albert had left for the access point Kathleen regretfully changed into a long-sleeved shirt; all citizens were expected to follow official health guidelines so allowing the Inspector to see her with the skin of her arms exposed to potentially cancerous sunlight would not be advisable. She even spent a couple of minutes brushing her mop of wavy black hair, in need of a trim at the moment for she normally kept it short for convenience. Any suggestion of scruffiness could be regarded as lack of respect, of course. The new man would probably be accustomed to working from an office in one of the urban conglomerates. She had seen the type before, immaculately dressed, their first act on arriving at the farm to don a disposable anti-contamination garment and the obligatory white plastic hard hat.

Barney had disappeared somewhere, off to one of his secret hidey-holes no doubt. Kathleen envied him as she made her way to the fields, checking the hour on her wrist, hoping the Inspector would not be late so as not to waste too much of her precious time.

Though still comparatively early it was clear that today would be a scorcher. As she moved about the fields testing the ripeness of the grain here and there, the heat of the sun burnt through her shirt and she occasionally stopped to fan herself with her hands. There wasn't a breath of movement in the air and she started to worry a little. Barney could be right, she thought, maybe there is just a trace of something; not exactly sultry but the merest hint of heaviness that could be moving in their direction. It was common enough after all for a really good spell of heat like this to be followed by a downpour.

That was the trouble with all the controls that they worked under now she reflected. Instead of being able to make your own decisions you had to have official approval before commencing any of the important operations on the farm. A few of the Inspectors were reasonable enough, acknowledging the experience of someone like herself but too many of them were so full of their own importance and paper qualifications that they seemed to take a delight in contradicting the opinion of a mere manager!

Glancing at the time again, she sighed and made her way back to the 'homestead'. Using a handkerchief to mop perspiration from her face and neck she resigned herself to waiting around until the Inspector arrived.

CHAPTER TWO

There was mud on his boots! Unsightly splodges must have oozed on to the highly polished uppers when he trod on the soft verge of the lane. He was grown up now, his mother long since passed away but still the familiar sickness returned to the pit of his stomach.

Stephen's mother had always insisted on absolute cleanliness. Time and again during his childhood she had impressed on him that keeping himself clean in every respect was an essential part of their relationship. He still trembled at the memory of her anger when, on one of the rare occasions that he had been allowed out of her sight, he had returned with his clothes rumpled and stained. The interminable days that followed during which she wouldn't speak to him, wouldn't touch him, wouldn't even acknowledge that he existed. He'd scrubbed himself again and again, washed and cleaned anything that he could lay his hands on, all the while begging for the forgiveness which eventually came with a stern warning that if anything like that happened again she would put him out in the street to fend for himself.

When he had reached his teens she had extended her strictures to include cleanliness of mind. 'Dirty thoughts are as bad as a dirty body' she had declared. 'When you get older, people will try to get you to do dirty things but you must always fight them. There are girls that will smile at you and want to touch you; all they really want is to make you as dirty as themselves, but I know that my nice clean boy will never have anything to do with them'.

She had never mentioned his father or indeed acknowledged the existence of such a person. Once only, after hearing other children discussing their parents he had touched on the subject in conversation. His mother's face had stiffened, she had told him he was disgusting and locked him in his room as a punishment; from that day until she died he had never dared to return to the subject.

No, dirt of any kind was simply not permitted to impinge on Stephen's life, he took good care to make sure of that!

His mother had been right about the girls though. He now knew all about the sneaky ways they would try to drag a man down. The brazen ones were easy to deal with. The way they flaunted their bodies, giggled and made suggestive remarks almost brought him to the point of vomiting. It was the quiet ones who gave him the greatest difficulty, he knew they were only pretending to be shy and demure while secretly trying to put hot dirty thoughts into his mind. It was all the fault of one of those quiet ones that he was here now, in this filthy countryside instead of in his pristine office giving advice to young citizens in one of the big training centres.

His job had been counselling those who were nearing twelve, the legal age of consent in the new enlightened society and he had been good at it. It was important that these youngsters were fully informed and aware of the various forms that sexuality could take before they could decide on their own orientation and it was his responsibility to ensure that they had all been given the appropriate instruction before they came of age.

Some of these youngsters were reluctant to take part in all the practical demonstrations which were necessary before they could be issued with a Certificate of Adulthood; they needed encouragement and this was where Stephen's ability became invaluable. He had the knack of gaining their trust and, nearly always in one-to-one sessions would explain, cajole, flatter and generally overcome their objections. In most of the cases he was able to send them back to their classes, willing, or at least resigned to doing their duty. He genuinely regretted his few failures who would then have to be prescribed medication to enable them to become proper citizens.

Occasionally he had been asked to select a group of youngsters who would be enthusiastic participants at private 'coming of age' parties, where his superiors and other high officials would welcome them into adulthood. This was a strictly unofficial task but he was glad to oblige; knowing that these people relied on his discretion gave him a warm feeling of belonging and being appreciated. He had been assured that he was likely to gain promotion in the near future, so he had every reason to be satisfied with his life.

But then there had been a problem girl. She was small and skinny and hardly spoke in the class. Others said she was shy but Stephen, with his superior insight could tell that she was only pretending; she didn't speak because her mind was too busy with dirty thoughts. He arranged a special counselling session to try to get her to change her ways, putting on his easiest manner as he spoke at length about her duty to comply with the curriculum, but he could tell that she wasn't paying any attention, she just sat there looking at the floor. Foolishly, he gripped her head to force her to look at him and was immediately overwhelmed as a wave of dirty images poured out of her big eyes into his unprepared mind. He had resisted of course but she kept doing it and he got angrier and angrier. She had to be punished for her behaviour, to be hurt enough to stop the mental bombardment, so he started hitting her but that only made the images stronger. He tore at her clothes, exposing naked flesh on which he could inflict more pain but still the images persisted. He was banging her head on the floor when at last his mind cleared and he found himself wet with relief. He must have overdone the punishment however, because she never moved again.

His superiors had done their best to cover things up but Stephen was forced to leave the training establishment and accept a transfer to a post that would allow him to keep out of circulation until the episode could be decently buried. And that was how he came to be standing by a Transi in a muddy lane with dirt on his boots!

It was the bridge which had made him stop and alight from his vehicle, but even before that his temper had been steadily worsening. Somehow he'd taken a wrong turning, ending up on this track that meandered through the fields, the soft verges making him afraid to turn or reverse. He had no choice but to keep going but then he had come to the bridge..!

It had no right to exist! It was built of old grey stone slabs for goodness sake and there was no Grading sign on it; how was he supposed to know whether it would take the weight of his vehicle? It belonged to the discredited past, to history; it should have been swept away along with all the other outmoded artifacts and traditions which were demolished during the re-shaping of the land that had taken place when he was only a boy. If this waterway required a bridge it should be one of the types authorised by the Central Transport Department; it should be made of steel and concrete; it should have a number code on it so that it could be checked against the file which was accessible through his persaCom. He made a note to report the error to his superiors, but that wasn't enough to satisfy him now. He urgently needed to find some underling to tongue-lash into quivering abasement in order to alleviate his own displeasure.

He looked again with disgust at the brown splodge his otherwise immaculate boots had picked up from the side of the lane. Swearing, he got back into the driving seat and gunned the Transi engine to take a run at the bridge. He managed to avoid the low sides but there was a clang as some part of the vehicle's underside hit the uneven surface and his anger developed into a seething rage. Suppressing it only until the opportunity for release came, he continued along the winding lane until it ended at a wall adjacent to some farm buildings.

"Good morning." The call came from a young female approaching from the direction of an ancient looking outbuilding.

"Are you the Manager here?" he demanded brusquely, glad to see her flinch a little at his tone.

"I'm Kathleen Pierpoint," she agreed.

"Where's the other manager, Albert Arden?" His question was peremptory.

"He had to go to the Depot this morning," she made the excuse. "I'm sorry he's not here, but I'm quite able to deal with this."

"I suppose you'll have to do," he snapped, secretly feeling a frisson of satisfaction. If he was going to release his temper on someone this woman here on her own looked a suitable candidate.

"It's a lovely morning isn't it," Kathleen ventured cautiously in an attempt to lighten the mood.

"It would be a better morning if you had a decent access road. I may have damaged my Transport on that bridge." He glared at her and continued. "I can't understand how you are allowed to produce food in such primitive surroundings.

"I'm afraid you must have missed the proper entrance," she replied, forcing a rather tremulous smile to disguise her misgivings about his manner. "This is only a lane that we use with the ForTrak to take stuff to the far boundary."

It was the smile that did it. That and the hint of trepidation as she spoke. Up until now, he had only intended to be as domineering and unpleasant as possible to instil a measure of fear into the woman but he suddenly realised that she was one of the dangerous ones. There would be dirty thoughts in her head, thoughts she would try to share with him, to contaminate his purity. She would have to be physically punished he decided, as well as being degraded to compensate for all the aggravations which had brought him into this filthy dump. Oh, he would bring her down, she would realise that she was no better than any other stinking farm animal as far as he was concerned. She can pay for the damned bridge and the muddy lane as well as her own wickedness. She'd be sorry she was ever born by the time he'd finished with her.

His mind went in to overdrive for a moment as he assessed the best way to go about his intention. She was wary of him at the moment, he decided. It would be better to reassure her, to build up her confidence so that her downfall would be all the greater.

"I suppose it's my own fault for being stupid," he admitted with one of his special genuine smiles. "You'll have to forgive me, I was just worried that I might wreck the Transi. I'm new to this job you see so I really need you to help me as much as possible. Will you please excuse my bad temper and lack of manners?"

Kathleen expression lightened with sudden relief. Confronted with that pleasant smile which had a touch of little boy pleading in it, her earlier misgivings evaporated completely.

"Of course I'll help you in any way I can. I've been on this Unit all my life so I'm pretty sure of when the grain is ready. The test should just be a formality."

Arrogant too, he thought as he meekly followed her into the fields, stumbling a little on the uneven ground. Watching Kathleen's natural grace as she strode along only increased his determination to see her humbled.

"How many tests do you need?" she asked as they reached the first of the barley.

Stephen consulted the file on his persaCom.

"Ten," he announced. "Does that sound about right?"

"Yes, that's the usual requirement. Shall I pick the first one?"

Without waiting for a reply, she proffered a handful of ears that she had plucked from the golden crop. Stephen unhooked the test kit from his belt and took the sample from her, suppressing a shudder as he accidentally touched her hand. Carefully he went through the procedure he had practised during his training; it was simple really, the tester was linked to his persaCom so the data was entered automatically. He pressed the key for a read-out.

"Well, you're right about that one," he announced with another of his special smiles. "I suppose we'd better go through with the rest of them, though I'm sure it's not really necessary."

"Certainly," Kathleen agreed. "We don't want you to get into any trouble." She was rapidly warming to this pleasant and obviously genuine representative of officialdom, thinking that if only they were all as nice, life would be so much easier.

Slowly, they made their way through the fields, taking it in turn to select samples as the regulations required. Stephen, trying hard to hide his detestation of the whole procedure was further aggravated by the midday heat.

Clad in his normal attire of suit, long sleeved shirt, collar and tie and also the standard anti-contamination coverall, he was sweating profusely. I'll have to take extra care washing myself tonight he thought with disgust, bringing out a sanitised tissue to mop the moisture off his face.

"It's hot isn't it," he complained, giving Kathleen a rueful smile. "I'm not used to this."

"Yes, it is hot," she agreed, languidly stretching her arms upwards and and tilting her face back to glance at the cloudless sky. "But I love it when it's like this. You can feel the warmth soaking into your body and into the crops and the land."

Stephen stared for a moment as the woman's shirt stretched over her breasts, the light material delineating the proud outlines almost as clearly as if she were naked. It's deliberate he raged, turning away in disgust. She wants me to notice, she really is one of the wicked kind, not content with dragging a man into filth that would contaminate his body, now she was trying to get dirt into his mind. He was strong enough to withstand her, he assured himself, but the image of firm curves persisted; his hands clenched momentarily as he imagined his fingers digging into soft flesh, inflicting pain until agony became her only sensation. It was imperative that she should be punished, be made to grovel in her own dirt, but how to go about it? He had hoped to be able to find fault with the grain samples but his persaCom was linked with the central computer and he couldn't risk fiddling the test results. He fanned his face for a moment to give himself time to think.

"How important is it to get the Harvesting Approval today," he asked idly.

Kathleen grimaced. "Very important. I suppose the crop would be all right for another week but I don't trust the weather. If we don't harvest before it rains we could lose half of it. That would mean we wouldn't meet our Target."

"The official forecast is for dry weather continuing, isn't it?"

"I'd sooner trust my own senses." She smiled as she wondered what this man would say if she told him that the forecast came from Barney.

"And what happens if you don't meet your Target." He made it sound like polite conversation.

"The end of the world for me! There would be new Managers appointed and we'd be put into a Produnit." The desolation in her voice was unmistakeable.

Stephen could hardly contain his delight. The silly creature had just handed him the means to destroy her. There was genuine pleasure in his smile this time as he told her.

"Well, we'd better make sure that you meet your Target, hadn't we?"

Once they had completed the tests they made their way back to the outbuildings. Stephen was sticky with sweat but the woman managed somehow to look comfortable in spite of the heat.He flinched as he accidentally touched the hot metal of his Transi.

"Can we go into the shade while I record the details," he begged her.

"Of course." He detected a trace of sympathy in her smile which incensed him even more.

He followed her into the big barn, swallowing his disgust at remnants of straw and other dirt on the floor. But he had to admit that it was better than the relentless glare of the sun outside. He fiddled with his persaCom, calling up the file while he finalised his plan for this woman's debasement.

"Right," he told her eventually. "Your crop is approved for harvest. Now let's see how soon the machinery can be here."

Kathleen felt a wave of relief flood over her. Everything was going to be all right after all. She allowed herself a smile of satisfaction.

Watching her with barely concealed anticipation, Stephen called up the appropriate file; entering the details he merely substituted a three for a one in the priority section. The main computer would certainly pick up the mistake but there would be delay before it automatically re-allocated the machinery; this woman would believe what he told her in the meantime. He read off the results and smiled at her.

"I hope for your sake your weather forecast is wrong," he announced. "The harvesting machinery has been allocated for the middle of next week."

He gloated as a look of alarm wiped away her smile.

"That's crazy," she protested. "The whole schedule is geared to having the machinery available at the right time."

"I know it sounds crazy," he agreed. "It seems to be a matter of priorities."

"But ripe barley carries a Number One rating. We have to have priority."

Stephen shook his head, loving every minute.

"Someone must have decided otherwise in this case. Look, you can see for yourself."

Kathleen gazed at the persaCom screen.

"I don't understand it." She sat down heavily on a wooden bench. "I'm certain in my own mind that if we don't harvest in the next couple of days we are going to lose the crop."

"I'm really sorry, but that's what the figures say." He was secretly gloating at her misery; she seemed to have physically shrunk and he was sure she was close to tears.

"If the worst comes to the worst it can't be too bad in a Produnit; it's clean, all your needs are catered for and I'm sure lots of people are perfectly happy in them." He was comforting her with a twisting knife.

"I'd sooner be dead!" She lifted her face and he was gratified to see moisture on her cheeks; her eyes were filled with anguish but she wasn't suffering enough to shut down the images of filth emanating from her.

"Isn't there anything you can do?" she appealed to him.

Stephen felt the tension mounting in him as he revelled in the thought of the punishment he would soon administer.

"I suppose I could...." he let his voice trail off for a moment....."No, that would be a violation, I'd be finished."

"What couldn't you do?" There was a suggestion of hope in her voice.

"I'm allowed to do an emergency override in exceptional circumstances but it's only meant to be used if there's a major glitch in the computer system. If I used it irresponsibly I'd be in terrible trouble. I might even end up as an Impy."

This was all pure fabrication but Stephen was sure that she was stupid enough to believe him as indeed she did.

"I couldn't ask you do it then." She was back in the depths of dejection.

"There might just be a way," he told her after a few moments silence. "But it could be risky for you."

"I don't care," she came to life again, with hope in her eyes. "If we lose the harvest I'm finished anyway so I'll do anything that gives me a chance."

"Well, if you're really sure." This is going to be so easy, Stephen thought smugly. Even his young clients at the training centre were more astute, more wordly-wise than this peasant.

"If I override the harvesting priority on my persaCom and then we verify it with your individual piCode instead of mine I could say that you must have done it when I let you look at your Unit file on the screen. I would only get a reprimand for being careless. And if the weather does break as soon as you think, you would probably be excused from punishment because of the importance of food production."

Kathleen took a few moments to consider the implications. She knew of only one reason you would put your piCode into someone else's persaCom. Laws of such severity had been brought in to protect citizens from unwanted sexual harassment that anyone so accused was automatically found guilty unless their persaCom showed that Consent had been obtained. This was signified by each of the putative partners entering their absolutely private number into the other's persaCom under the appropriate file heading. The scheme proved to be effective, the only disadvantage being that although intimate relations could come in considerable variety there was only one level of Consent; once this had been agreed, practically any form of physical behaviour could be regarded as acceptable.

She couldn't imagine that this pleasant young man had any covert intentions as regards her body. There must be a system with officials that they could use their number for some kind of authorisation she assumed; anyway, she could make sure that it wasn't the personal relations file on his persaCom before she entered her private code.

"You're sure that my piCode will be acceptable to the override instruction?" she asked.

"I don't see why not," he assured her, sniggering inwardly. "It works all right on an inter-official basis."

"I'll do it then," Kathleen declared.

"Just a moment while I find the relevant section." Stephen turned away, ostensibly to concentrate on his persaCom but really to hide the sneer that he was sure must be visible on his face.

Before his 'error of judgement' Stephen had accidentally become aware of seriously inappropriate behaviour by his Departmental Head; in return for a promise of absolute discretion he had been rewarded with a secret code known only to a privileged few. This code had the ability to temporarily substitute one filename on a persaCom for another without changing the contents. Stephen called up his personal relations file, erased the filename and replaced it with a random series of numbers. Now the slut wouldn't recognise the file heading and once her piCode was entered he could do what he wanted to her without fear of repercussions. It took a few moments until he was satisfied.

"There you are," he held his persaCom towards her. "I'll look away so that I don't see your piCode," he added with a disarming smile.

Kathleen took the proffered hand and studied the read-out. She certainly wasn't familiar with the file heading so the offer must be genuine, she decided, hesitating only a moment before tapping a sequence of keys.

The pounding in Stephen's head accelerated as he felt the pressure of warm fingers. 'You mustn't let them touch you,' his mother's warning echoed, 'they can put their dirty desires right through your skin if they touch you.' It was true too, he could feel them flowing into him from her touch, sending hot blood throbbing throughout his body. He had to make her stop!

"Have you finished?" he couldn't keep the harshness out of his voice.

"Yes." Her eyes widened a little at his change of tone.

"I'm going to beat the filth out of you!" he shouted, and her expression changed to bewilderment. Without warning he swung his fist into her face as hard as he could, knocking her off balance so that she fell heavily to the floor.

"Wha..." she cried out, but he didn't give her a chance to continue. He hit her face again and again until blood welled from her mouth and nose then grabbed her shirt, the buttons flying as he ripped it from her body and tossed it to the ground. The whore made a pathetic attempt to cover herself, but he brutally kicked her arms out of the way so that her corrupting figure was exposed, inviting him to inflict the necessary pain; hot excitement welled within him as he attacked the firm flesh, wrenching, jabbing, scratching, nipping, squeezing, until red weals appeared and rapidly merged together into ugly mottled patches of dark bruising.

"You've got to stop," he shouted, tearing off the rest of her clothes as she lay, screaming and helpless on the filthy ground. The sight of more pale and as yet unmarked flesh added to the vile images she still forced into his mind and drove him into an agony of frustration; his knuckles were sore so he used his feet, kicking and grinding his boots into the crumpled form until at last he gasped as relief floooded through his body, his senses clearing as he realised that he had achieved his purpose. He had punished the bitch enough to stop her! No longer was she trying to contaminate him with her filthy desires, his mind was clean and pure again! No matter that his body was dripping with sweat and that a warm wetness spread from his crotch; that could be remedied by a good scrub under the shower; his clothes would have to go for re-cycling but that was unimportant too. What mattered was that he had lived up to his mother's expectations.

As he collected his breath he looked at the carcase lying on the dirt floor with a mixture of disgust and pity. Curled up into as small a ball as possible, her screams had subsided, but little sobbing moans and whimpers still issued from her bruised and swollen mouth. She reminded him of wounded animals he had seen in some show on the Vidcom, but of course that was all she really amounted to. If only those like her wouldn't put their dirty ideas into clean people's minds they wouldn't have to be punished. Maybe, he thought with a warm glow of satisfaction, this was to be his mission in life; perhaps he had been chosen to bring retribution to those who needed correction. He was sure to meet plenty of them in the unhealthy environment in which he now worked.

Flinching with distaste, he held her persaCom so that he could enter his side of the Consent procedure. Then, full of new-found purpose, he swaggered out to his Transi and stuffed his coverall into a self-seal bag for Contaminated Waste Disposal. After looking in vain for a gate that would let him through to the proper farm entrance he resigned himself to the fact that he would have to retrace his route along the muddy track. Revving up the engine, he cautiously bumped along towards that miserable excuse for a bridge.

Barney was lying in a hollow in one of the thick hedges which separated the fields. He was deeply engrossed in the activities of a number of ants which were trying to drag a leaf over the dry and dusty ground. What they wanted with the leaf, or where they were taking it no-one would ever know, but Barney was totally absorbed in their efforts as they scurried round and round, moving the leaf a tiny fraction of an inch each time a number of them managed to pull in the same direction. His concentration was shattered however, when the stillness of the air was broken by a scream, then another. He leapt to his feet, searching for a direction. Another cry pointed him towards the outbuildings in the distance and galvanised him into the fastest run of which he was capable. That was his 'missa' in pain without any doubt and any hurt to her was an equivalent hurt to Barney himself. As he neared the barn however, panting with effort, he was horrified to see the figure of a stranger emerge. It must be the Inspector 'missa' had warned him about and after years of injunctions to keep out of sight of Officials it was second nature to throw himself down among the barley. Cautiously parting the stems he was able to see the man busy at his vehicle. Barney crept carefully sideways until he could be sure of being hidden by the building, then hurried to where a damaged board would let him see inside. There was his 'missa' lying curled up on the floor and her sobbing cries told him more clearly than words that she was hurt.

What had happened? What had this stranger done to hurt 'missa'?

Although Barney could be tender with injured animals he was at a loss when it came to people. His 'missa' needed help. The stranger who was now leaving in the Transi didn't seem to care but he was the only person within reach; he had to be brought back to help 'missa'. Surely under the circumstances all the strictures about keeping out of sight could be ignored!

The Transi was already some distance down the track and couldn't be caught in a straight chase. However, the lane wound its way between the fields until it came to the bridge over the stream and that was where Barney headed with his peculiar lolloping gait. He splashed through the water and, with his breath coming in short gasps, reached the top of the bridge from one direction just as the Transi started to ascend from the other.

Stephen braked sharply as a figure appeared in front of him. What on earth was this yokel doing blocking the way? Was he trying to tell him that the bridge wasn't safe? He stopped the engine, but still couldn't understand what the fellow was mouthing so with more than a little exasperation he got out of the Transi. He had to suppress a surge of revulsion as his boots sank again into the soft edge of the ditch.

"'Missa'. Hurt." Barney was trying to shout but shortage of breath made him more incoherent than usual and also, fear at the sight of the dreaded Inspector constricted his throat until all he could utter was a few strangled grunts.

'An Impy!' Stephen thought incredulously. 'An Impy that's escaped from his control somehow.' But there was no collar on this fellow's neck. There was no persaCom locked on to his wrist either and that meant that he was definitely an illegal, and there would be a reward for his capture. He would have to be taken in to the Registry for identification and assignment.

"Come on now," Stephen put on his most soothing tone as he reached into the Transi for a restraining leash. "I'll look after you. You just come in the Transi and I'll take you to a place where you'll be taken care of." He cautiously approached the wildly gesticulating figure.

The appearance of the leash added to the panic in Barney's mind. The sight of tethered animals had always upset him, sympathy for their lack of freedom his overwhelming emotion. Why did this stranger want to tether him. He had to be made to understand that he must go back and help 'missa'. Barney stepped forward and put up his hands to try to push the stranger back towards the Transi.

Stephen dodged to one side. Did this madman mean to attack him. He reached into his pocket for the tranquilizer gun which was issued to all field operatives.

Barney pushed harder, trying to show this stranger that he must go back to the barn and Stephen staggered against the low parapet of the bridge. One hand was trapped in his pocket holding the gun and although he grabbed desperately at the stone wall with the other, he failed to get a grip and, almost in slow motion, overbalanced and toppled over the edge. As he fell, his hand clenched involuntarily on the tranquilizer gun, jerking the trigger. The dart penetrated his clothing, the point burying in his thigh and the fast acting drug ensured he was unconscious before he hit the ground.

It wasn't a big drop, and it was only a shallow stream below but Stephen fell face down into the water and lay there unmoving.

Barney looked over the edge and uttered a strangled sob of terror as he saw the prone figure. It was all too much for him and his overloaded mind shut itself down. He fled along the bank of the stream until he reached one of his secret places where the continual chuckle of the water over a rocky sill would soothe his ragged emotions. A solitary beech tree spread its welcoming shade and he curled himself up among its roots and went to sleep.

CHAPTER THREE

The sound of the Transi had faded into the distance before Kathleen stirred. Slowly, wincing with every movement, she managed to raise herself on to hands and knees; there she remained until the swaying barn had settled into something approaching its usual immobility before finally struggling to her feet.

Her mind numb with bewilderment, she tried to fathom out the reason for such a savage assault. The way he had torn off her clothes pointed to some kind of sexual motive but he surely would never have dared to touch her without her Consent. A sick feeling in her stomach came with the realisation that she had almost certainly been tricked with that piCode business. And was the problem with the Machinery Allocation part of the trick or would the harvest really have to wait till next week? There was no way to find out because CenCon was so inaccessible that it would take weeks to get a reply to a query from one of the outlying regions.

Wincing, she wrapped herself as well as possible in her torn garments, trying not to cry out as her injuries objected to the movement. With frequent rests, she managed to stumble to the farmhouse though at times she thought it would have been easier to crawl. Careless of the drain on their energy allocation, she soaked in a hot bath for over an hour, trying to close her mind to the nightmare scenario that confronted her. Later, a sense of impending doom threatened to overwhelm her as she slumped in front of the VidCom. There was work that she should be doing outside but her body wasn't capable of anything remotely physical.

She flicked from channel to channel in a vain attempt to find something that would interest her. She rarely bothered with the VidCom, regarding the vast majority of its offerings as trash; the few leisure hours that farming life offered she preferred to spend with a book from the stock which her parents had accumulated. By contrast

Albert would, if given the chance, spend all his waking hours in front of the screen.

The waning brightness of the sunlight made her realise she should be preparing the evening meal; last night's leftovers would have to do, she decided, managing to swallow a little though she didn't feel at all hungry. There was no sign of Barney but on summer days like this it was not unusual for him to forget about mealtimes. She wondered for a moment what he was doing; perhaps he'd found an injured fledgeling and was standing guard over it. Albert had been a long time too, he should have been back from the depot by mid-afternoon at the latest. Maybe there had been another glitch with the transport allocations, she thought resignedly. It was late before she eventually heard him at the door.

It was immediately apparent what he had been doing. Kathleen swore inwardly as she noticed his unsteady gait and flushed face. She realised now why he had wanted to go to the Depot himself; as if credits weren't scarce enough already'

"Everything go all right with the Harvest Approval Kath?" His slurred words were accompanied by an attempt at an ingratiating smile.

"I don't really know," she replied, her voice tight in her throat.

"How don't you know. Either it is or it isn't. How stupid can you get? She glared at him in reply and his eyes shifted uneasily to the cooker.

"Not stew again," he said disgustedly. "What the Hell have you been doing all day, and what's happened to your face?"

"I've been getting beaten up, that's what I've been doing," she flared at him.

Albert gazed at her with puzzlement, his eyes widening a little as he noticed the extent of her bruises. She wasn't prepared for his reaction.

"You cow," he swore and then started to laugh. "Did you think you'd get Harvest Approval by letting the Inspector have a fuck? I suppose he roughed you up to try to get your motor going did he, you frigid bitch?"

A different expression came into his eyes and he leered at her. "Did it work? Did he get a bit of life out of you? Maybe I should try that myself!" He moved towards her, slack-mouthed, drunken lust filling him with bravado.

Horrified, Kathleen backed away for a moment before rage and revulsion took over from fear. Glancing about her, she grabbed the breadknife from the table and pointed it in his direction.

"If you come any closer you bastard," she warned him coldly. "I promise you won't have anything left to bother me or anyone else with!"

He must have thought she meant it for the lust faded from his eyes and he turned away to slump into a chair.

"Whore of a bitch," he mumbled in an attempt at defiance. "You deserved everything you got. I only hope the Inspector enjoyed himself."

Overcome with disgust, Kathleen limped up the stairs to her bedroom. She was pretty confident that Albert wouldn't bother her again but she wedged a chair against the door as a precaution. She put the knife under her pillow and without undressing, pulled the covers over her. Only once before had she felt so hopeless and alone, but the travails of the day took their inevitable effect and she fell into an exhausted sleep.

It was dark when she was wakened by banging noises outside. Panicking for a moment that Albert had decided to try his luck, she reached for the knife and swung her feet on to the floor. At that moment the door crashed open and a bright light shone into her eyes. Dimly, she discerned more than one figure in the shadows.

"Kathleen Pierpoint? We are Police Officers and you must come to Police Headquarters with us. At once!"

"Whatever for?" her mind was groggy with sleep, but she had enough sense to put down the knife.

"You'll find out when we get there!"

That was all they would say. She was still dressed from when she had collapsed on to the bed so they grabbed her arms and hurried her down the stairs. Clamping her mouth shut, she managed to suppress the cries of pain as her bruised and battered body was manhandled out into the yard. There, Police vehicles were parked with their lights shining on the farmhouse and she saw Albert being hustled into one of them while she was taken to another. She was strapped into the rudimentary seat, the doors of the secure compartment closed around her and once the shutters snapped into place she could see nothing more. Heart thumping, she flogged her weary mind to consider what this could be about. Had Albert done something wrong while he'd been drinking? Had Barney got into some kind of trouble. If they had been caught breaching one of the thousands of regulations that governed their lives and the operation of the farm there would hardly be this weight of reaction. Her ordeal earlier in the day was pushed into the back of her mind as she fretted about her current situation.

She didn't see Albert at the Police headquarters. After her persaCom data had been downloaded into the Station terminal she underwent a brief Mediscan and was then locked into a small holding cell. After what seemed an interminable time she was taken to an interrogation room where, after formal identification proceedings, she soon found what it was all about.

"Did you receive a visit from AgriDept Inspector Stephen Lock today?" was the first question.

"Yes, but I didn't know his full name," she agreed.

"What time did he leave?"

"I never checked the time. It must have been after midday though."

"Stephen Lock never left your Unit citizen. His body was found in a stream there in circumstances that appear suspicious. We have reason to believe that you may have been involved."

Kathleen was flabbergasted. The man's body found in a stream must mean that he was dead; a small part of her mind exulted in the knowledge but the drift of the questions seemed to point to serious trouble for her. She had better be careful what she said from now on.

"Why would I want to harm him? I never saw him before today," she stated adamantly.

"You are positive that you never saw him before today, citizen?"

"Yes, I'll swear to it."

"Your persaFile doesn't show you as promiscuous, Citizen Pierpoint, yet you gave Consent to sexual congress with Mr Lock less than an hour after meeting him for what you claim was the first time. Was he so incredibly desirable, or were you offering a bribe for a favourable report?"

Kathleen's shoulders sagged and her face burned with humiliation. So she *had* put her piCode into the Inspector's consent file. How could she explain it? If she told them what had happened she would be seen to have a good reason for wishing the Inspector harm. If she didn't, even if she was cleared of any involvement in his death, the assumption would be that she was prepared to use her body to corrupt the proper adminstration of regulations. It wasn't likely that she would be allowed to continue in charge of an AgriUnit under those circumstances.

Who could have done it if not her? Albert was surely too craven to attack an Official and anyway, he had only too obviously been elswhere; apart from him who else was on the farm? Her breath caught in her throat as she remembered Barney; could it have been dear simple Barney, who wouldn't tread on an insect if he could help it? Her face burned with shame again. Could poor Barney have seen what happened in the barn, could it have made him angry enough to confront a dreaded Inspector?

"The Mediscan report shows that you have undergone violent treatment. Was he too rough for you, citizen, so you decided to take revenge. It appears that you were the only person on the Unit at the time. Don't you think that it will be easier for us all if you make a full confession?" The questioner was relentless.

Kathleen shook her head. She would not say another word until she'd had time to think. After a little while they gave up; she was formally charged with the murder of one Stephen Lock. She was stripped of her clothes, zipped into a standard prison coverall designed so that it could not be used to harm herself, her persaCom was removed from her wrist, and she was locked up in a cell.

David pushed his chair away from the desk and massaged his forehead with his fingertips. There was something wrong, some tiny thing that teased at the back of his mind. All the information cross-checked, all the figures were right, there was nothing to be worried about. Still the doubt persisted; with a sigh he restored the file to his screen and forced himself to re-examine every detail.

He shouldn't even have been here at this time of night. His job now required only a simple daytime stint, it was a sinecure or more truthfully an excuse to keep him out of the way but within reach should something happen that required his particular talent.

He had been an ardent fan of the concept of the Uropian Federation and, as one of the foremost experts in software design, had been happy to play a major part in creating the computer program which made the centralised control of all aspects of life in the Federation into a practical possibility. It was only during the final stages, when extra requirements had been introduced, that small misgivings had graduated into serious doubts. Even then, unwilling to believe that the dangerous implications of what he was doing were intentional, he had confined himself to building secret access codes into the basic system. Codes memorised, known only by himself, never to be used unless it became evident that the operation of the entire project was flawed beyond redemption.

The Authorities kept him on a string as an insurance should there ever be a major failure in the software, but there was no challenge in his allotted task so to stop himself from going mad he spent much of his spare time delving into random files, using his codes to bypass restrictions and to erase any record of his activities.

Tonight he had been looking at Police operations in this area. Murder was unusual and the case of Stephen Lock had caught his interest for a moment; he had run through the file in a routine check of the procedures but it all seemed to be in order and he was about to move on when this nagging doubt surfaced. He read through the file again without finding anything wrong but the feeling was stronger.

There it was! The read-out from the dead man's persaCom was on the screen and there was a momentary flicker on the man's Consent File heading. There had been mention of the Consent File in the case exposition. Yes, he had apparently made an agreement with the Unit manager who was the chief suspect. Not in itself exceptional, though it could indicate malpractice, maybe an attempt to get approval for a substandard crop. But what was the reason for that flicker?

What kind of person was this Stephen Lock? David accessed more files, noting the salient points. Only son of a single mother, good educational record, Counsellor in an Educational Centre, transferred to AgriDept and promoted to Field Inspector. Promoted! Surely that was an anomaly. AgriDept ranked much lower than Education, this fellow should at least have been at Administration level rather than a field operative. Clearing the screen and using another of his secret codes, David entered the officially non-existent section of deleted files where he initiated a search for any relevant information.

He was pleasantly surprised to see a file appear but anger mounted as he absorbed the contents. 'Brutal attack resulting in death;' he read, 'violence stemming from repressed sexuality; likelihood of re-occurrence; association with vulnerable females inadvisable; medical treatment recommended, if ineffective implant should be fitted to ensure the safety of the public.'

Who had buried this file and allowed such a monster to be at large? It was a simple matter to find out and the name teased at David's memory for a moment. All at once, he had a good idea of what had caused that flicker in a filename.

Carefully he checked his theory. Yes, the one who had deleted the information from Stephen Lock's file was on a short list of those who, under certain circumstances, were permitted to substitute filenames. And that flicker, he recalled, was an indication of this happening.

What could he do about it. If he took his suspicions to the Police Investigators he could not produce evidence from deleted files without admitting that he had access to the whole system. They would almost certainly consider him such a threat to Administration that he would immediately be fitted with an implant. If he did nothing it was likely that, however unjustly, the same fate would befall the woman. He had to face up to the fact that what he had uncovered was unlikely to be an isolated case and that the system he had helped to build was being used to facilitate abuse of power of the most evil kind. Almost reluctantly, he typed commands for a moment then sat back with his eyes closed while he tried to work out a plan of action.

Kathleen expected to have at least the rest of the night to try to gather her thoughts and formulate some kind of defence but was disturbed in less than an hour. She was marched outside and put into a Transa with only the driver for company. This took her to an anonymous looking building where she was led along passageways and finally pushed through an open door. As it closed behind her she heard her escort's footsteps receding down the corridor.

At first glance it looked too cosy to be an interrogation room. There was a desk certainly but there were also soft furnishings, comfortable chairs and a large window looking out over the street. She took a cautious step forward and a rather tired looking man of about her own age rose from behind a terminal and indicated a chair. Gratefully she lowered her body into it while adjuring herself to be on her guard. This seemed suspiciously like the softly softly approach.

She assessed him cautiously while he sat fiddling with an ancient-looking wooden ornament. An untidy thatch of brownish hair surmounted a strong face but his eyes looked tired and his entire demeanour suggested weariness; he was probably quite tall - it was difficult to tell while he was sitting down - lean and fairly muscular although his skin was pale as though he spent most of his time indoors. His gaze did not appear hostile, neither did his voice when he spoke.

"Kathleen Pierpoint, perhaps I should start by introducing myself. I am David Brook and though I am called an Area Co-ordinator, I have nothing to do with Police investigations. I've broken a few rules to be able to talk to you, purely because I'm disturbed by certain aspects of today's, no, it is now yesterday's events."

Kathleen made no reply. 'The nicer they sound, the more dangerous they are' she told herself.

"Miss Pierpoint, I think I should tell you that Stephen Lock was transferred to the AgriDept after unacceptable behaviour in his previous position. I have reason to believe that this behaviour re-occurred when he visited your Unit and I would like you to tell me the truth about what happened yesterday."

She put all her effort into keeping expression from her face and said nothing.

David Brooke sighed; rising from the desk he crossed to the window. He beckoned her to join him.

"What do you see, Citizen Pierpoint?"

Kathleen looked down at the street. The lights were still on but there was nothing moving apart from a gang of Impys cleaning out bins and sweeping rubbish from the gutters. She shuddered at the sight of the pathetic creatures with jerky uncoordinated movements, their control collars and faded blue overalls emblazoned with yellow stars. Mercifully, she could not hear the monotonous dirge they chanted as they worked.

"Do you know what will happen to you if you're found guilty of being involved in a murder, Miss Pierpoint. You'll have an Implant put into your brain to make you programmable and you'll spend the rest of your life like those poor creatures. It probably won't be a very long life; not many of them seem to last for long, but I'm told that they still have their original thoughts. Imagine spending the rest of your life with all your present feelings but with your physical actions dictated by electrical impulses into the lower part of your brain." He turned to face her and his voice hardened. "And not just you, Miss Pierpoint; Barney is undoubtedly an illegal and will get the same treatment even if he isn't guilty of any offence."

The blackness which had hovered at the edge of Kathleen's consciousness since her arrest now took command; her legs threatened to give way and she was thankful for the supporting arm leading her back to the chair. 'They know about Barney'! a voice screamed in her head. Maybe she said it out loud because David Brooke continued.

"Yes, Miss Pierpoint. Albert Arden, your co-manager was interrogated too and he has told the police about Barney. There will be a hunting team going to your farm in the morning." His voice hardened again. "Have you ever seen one of those teams at work? It's a bit of fun for them so they make sure that they take their time, chasing and chivvying until their quarry is exhausted before they use the stunners."

Kathleen looked at him for a moment in utter misery. Was that a gleam of pity in his eyes? Was he trying to trap her by using the word 'farm'. She thought of Barney being hunted by a team of men with tranquilizers; she thought of his simple spirit, free and birdlike, being trapped into a robotic existence. She had suffered purgatory in the past to save him from just that fate and the realisation that she was now powerless to protect him any longer brought a dry sob to her throat; *her* life was finished she knew, but if Albert had only kept his mouth shut Barney would at least have had a chance. The crushing inevitably of what was happening broke her reserve.

"What do you want to know," she murmured, looking at the floor.

"Everything you can tell me."

So she told him very nearly everything. When her voice cracked he brought her a glass of water. She told him about her parents and 'The Beeches'; about Barney and his empathy with the land; about Stephen Lock's visit, and how he had manipulated her fear of losing the farm; of the frenzied attack she had been subjected to; about Albert's reaction to her treatment. She showed him some of the spreading purple bruises on her flesh.

When she had finished she lifted her head to try to guess his reaction. He wasn't looking at her though, his gaze fixed on the window and she noticed that the ornament he'd been playing with was lying in splintered pieces on the desk.

"Let me kill myself," she begged. "If you think I don't deserve such a dreadful end then do that for me! Don't condemn me to the hell that's out there."

After a moment he turned to look at her face; the expression in his eyes was unfathomable.

"It would be merciful," his voice was soft, almost as if he were speaking to himself. "The truly awful thing is that it would be merciful."

As though he had reached a decision he pushed his chair back and stood up.

"Kathleen Pierpoint, I know you've gone through a terrible experience but there is more I must ask you to do. You have no reason to trust me, but to be honest you have nothing more to lose. I want you to come with me to the farm to get a hold of Barney before the hunting team arrives."

"What will you do with him?" Her whisper was hardly audible.

"He can't stay at 'The Beeches' anyway. I think I know a place where he could be safe but I doubt if he would go without your encouragement."

"How do I know that this isn't another attempt to trick me," she asked bitterly, regretting her tone immediately as a look of genuine hurt flashed across David Brooke's face

"You don't," he admitted sadly. "I honestly want to help, but after what you've been through I have no right to expect you to believe anyone."

"And after we've got Barney? Do I go back to my cell and wait for them to give me an Implant?" Resignation dulled her voice

The hurt look reappeared for a moment.

"That is not my intention," he assured her. "But I would prefer not to say any more at present."

Kathleen considered for a moment. 'I haven't any choice,' she thought bitterly, 'this may be a ruse to get

Barney to come quietly but it will still be better for him than being hunted down in the fields. And if it is a way to implicate me, I'm already in so much trouble that it won't make any difference.' She was too numb, too washed out to put up any kind of fight.

"Okay, I'll come with you," she consented.

David studied her for a moment, then nodded before sitting down again at his desk. She watched as he punched in commands and sequences of numbers, scrutinising the read-out intensely as he did so. Eventually he gave a grunt of what might have been satisfaction, stood up and rubbed his eyes.

"Time to go," he announced.

Meekly she followed as he led her out of the building, walking in the direction she was pointed, sitting where she was told in the Transa, wondering vaguely how he knew the name 'The Beeches'. She only started to come to life when she recognised familiar surroundings in the headlights.

"Have you any idea where he might be?" David Brooke sounded dubious.

She nodded. Her throat had closed up making speech difficult.

He parked in the yard, making no move to follow her as she got out. There was enough light from a sliver of moon to show her the familiar route to the barn; strange, was it really less than twenty-four hours since she had stopped to admire that glorious sunrise? Switching on the loft light, she wearily climbed the stairs to the niche that Barney had claimed; there he was, pressed into a corner with a blanket pulled over his head.

"Barney," she said softly. When there was no response she touched his arm and spoke his name a little louder.

Inch by inch, the blanket slipped down his face. Kathleen heart twisted in her chest as she saw the haunted look in his eyes.

"It's all right Barney," she soothed. "Everything's going to be all right."

"Missa," Barney's mouth worked desperately. "Missa... Bad man... Hurt missa."

"What happened to the bad man Barney?" she tried to be matter-of-fact.

He swallowed painfully, then again. "Barney.. bad man..water," he managed with a great effort. "Barney bad?" he continued, looking at her pitifully.

"No, Barney not bad," she assured him giving him a hug and turning her face away so that he would not see the fresh tears on her face. She blinked them back angrily. This was no time to start crying.

"We have to go away Barney," she told him. "Away from the bad men who will come looking for you. Will you come with 'missa' now?"

He looked at her doubtfully. Kathleen stretched out her hand which he clutched as though it was a lifeline. She led him, childlike, down the steps and into the yard, much as he had led her through the fields thirty years ago, she thought ruefully. He baulked as they approached the Transa and she had to cajole him to get into the rear seat; then she had to sit beside him so that he could hold her hand.

"I was going to suggest that you collect some personal items from the house," David Brooke suggested. "You have to accept that you probably won't ever see it again."

Never see 'The Beeches' again! The finality expressed in the remark gave her a fresh shock. Where were they going and what was to happen to her? Was this all an elaborate pretence? Somehow she didn't think so. Anyway, as he'd said, she had nothing to lose any more. If there was a chance that Barney could be protected she would grab at it irrespective of the outcome for herself.

"I don't think I can leave Barney in the Transa on his own even for a few moments," she demurred.

"It might be better to take nothing anyway," David reflected. "If you are to disappear completely it would look a bit odd if some of your things were missing. I don't suppose it's any use relying on Albert Arden to cover for you.?"

"I don't know any man called Albert." She chose the words deliberately, her voice as expressionless as her face.

David glanced at her before switching the vehicle into drive. She felt Barney trembling beside her and soothed him as best she could while she struggled with her feelings. She should be breaking her heart at leaving her home, the only home she had ever known; leaving the land that she loved so intensely. 'I haven't got a heart to break any more,' she decided. 'I'm just a shell of a person, nothing can bring joy or despair into whatever existence I have from now on. All my emotions have been destroyed during the last twenty-four hours.' Her melancholia was almost comforting and she lapsed into a kind of trance, hardly noticing that the sky was lightening; it was full daylight although the sun had yet to rise when David pulled off the road and braked to a halt.

"I daren't take the Transa any further," he explained. "They are all fitted with transponders so that they can be located, and if one crosses into another Region it automatically sends out a signal. We'll go the rest of the way on foot. It's not too far to a place where I think you'll be safe for a while."

They left the road and kept to rough paths and beside hedges as much as possible for though nobody should be looking for them yet, it did no harm to be careful. Walking soon exacerbated the pain from Kathleen's bruises and she had to exert all her will power to keep going while her body cried out in agonised protest. The sun had just cleared the horizon when David led them through a farmyard and, after knocking, into the farm house.

Exhausted with pain and lack of sleep, Kathleen was grateful to be able to sit with a cup of tea at the scrubbed wooden table that still declared 'farm kitchen' to the world. Barney had become more like his old self during their walk over the fields. He'd stopped trembling as soon as he was out of the Transa, and had paused a couple of times to pick a blade of grass or a twig to chew at. Now he was on the floor with a contented look on his face as three black and white kittens conducted exploratory trips across his body. David Brook was at the far end of the kitchen with George and Nellie, a stout, weather-beaten couple well on the wrong side of middle age, who were looking at him with a mixture of horror and suspicion. Every now and again Kathleen would hear a sharp exclamation or catch a quick glance from them. She assumed they were being told of the events which had led to her and Barney being fugitives; she didn't want to know, she was quite happy to drink tea and let her mind go blank. Eventually, the three of them joined her at the table.

"What you've told us is an appalling story," the man's voice was a deep rumble. "But why have you come here? We are good Federation citizens, surely what you must do is to surrender to the Police!"

David Brooke gazed at him steadily as he spoke.

"I've told you that I am a computer expert. I've done a lot of research into all sorts of records and I know that your two sons have disappeared, probably out of the country. I think that you may know of a way to help this girl here to a place of safety."

The couple looked at each other, fear the most obvious component of their expressions.

"That's nonsense," George stated firmly. "I told you, we're law-abiding Federation citizens doing our best to manage this Unit. Our boys just vanished after the Troubles, we have no idea what happened to them."

Nellie murmured in concurrence.

David shook his head with a fleeting smile. Taking a scrap torn from a page of printout out of his pocket he placed it on the table so that they could both read what it said.

"That doesn't mean anything to us," George protested weakly, but his face betrayed turbulent emotion. Nellie reached out and squeezed his hand briefly before she turned to David.

"Perhaps if you tell us what you want, and what your position really is, we might be able to offer some help."

"I told you the truth when I said I was an Area Administrator. It is also true that I am an expert on the entire Com system and, though the Federation Authorities don't know this, I can obtain access to every scrap of information that the network contains. If it were known what I had done I wouldn't even get the pretence of a trial.

I brought Miss Pierpoint and Barney here in the hope that you might be able to look after them so that I can get back to my office before any questions are asked. Helping fugitives to escape makes me as bad a criminal as they are and if you decided to hand all three of us over to the Authorities you would certainly be able to claim a reward!"

He went on to explain how his concerns about misuse of the system had caused him to spend countless hours monitoring records; how he had chanced upon the murder file; discovered Kathleen inevitable fate as a result of Stephen Lock's brutality and realised that he had to take action to prevent such injustice.

Kathleen didn't want to be reminded of the events on the farm; she shut herself away from the conversation but it was already too late. Images formed behind her eyes, vivid and terrifying images which grew in intensity in spite of her efforts to dismiss them. Clenching her hands so that the nails dug savagely into her palms and clamping her teeth together she fought to control her emotions; she even thought she was being successful until Nellie's arm went round her shoulders.

"You poor dear, you've had a terrible time and all these men can do is talk until the paint comes off the walls. You come upstairs with Nellie and get a bit of rest."

The words of comfort shattered the last fragile chains of Kathleen's strength. Up until this moment she had been too sick with worry, too numb or too angry to give way to tears but the plump woman's sympathy broke through all her barriers and the tightness in her chest rose inexorably into her throat until it burst out as a childlike wail of grief. Held securely in the big woman's arms she gave way to a paroxysm of wild sobbing. Helplessly, she allowed herself to be half-carried upstairs, undressed and placed between cool sheets.

"I'm - so - sorry!" she managed to gasp between spasms.

"Lovie, Lovie, don't you say a word. You've had an awful time and it'll do you the world of good to cry."

Nellie's hand gently caressed her forehead. "You just go off to sleep now and don't worry about a single thing."

CHAPTER FOUR

Nellie's expression could have hewn logs as she re-entered the kitchen and the two men fell silent under her gaze.

"Are you quite sure that this Inspector fellow is dead?" she demanded.

"Positive," David assured her.

"I suppose it will have to do," said Nellie sitting down with a sigh. "Though I would dearly like to put him to swim in a dung-slurry pit and keep pushing him under with a stick till he stayed down for good." At her husband's shocked expression she continued. "The state of that poor girl's body beggars belief. I doubt she could even sit down without being in agony. And you made her walk from the Area border." She glared at David and her husband, irrationally angry at both of them merely for the fact that they were men.

"I couldn't bring the Transa any further," David protested. "You must know that if it was traced to here you would be implicated. I offered to help her but she said she could manage."

"Do you think she would want any man's hand on her after being treated like that." Nellie's glance was as scathing as her tone and a flush of embarrassment spread over David's face.

"How can a human being be so twisted, so evil?" George tried to distance himself from the implied association.

"It's the system that's at fault," David replied sadly. "There will always be maniacs in society but the system we live under has no safeguards. Those in power will look after their own compatriots irespective of their faults and if there is corruption at the top, it will spread down into all levels of Administration until nobody is safe. I've come to the conclusion that the only answer is to destroy the whole thing."

"What possible hope is there of doing that?" Nellie

demanded.

"I don't know," David shook his head. "I have wondered what would happen if I introduced a virus into the core programme that would cause the entire Com network to collapse."

"You could do that?" George was astounded.

"I could do it all right but I'm afraid that it would lead to terrible hardship. Virtually every aspect of life is now administered by CenCon and if the program went down there would be no food supplies, no policing, probably no power after a day or two. Millions would suffer and a lot of people could die before there was any effective authority. Even then, there would be no guarantee that the Federation would be displaced."

George and Nellie exchanged glances and asked to talk privately for a moment. When they returned they seemed more animated.

"If we wanted you to meet someone we know, how soon would you be available? What do you intend to do at the moment."

David thought briefly.

"I going to take the Transa back to the Depot and erase the record of my journey with Citizen Pierpoint. Then I'll have to sit tight and see if anyone connects me with her disappearance."

"What are the chances of that?"

David shrugged. "I can't be sure. I can alter the records but I can't erase people's memories."

"What will happen if you are implicated?"

David shrugged again and used his hands to make a circle round his neck.

George shook his head. "It would be stupid to take the risk." he said adamantly.

"If you think that we can find a safe place for these two, why shouldn't we do the same for you?" Nellie added.

"You may not know it, but the position of every persaCom can be tracked. When I get back to the office I can alter the record of my journey here but if my absence is noticed, any inquiry will find out where I am immediately."

"We can find a way round that problem." George sounded confident.

"I've already put you in enough danger." David's tone was blunt. "If there's to be risk it is only right that I take it. I told you that I am largely responsible for the programme that enables the Federation to control everything. I am carrying a lot of guilt and I would almost welcome a chance to make atonement."

"Fiddlesticks!" George and Nellie burst out almost simultaneously. They smiled at each other before George continued.

"If you feel so guilty, wouldn't it be better to make recompense by fighting to overthrow Federation control? Would you be prepared to do that?"

"What could I do on my own?" David asked hopelessly.

"You might not be on your own."

David raised his eyebrows in surprise.

"No, I won't say any more at the moment," George continued and put on a more business-like manner. "Now, after you've returned the Transa and fiddled the records can you get back here without leaving a trail?"

David reflected for a moment then nodded in assent.

"I think I could manage that all right but..."

"No buts please," George told him firmly. "And the sooner the better. I'll take you to the area border in the ForTrak to save a bit of time."

"I would need the transponder code of your ForTrak to delete that journey as well."

"There won't be anything to delete." George said confidently and winked at his wife. "Come on now, let's get going."

Kathleen woke briefly sometime in the afternoon; she lay there disorientated but as the events of the previous day came crowding into her mind she curled herself into a ball and screwed her eyes shut in an attempt to drive the memories away. It was dark when she woke again and a momentary panic made her throw back the covers. What had happened while she slept; where was Barney and what was David Brooke doing?

She swung her feet on to the floor, suppressing a groan at the stiffness in her body. Padding barefoot to where a thread of light outlined the door she fumbled until she found a light switch; inspecting her surroundings she found no trace of her coverall but there was a voluminous dressing gown hanging on a chair beside the bed. Feeling filthy and unkempt she wrapped it around her and, venturing cautiously down the stairs she paused at the kitchen doorway.

Hearing no conversation, only a comforting clatter of pots, she eased the door open to see Nellie busy preparing a meal but not so busy that she didn't catch the movement

"There you are Lovie, are you feeling a bit better?"

"Much better thanks." Kathleen smiled her appreciation. "But I think I'd be better still if I could have a good scrub."

"Of course you will, Lovie. I've washed that nasty thing you had on but if you don't want to wear it again there are some things of mine here. Lord knows they won't come anywhere near to fitting you but you'll maybe be able to pull them together enough to do for the moment. There's a towel warming by the stove here so you go and have a nice hot bath and you'll feel like a different woman."

"Where's Barney? Is he all right?" Kathleen enquired anxiously.

"He's out in the barn, Lovie," Nellie beamed at her. "It's the oddest thing; when the boys were young they had a little den out there and as soon as he saw it you could see it suited him. Is that where he stayed at your place?"

"He never fancied being in the house very much," Kathleen admitted. "I think that he doesn't like to feel closed in."

"Ah, the poor dear." Nellie's voice was full of sympathy. "Now I'll just show you the bathroom, there's plenty of hot water so you can soak as long as you like and I've got a jar of salve here that might ease your bruises. We'll wait for the men to come back before we eat."

"Where have they gone?"

"Some things they seem to think are important." Nellie shook her head as if to indicate that the preparation of a meal ranked considerably higher in her opinion. "No doubt they'll want to tell us all about it when they get back."

Kathleen did take her time, luxuriating in the hot water until she started to feel a little guilty. After drying herself she inspected the jar she had been given. Noting the lack of a lable, she gingerly tried the ointment on her arm and was pleasantly surprised by the almost immediate soothing effect. Quickly applying it to the rest of her bruises, she inspected the garments she had been given, having to suppress a chuckle as she tried them on. They were certainly on the large side but with the aid of a stout leather belt she managed to gather them together enough to be decent. 'Anything's better than that horrible prison shroud,' she comforted herself as she returned to the kitchen.

Nellie and the two men were sitting at the table when she entered; David immediately inquired after her health and looked relieved when she assured him that she was feeling much better.

"We've been waiting for you before discussing the situation and making any plans," he announced.

"I'm glad to know that we have a future we can make plans for." The hurt look that crossed David's face made her add hastily, "I'm sorry, I didn't mean that to sound nasty."

"I wouldn't have got myself involved if I didn't believe that I could help you," he assured her with an attempt at a smile. "Now, I suggest we bring you up-to-date with what has happened while you've been asleep." A genuine smile this time robbed his words of any implied criticism.

"Should we bring Barney in?" Nellie suggested.

Kathleen shook her head. "He really only understands simple things to do with the land and animals. He wouldn't know what we were talking about."

"He's just a big child," Nellie beamed. "I'm sure there isn't an ounce of harm in him."

"Barney wouldn't hurt an insect if he could help it.. "

Kathleen's voice trailed off as she realised what she was saying. She shot an anguished look at David, who came to her rescue.

"I managed to get a look at the updated report on yesterday's events. Apparently Stephen Lock was unconscious when he fell into the stream, so his drowning was something of an accident. It seems that he managed to shoot himself with a tranquilizer gun while it was still in his pocket."

Kathleen's heart gave a leap. "Does that mean that it wasn't anybody's fault? That they won't blame me?"

David shook his head sadly. "I'm afraid you're still on the wanted list. They're positive he was pushed and that would be manslaughter; because they've been informed about Barney he's obviously another suspect but you would be guilty of harbouring an illegal who was also a dangerous maniac. They'd still give you an Implant I'm afraid."

Kathleen gulped as the brief flare of hope died. That was it then, her previous life was over, there was no going back. She piled her memories into a heap and slammed a shutter down on them. Her face hardened, her voice became firm.

"It seems you changed your mind about going back?"

David glanced at George, who gave him a brief nod. As he turned to Kathleen he linked his fingers together and she noticed with surprise that he had a heavy glove covering one arm to the elbow. She was just about to ask if he'd hurt himself when he spoke.

"George persuaded me that if I don't like the system I have to fight it," he said simply.

"How will you do that?"

Again he glanced at George for approval.

"It seems that there is some kind of underground Resistance movement. George is connected with it and can arrange for me to meet them."

She gaped at him for a moment.

"Do you really think that there is any chance of changing the conditions that we live under?"

David turned to George who gave a slight shrug as he

spoke.

"Maybe there is, maybe there isn't. Perhaps it's just a foolish dream of a few folk who can remember the days when we had at least a form of democracy and could change our rulers by voting at an election every few years. Whatever way it is, nothing will get better unless people fight for it."

"I've got nothing to go back to now," David explained. "I'd been getting more and more disillusioned with the situation and when I discovered what had happened at your place I had to do something. I knew I would have to get you a place to hide and then I thought of George and Nellie here."

"What made you think that they would take me in?" There were so many questions she wanted to ask.

"They are both old enough to remember this land before it became part of the Federation, when it had its own Government, and I discovered that their two boys got out of the country after being involved in the 'troubles'. They would need to have had contacts to do that and I was banking on them being sympathetic to someone in your situation."

David smiled at the couple before continuing.

"It seems that I was right and that they think that they could keep you out of sight here for as long as you like. Me too if I wanted, but if there is a chance of doing something worthwhile against the Federation I would prefer that to hiding out as a non-person."

Kathleen tried to make some sense of what she was hearing. David had turned to George with some remark that she didn't catch and Nellie was fussing over the cooker. This talk of a Resistance movement seemed fanciful yet it caused a little stir in her heart. What if it were true; would it really be possible to strike a blow against those who had caused her such torment, who had treated her almost as sub-human merely because she loved the land she was born on.

"Would I be allowed to join this Resistance?" She threw the remark at all of them.

"Kathleen, it's likely to be dangerous and thankless

work," David responded hastily. "And it'll mean moving to the more northerly regions. Much better that you stay here where you're welcome." George nodded in agreement.

"That's men's work, Lovie." Nellie turned from the pot she was stirring. "It'll be no place for a woman."

Kathleen made her voice sound as hard as she could. "What makes you think I'm a woman? I've had all the womanhood beaten out of me! I haven't got a home, I haven't got a friend, I haven't got a future. I'm a non-person who'll be made into an Impy if I ever get caught. I begged David to let me kill myself yesterday and I meant it! He told me I was at the bottom of the pit and had nothing left to lose and he was right. I'm an ideal person for your Resistance because I'm as good as dead already!"

There was a shocked silence for a moment. George and Nellie's eyes reflected sadness while David's showed anguish mixed with a trace of what could have been admiration.

"Well!" She kept her voice hard. It hurt her to be so abrupt with such kindly people; to tell the truth the thought of being cossetted by them for a while was tempting though she knew that eventually she would find it suffocating.

"There's no denying the movement needs all the help it can get." It was George who spoke. "Though it's a shame for someone so young to have such a bleak outlook on life."

"I'm not as young as you seem to think. Before yesterday I was thirty-five, now I'm at least ten years older.

"Whoa, lass." George started with a smile. "You'll soon be too old to join the movement if you are aging as fast as that!"

The atmosphere lightened a little and Nellie chose that moment to send George to bring Barney in for some supper. Kathleen hadn't realised how hungry she was; when she thought about it, she realised she hadn't eaten for twenty-four hours. Nellie beamed when she asked if she could have a second helping.

"That's my girl," she teased. "You stop with me for a

while and you'll be as big as I am."

Pleading tiredness, David refused to discuss any more plans until the morning. Kathleen accompanied Barney to the barn to inspect his new den which, though on the small side, was cosy enough. She tried to introduce the thought of her departure to him

"Will you stay here and help George with the farm, Barney?"

A vigorous nod indicated his assent.

"Will you stay here if I go away with David?"

"No bad man?" Barney looked troubled.

"No, Barney, he's not a bad man. We are going to try to make everybody safe from bad men. But I want to be sure that you will be all right here and that you'll keep out of sight of strangers."

"Land here good." Barney was emphatic. "Good water."

A little easier in her mind she returned to the farmhouse.

"He's not much trouble and he's quite capable so long as he knows what you want," she assured George and Nellie.

"I'll be glad of a lift now and again," George conceded. "What about you, are you set on this idea of going off with David?"

"With or without him," she insisted. "Now I know that people are trying to change things I'm determined to help. It'll give me a purpose, a reason for living. Can you tell me more about what they do?"

"We'll leave that until the morning lass." He heaved himself up and headed for the stairs. As Nellie obviously wasn't going to oblige with answers to the questions still buzzing in her head she resigned herself to waiting till tomorrow. She said goodnight and retired to her bedroom.

Having slept through the afternoon she expected to be able to lie awake to consider the astounding news she'd heard; however, emotional exhaustion had taken a severe toll of her and it wasn't more than a few minutes before she drifted into sleep.

She woke with first light however; hearing sounds of

movement she dressed herself hurriedly, wondering how non-persons would acquire clothes or even sustenance. Credits were obviously out of the question owing to the extensive controls which governed their use. Maybe it would have to be something like the 'barter' that her parents had mentioned. There were so many things she would need to find out, but when she went down for breakfast it seemed that she would have to wait for more information.

"We'll set off in the ForTrak as soon as you've eaten," George was saying to a bleary-eyed David. "It seems that there's a search of some kind going on in Region Four with all non-essential movements stopped. When they draw a blank there they will likely extend it to the adjoining Regions so I reckon the further away you are, and the faster, the better."

"There are likely to be check points on the roads in that case," David warned.

"We won't need to go near any roads for most of the way," George sounded confident. "We'll be on the farm tracks and over the fields for the best part of the distance."

It all seemed to have been decided for them. Kathleen accepted a bag of 'bits and pieces' as Nellie called it and was hugged to the point of submersion against her generous bosom. Barney watched the preparations with increasing uneasiness. Eventually he screwed himself up to approach David.

"You..'missa'..go?" he demanded.

"I'm afraid so, Barney," David responded seriously.

Barney's mouth opened and shut a few times as he tried to transfer his thoughts into the words he found so difficult.

"No hurt 'missa'," he burst out.

David solemnly scooped up a handful of soil; he gripped Barney's hand, pressing the soil between their two palms. "I faithfully promise on the land itself that I will never hurt 'missa'" he intoned gravely.

Barney's face broke into a delighted smile as he turned to Kathleen. "No bad man" he assured her.

As they boarded the ForTrak and George settled

himself behind the steering bar, Kathleen again noticed that David was still wearing the heavy glove.

"Why have you got that on?" she demanded. "Have you hurt yourself?"

"No, nothing like that," he assured her. "You probably don't know, but every persaCom transmits signals which mean that the wearer's location can be pinpointed. Of course, there are far too many of these to be monitored all the time but in the case of an investigation it's a simple matter to call up a piCode to find that person's whereabouts. That's how they found Stephen Lock so quickly. When he failed to log in at the end of the day they could immediately send a team to pick him up. This glove is a screening device that stops the signal getting out."

Kathleen involuntarily glanced at her own naked wrist. She had been too overwrought since her persaCom was removed to pay much attention to the lack of the familiar band but now she thought about it, it felt undeniably strange.

"Why did they take mine off at the Police station?" she wanted to know.

"Standard procedure with suspected criminals under lock and key, so that they don't have access to any information. Normally you would have an electronic restraint fitted before being removed from the cell but I was able to bypass the requirement. In the unlikely event of someone escaping they would soon be reported because there is a reward for such information."

"How could you bypass a 'standard procedure'," Kathleen wondered.

"People in the lower levels of Administration don't think for themselves now. If they receive an instruction they do exactly what it says, nothing more, nothing less, then they can't be blamed if something goes wrong."

She nodded her understanding and sat quietly for a while; what she had thought of as just a handy little communicator and computer link obviously had more sinister uses. She shuddered, wondering if the device could eavesdrop on conversations or maybe even watch you through its miniature screen.

"No, a persaCom can't do anything like that," David assured her, when she voiced her concern. "But if you're using the VidCom you can be identified because the two of them automatically link together."

George wasn't far wrong when he called me 'child' Kathleen thought to herself. There I was, thinking I was a free woman, that so long as I met the targets I was avoiding the disciplined toil that I hated; content to live out each day tending to the land while in reality I was only one of a mass of mindless robots being manipulated by the Federation. Could I be content to go back to my old life now even if it was on offer, she reflected. Knowing that the dreaded Implant would be waiting for me at the first sign of independence, could I meekly conform to the system? A spark of anger started to burn, giving life and meaning to the emotionless construct that she had shown to the others last night.

"George hasn't got a glove on," she observed after a while.

"I gather his persaCom has been modified. That's one of the things I hope to learn more about," David smiled at her. "He assures me that we are quite safe."

Kathleen resolved to stop worrying over matters of which she was ignorant. I have to trust these people, she told herself, they seem to be genuine in their desire to help; every day, every hour is really a bonus when the alternative is to have an implant in my brain. She shuddered at the thought and drew her jacket closer.

"Not cold are you?" David was solicitous.

"No, no," she assured him. "Just cold thoughts." He reached for her hand and clasped it in an attempt at reassurance.

Indeed she had no excuse to be cold. It was still early but there was plenty of heat from the sun with the promise of a scorching later on; there was the merest haze in the sky though, and Kathleen counted back the days before deciding that Barney's forecasted change was likely to be proved accurate.

She called to George over the noise of the engine. "Barney said that there would be rain coming sometime today."

George looked at the sky before nodding agreement. "He could be right at that. Is he good to tell the weather?"

"Pretty good." Kathleen admitted. "It was two days ago that he told me."

"Sounds like a handy lad to have around a farm." He smiled at her before turning his attention back to driving.

The ForTrak was an all-terrain vehicle, a cross between a heavy farm tractor and the little Quads which had been fashionable for a while in the past. Popular for general farm duties for quite some time, they were capable of a reasonable speed on good surfaces, could also cope with incredibly rough ground and in addition had sufficient power to tow virtually any agricultural implement. They could not, however, be described as economical; though Kathleen had used one often enough on her own place it had only been for essential heavy work. She wondered how George managed to account for the amount of Ectol that a trip like this would require.

Originally the vehicles had been fitted with transponders as were the various types of road Trans but so many were lying about farm fields cannibalised to keep others going that no checks were made on them any more. The ride was not particularly comfortable, better for the driver who had a sprung seat, not so good for any passengers who were only insulated from a metal bench by totally inadequate and usually disintegrating cushions. George had explained that there was a network of usable tracks alongside the hedges; most often these continued from one farm to another with only a gate or a movable bit of fence as a barrier. Occasionally though, he had to cross boulder-strewn areas and ditches and when this happened Kathleen and David were bounced mercilessly up and down and from side to side, frequently having to hold on to each other as well as the grab handles for support. The sun had further to climb yet but the already scorching heat, exacerbated by the ForTrak's plastic canopy, made conditions thoroughly miserable.

Kathleen had discarded her jacket but her oversize shirt was sticking to her perspiring skin with dark patches spreading under her arms and between her breasts. Her hair hung in lank strands around her neck and over her forehead despite all her attempts to push it back.

"Do you know how far we have to go?" she asked David on one of the quieter stretches.

He shook his head. "I think that George expects to be back home tonight so I would assume that some time after midday should see us there."

Kathleen glanced automatically at her wrist and shrugged; no persaCom, no clock read-out. She tried to judge the position of the sun and, deciding that it had further yet to climb, resigned herself to at least another couple of hours of discomfort.

Apart from opening the various gates or peeling back and replacing the occasional bit of fence there was nothing much for her and David to do; idly she wondered if the Depot had sent machinery to harvest her barley; if Albert was back at the farm, and what he would do now; what action the authorities would take about her disappearance; how Barney was getting used to his new surroundings; she had a vision of him being called in from roaming the fields by Nellie to face a mountainous pile of food. Remembering her bag of 'bits and pieces' she ventured a quick look at its contents, finding soap, flannel, toothbrush etc. and a small jar of the soothing salve. Dear Nellie, she smiled fondly but the overpowering heat turned her smile into a yawn.

"I'm not used to sitting about doing nothing," she defended herself against David's amused enquiry.

"You'd better make the most of it," he advised her. "I still wish that you would go back with George instead of the uncertain future that we face."

"Why should I be different from you?" she argued. "I never expected other people to fight my battles for me and I've got at least as much reason as you to want to strike a blow against the Federation."

"It's not the same," he insisted. "Kathy...you don't mind if I call you Kathy?"

"I don't mind Kathy but don't ever call me Kath," and in response to his raised eyebrows, "Albert called me Kath sometimes when he'd been drinking!" She wouldn't allow herself to remember those times.

David nodded in acceptance. "What I was going to say was that I worked for the very system that I see now has done so much harm. When I said I was going back prepared to take the blame for my actions I felt that it would be a grand gesture and would assuage some of my responsibility for helping to make such iniquity possible. George here persuaded me that it would be more meaningful to do something practical."

"I would think so too," she was indignant. "If you intend to sacrifice yourself, why not get a weapon and take as many of them with you as possible."

He shook his head. "Most of the ones we work with aren't bad people Kathy. They are doing a job without thinking too hard about it; some of them are probably misguided enough to believe in what they're doing. The really evil ones are those at the top, the ones who crave power for its own sake and they're too well protected for us to get anywhere near them."

Kathleen said nothing in reply. She was sure that there must be others of similar morality to Stephen Lock who did not deserve any kind of consideration.

George drove the ForTrak up a steep bank and turned onto a lane with a Tarmac surface. Although he increased speed it was still bliss compared with the previous terrain; Kathleen leaned back and tried to relax her aching muscles.

David bent forward to speak to George.

"Won't some of the newer managers be suspicious when we cross their land?"

"Most of us in this Region had enough warning to manipulate the records when the land grab took place," George explained. "We had a sympathiser in the Registry and he managed it so that the locals were at the top of the list for allocations. We're careful with any outsiders until they've had a year or two to settle down. It can happen that they need a bit of help to meet the Target and we're able to provide that help and maybe drop a few hints that the Federation doesn't always know best. The new people come to think that some kind of secret club exists to look after its members and don't want to do anything that might stop them from being allowed to join."

"I never heard of anything like that where I come from," Kathleen interposed.

"It will be there, but probably very low-key," George was quiet for a moment. "Over your way has always had a reputation for officiousness even before the country was broken up into Regions. It's maybe because the main Admin Centre was close by; the further north you go you'll see that things aren't so strict. Some of the Inspectors are from the land and I've even heard that there are one or two above them that would like to see changes."

"How can it be so different?" she wondered. "It's still part of the Federation isn't it."

"I could try to explain, but there's one who knows far more than me and will make a better job of it; you'll meet him when we get to where we're going.

There was little attempt at conversation from then on for the heat became enervating as the sun neared its zenith; it was now obscured in a thickening haze however and the air became increasingly sultry and oppressive. While the ForTrak ran on another short stretch of smooth roadway, Kathleen took the opportunity to fan herself with her hands.

"Sorry," she apologised to David with a grimace. "I don't think I smell very nice at the moment!"

"I'm surprised you haven't passed out sitting this close to me," he rejoined, and together, they laughed ruefully.

"We're turning off here." George's call intruded on their amusement. "Just brace yourselves for this next bit!"

Kathleen yelped as the ForTrak dropped bodily down into another field; David grabbed her in mid-air, holding her steady but not able to reduce the impact as her bruised bottom landed on the unyielding seat.

"Owww," she groaned. "I'd even feel sorry for a sack of potatoes treated like this!"

"The end could be in sight," David comforted her, pointing ahead to where a cluster of farm buildings had come into view.

"It's my end that I'm bothered about," she joked testily, leaning against him as she tried to massage some feeling into her posterior. Relief was her primary emotion when George braked the vehicle to a halt under a lean-to roof and switched off the engine.

CHAPTER FIVE

George hurried them across a yard and into a rambling and ancient looking farmhouse on which tendrils of ivy had grown unchecked until a large part of the stonework was concealed. After a cursory introduction, he hurried off saying that he wanted to get home before dark otherwise Nellie would be worried. Kathleen and David found themselves sitting in a comfortable kitchen that seemed pleasantly cool after the sultry heaviness of the day outside.

"Well," Richard Green smiled at them. "I suppose you'd better tell us a bit about yourselves."

He looked to be in his fifties, lean and wiry with a sparse covering of short-cropped grey hair. His wife Hazel was slender without appearing in the least frail; though of average height she seemed almost birdlike with the sharpest and most penetrating eyes Kathleen had ever seen. 'I don't think you would get far telling lies to that woman' she thought.

Aloud, she said. "I think David had better tell it, he knows more about the background. I'm just a simple farm manager really."

"Simple people don't get to manage farms for long nowadays," Hazel observation was so quiet it might have been for her own ears only. "They very soon end up on the prodlines." Her husband waved her into silence however, as David started to speak.

Kathleen would have liked to shut her mind to the recital of the events of the last few days, but she felt that to appear disinterested would give the wrong impression; this was plainly to be an interrogation and on its outcome would depend their admission into whatever kind of organisation the Resistance turned out to be. In her mind she piled reinforcements against the hard wall which Nellie's kindness had so easily breached; David glanced at her apologetically as his narrative reached Stephen Lock's visit to 'The Beeches' and she dug her nails into her palms in readiness.

"Hold on a minute." Hazel interrupted. "It sounds as though you've got a long story to tell and I think that Kathleen at least would like a chance to freshen up. You men can carry on without us if you want."

Gratefully Kathleen followed the older woman into another room, mentally castigating herself. She thought she had successfully suppressed any emotion but here it was bubbling just below the surface again. She blinked angrily as she felt wetness gathering in her eyes.

"Men! They've as much finesse as a bunch of bull stirks." Hazel sounded disgusted but she still stared at Kathleen as though to see into her very soul.

"I got the impression that the next part of the story was pretty unpleasant and you didn't really want to hear it spoken of?"

Kathleen nodded, not trusting herself to speak. Sympathy made the flimsiness of her mental barrier more apparent and she couldn't stop tears trickling down her cheeks.

Feeling tissues pushed into her hand she gave her face a fierce scrub.

"I'm sorry," she apologised, more than a little angry at herself. Was she going to make a habit of losing control?

"Nonsense," Hazel said briskly. "Now you're going to come upstairs with me and get a wash. Your clothes look as though they are sticking to you, and I don't suppose you've got anything to change into?"

"All I own in the world is what I'm wearing," Kathleen admitted with an attempt at a laugh.

"That's better," Hazel replied briskly. "Now, I have to confess to being a bit of a squirrel by nature; seeing that you look not far off the size I used to be, we'll have a root among my old stuff and see if there is anything that will fit you."

It felt almost surrealistic to be standing in a strange room trying on clothes. Her host had apparently stored everything in boxes and it was these boxes that Kathleen was invited to explore. Hazel held items up for her to examine while making apparently innocuous conversation, though Kathleen soon realised that a thread of interrogation ran through the seemingly inconsequential chatter.

Horrified by the sight of Kathleen's bruises and ignoring assurances that they were no longer painful, Hazel hurried off to find some ointment. Kathleen lifted a dark green dress embellished with some kind of glittery stuff on the hems and on the thin shoulder straps; letting it slip through her hands she marvelled at the silky softness of the fabric. Some impulse made her turn to the mirror and hold it against herself; she was surprised and maybe a little scandalised by the amount of bosom that would unavoidably be revealed.Hastily, she turned away as Hazel bustled back into the room,

"That colour would really suit you, my dear," she said enthusiastically. "Why don't you try it on?"

"I'd love to," Kathleen admitted, and added ruefully. "I don't know if I would have the courage to wear it in public though."

"Don't be silly," Hazel retorted. "That's a comparatively modest dress. You should have seen the skimpy things the girls wore in my day, not much more than a couple of wide belts!"

"Are you sure?" Kathleen queried then laughed. "I think that I had better wait until my bruises have disappeared before I put it to the test."

"Whenever did you get the chance to wear a dress like that," she asked as Hazel rubbed cream into her shoulders.

"Before I met Richard I trained to be a nurse and the crowd of us used to have rare parties; I was reckoned to be a bit of a beauty in those days and I used to plague my dad for money to buy the fanciest gear, like that dress. There may not be much of it, but it's made of satin and if I remember rightly he grumbled for weeks about what it cost."

"It would be lovely to wear something like that but I don't think I'll ever have a chance," Kathleen said regretfully. "I'll just take some of the more ordinary things if I may."

"I suppose you're right, but it's a shame to have to say

so. If you're ready now, we'll go and see how the men are getting on."

Richard glanced at Hazel as they entered the kitchen; some signal must have passed between them for he turned to David straightaway.

"Hazel and I need to get on with some work so we'll leave you with Jack; he'll give you a bit of a history lesson and try to explain the present situation."

'Who is this Jack?' Kathleen wondered momentarily, then almost gasped as an old man, older by far than anyone she had ever seen, appeared from a practically invisible doorway. Under Federation Regulations, when people reached the official retirement age they were taken to designated communities, located in the warmer southern regions where the elderly could be properly cared for. However, with social travel being almost unaffordable and strongly discouraged if not actually disallowed there was rarely any contact among families after the separation apart from a vid message now and again.

"I'm Jack," the old man greeted them in a strong clear voice. "As you can see, I'm walking, talking history. I remember what it was like before this wonderful Federation came into being so if you come with me to my quarters I'll do my best to answer your questions."

He led them through a short passage into to a small windowless room which seemed to be situated in the heart of the building; it was pleasantly furnished however and they were soon settled into comfortable chairs.

"This part of the building dates back more than five hundred years," he explained briefly. "Back then it wasn't unusual for there to be hidden rooms where people could be kept out of sight when the occasion demanded."

"It must have been a tough life in those days," David commented. "But even in the comparatively recent past the vids show us that everyday life was much harder and more dangerous, before the Federation took control. Do you remember those times, and was it really as bad as the vids show us?"

"Life was harder for some and easier for others; whether it was more dangerous would depend upon how you evaluate danger, but what you have seen on the vids is nothing more than Federation-glorifying propaganda. Let me tell you how it all began and then maybe you will understand what I mean."

The old man settled himself comfortably and started.

"Before you two were born, the Regions in this island formed one independent country with its own Government, similar to others which are now part of the Federation. However, a grand plan was conceived by a powerful group of idealists who claimed that prosperity and well-being would be enhanced if all these countries banded together into a Superstate. The general public didn't have much enthusiasm for the scheme but over a period of years they became worried as they were fed one scare story after. It practically amounted to brainwashing, with doom-and-gloom scenario's such as a world-wide Holy War, irreversible damage to the planet from industrialised society, a cataclysmic collision with an asteroid, the potential end of mankind etc. It was repeated again and again that the only way to ensure the future was for everyone to join the Federation, to give those at the top enough power to implement whatever policies were needed to avert these dangers. We were of course assured that we would all participate in the dynamic and beneficial future that was being created on our behalf. There were opposing views of course but these were decried as heresy and in the end we agreed to bring our government under the authority of the ruling Council. After a while however the economy started to suffer, at least in part as we discovered later from all the Rules and Regulations that were imposed on every activity. These Rules seemed very worthy, the reasons for them certainly plausible at the time but they all had the effect of taking away the right of ordinary folk to make their own decisions, one of the freedoms we had been accustomed to. As more and more businesses failed there was a big increase in unemployment; this was disguised by appointing vast numbers to oversee what the actual workers were doing. Millions were employed in this way but the economics obviously didn't make sense, taxes got higher and higher and everybody gradually got poorer. There were a lot of complaints, citizens were getting news from other countries outside the Federation via the VidCom and could see that people there had a much higher standard of living. You may remember the 'troubles' as they were called; although that rebellion was put down the Council realised that it would have to strengthen its control system. There was already an extensive cable network and a massive programme of development eventually ensured that any information from the outside world could only come from official Federation broadcasts. The explanation that this was to protect vulnerable citizens from the corrupting material which was widely available seemed reasonable, and indeed very laudable at the time.

"There is a huge Department at CenCon, that's the name for the Central Control building at the heart of the Federation, which monitors all international transmissions and only releases those which give a favourable view of the Federation. However, this still wasn't enough to satisfy the power-hungry who had clawed and lied and cheated their way into the top positions; the big breakthrough came with the introduction of a computer programme which enabled every aspect of production and recreation to be administered from a single central location. As soon as that was in place, wearing a persaCom became compulsory and CenCon's dream of absolute control of the populace was realised."

Jack stopped to sip from a glass of water before continuing.

"As regards the danger you mentioned, there was certainly far more crime before this all happened. A lot of men, especially young men had become increasingly resentful of a society which had more-or-less dismissed the entire male sex as either macho bullies or potential perverts, and treated them accordingly. It developed into a serious problem in the urban areas; Government policies were not only weak; they were continually challenged by clever lawyers and as a result, gangs of criminals roamed the streets with impunity knowing that if apprehended there was little chance of punishment as this might infringe their 'rights'. The persaCom, in conjunction with the fact that there was less and less to steal, brought all the lawlessness to an end and this was seen as a godsend by a large part of the population. It was not until later that the risks to liberty became apparent and by then it was too late to do anything about it.

"So the short answer to your question is that you are now less likely to be attacked or robbed by your fellow citizens, but have lost virtually all of your personal freedom to the State which, of course, can do no wrong! Back then we settled for the easy option and now we are suffering. It is only propaganda when we are told that most other countries are worse off than us and that it is the Federation that is saving us from all sorts of unpleasantness.

"It was at about that period when it became impossible for anyone to leave the Federation. The energy tax on all forms of transport added to a new embarkation tax made the cost of travelling too high for ordinary folk; anyone who managed to scrape together enough credits to apply for a ticket somehow would be found to have committed an offence one kind or another and the fine would wipe out their credits so they could never get away."

"I'm sure I remember my mother saying that the population was too high when she was young," Kathleen put in. "Why would the Council not want people to leave?"

"One of the ideas behind the Federation was that all the main production facilities would be more efficient if they were grouped together in the centre; I suppose it made a kind of economic sense, but it meant that there was a mass movement from the outlying regions to work in the large urban areas. A lot of the small towns and villages became almost derelict and were ultimately abandoned when this island group of regions was assigned for grain and Ectol production. The burden of bureaucracy means that the cost of production in the Federation is higher than outside, so there are virtually no exports; that means that we can't afford imports which is why it is so important to keep the farms in operation to feed the population. The situation's getting worse because the number involved in Administration keeps increasing; the birth-rate is falling; there are so few youngsters coming up that in spite of being officially retired, old folk now have to continue to work for the community."

"Surely the Council must see that it can't go on like this, that there will have to be changes?" David asked.

"It's quite possible that the Regional Assemblies would like to be allowed to adapt the rules to suit local conditions, but the Ruling Council has always been reluctant to derogate any of their powers; they like to keep control firmly in their own hands and always claim it is someone else's fault when things go wrong."

"What did you mean when you said that old folk have to work for the community now?" Kathleen asked, feeling a little apprehensive as to what the answer might reveal. And where do all the gangs of Impys come from?"

A look of distaste came over the old man's face. "The Impys are a perfect example of a good idea being corrupted. Back at the beginning of this century there was a fairly general belief that locking criminals away wasn't a humane way to treat them but none of the alternatives seemed to produce the right results. It had long been known that various chemicals affected different parts of the brain and when the research was taken a step further it became possible to fit an Implant linked to a collar that would release small amounts of the appropriate substance along with electrical impulses according to a preset programme. This meant that the criminals could pay their debt to society by doing useful work without supervision. Impy numbers increased when political dissidents were classed as criminals and got the same treatment. Then, as more and more of the workforce became supervisors there weren't enough left to do the menial drudge jobs. We'd stopped using machines whenever possible because of the high cost of energy and concerns over the environment; the Impys were cheap labour, but there were never enough of them to fill the demand.

"Our society at that time was far from perfect; a view had gained widespread acceptance that old 'nonproductive' people should not be allowed to be a burden on the State. It wasn't a big step from there to deciding that all citizens over a certain age should be drafted into the Impy gangs. That would have happened to me if I hadn't manage to disappear!"

"So old people never really went to retirement homes in the warmer parts of the Federation?" Kathleen said indignantly.

"You're supposed to think that but in fact the oldies only go to those places for long enough to make a vid saying how great everything is before they are given the Implant. The vid is then rehashed in the computer so that the family get what seems to be a different vidMail every year or so."

Kathleen was horrified by Jack's revelations. Her initial feeling of nausea blossomed into a ball of rage as she thought of her own parents shuffling about as semi-automatons.

"You said the Impys don't live for very long," she asked, her voice a little tight in her throat. "Why is that?"

"There is something about the human brain that the scientists haven't got an answer to. It seems that whenever the natural responses are blocked the brain tries to find a way round the block and in most cases it succeeds. Then the implanted person starts to be able to control their own actions again. That's why you see some of them moving in such a jerky fashion, their bodies are getting two different commands. The only way control can be kept is to increase the dosage of chemicals; this eventually overloads the brain and it dies altogether. As to how long, it varies from one individual to another; the older ones don't often last any more than five years."

At least Mum and Dad's suffering will have ended long ago, Kathleen tried to comfort herself. Sorrow and anger fought in her mind as she turned to the old man.

"Why did you.....the people allow these terrible things to happen?"

"The people never knew much of what was going on." Jack replied. "Those who did depended on the continuance of a massive bureaucracy for their future so they closed their eyes in return for security and fat pay packets." He held his hands up in admission. "We accepted too much of what we were told without question. As each new rule was brought in it seemed sensible and even caring; when it didn't work we were assured that minor modifications would solve the problem. We trusted the ones at the top, forgetting the way power can go to the heads of those who crave it. Everyone in Admin, even the lowest levels, know that if they obey orders they progress up the grades and hopefully achieve a post in CenCon itself. Plenty of credits, plenty of time for pleasure, sure of a lifelong 'productive' rating so no fear of being Implanted in old age."

"Doesn't that mean that it's hopeless to fight against the Federation?" David sounded despondent.

"I don't think so," Jack responded cautiously. "You have to remember that the Council cannot use massive military force to keep themselves in power like the other enforced Federations in history. World opinion has to be taken into account and it seems that there is widespread unease about the situation here. It is doubtful if Urfor would dare to use their weapons against a large scale popular revolt."

"Without wanting to sound nasty, why should we believe what you're telling us," David demanded.

"I expect you to have doubts," Jack gave them a weary smile. "When you get into the next Region you will be able to watch programmes and newscasts from outside Federation control." In response to their raised eyebrows he continued. "Yes, we have a few hidden receivers scattered about the country; in fact you can watch some recordings now if you like."

He slid a wall panel aside to reveal a small box with a curved screen.

"Before every house was linked to the VidCom network this is what we used to watch; it was called a Television set. We daren't put illegal recordings through the VidCom because it can be monitored by the authorities so we use this antique."

He loaded a recording into the machine and left them,

saying he was tired after doing so much talking. Kathleen and David watched the small screen, fascinated by the portrayal of a lifestyle so different from the drab and dreary existence they were used to.

"What do you think of it?" David asked when the screen had finally clicked into blankness.

"It's an awful lot to take in," Kathleen replied. "If it's all true then whatever it takes to achieve change will be worthwhile, even if the punishment for getting caught is to be made into an Impy. After all, we seem to run that risk merely by existing."

"I don't like to think of doing anything that would cause ordinary folk to get hurt." David seemed genuinely disturbed at the prospect.

"But people are getting hurt every day that this system of Government goes on. We can't afford to be squeamish about the methods, we've got little enough chance of succeeding as it is."

"I suppose you're right," he gave her a fleeting smile. "I've got this vision of standing at a barricade with a weapon and being told to shoot. I don't think I'd be very good at it."

"It doesn't sound as if that is what they are planning," she reassured him. "I don't suppose that people like us could get hold of weapons anyway. I imagine that whatever we're asked to do will be more undercover."

"I hope so." He was quiet for a moment then continued.

"It's strange that I never picked up anything about the retired folk being drafted into the Impy gangs, that came as a complete surprise to me; I'm sorry you had to find out in such a shocking manner."

"I'm feeling very angry about it," Kathleen said flatly. "You must be pretty upset too, knowing that the same must have happened to your parents."

David shook his head sadly.

"I never knew my parents Kathy. I was brought up in an Institution and all they would tell me was that I was an orphan. I don't know who my folk were or what they did or how they died. I've hunted through every file I can think of but of course this was long before CenCon came into being and I can only assume that if any information did exist it was lost somewhere along the line."

Kathleen was aghast, her own concerns fading immediately into insignificance.

"David, I'm so sorry. You must have felt so terribly alone when you were growing up."

"It helped that I wasn't the only one in that situation. There were around twenty of us in a group and we looked out for each other. I was quite close to a couple of them but once we started working we seemed to lose touch; any relationships I've had since then never lasted for long so you see Kathy," he paused to smile at her, "I'm just as much on my own as you are."

'At least I had a happy childhood,' Kathleen thought sympathetically. 'never to have had a family to love and care for you must be truly dreadful.'

She reached for his hand and held it comfortingly between her own. Rather to her surprise she heard herself say.

"We are both alone now aren't we, but we can try to make it better. I'll be your sister if you like and I would be happy for you to be my brother."

David studied her so seriously that she wondered if she had said something wrong; then, to her relief, his face broke into a smile of genuine pleasure.

"I would like that very much Kathy," he assured her.

They sat in silent reflection for a while, then David stretched his arms and yawned. "Let's go and see if it's all right to go outside. We might be able to help with the work."

Finding no-one in the kitchen they ventured cautiously into the yard to be greeted by a flurry of wind accompanied by a long rumble of thunder. The southern sky was a mass of dark cloud, pierced as they watched by a jagged streak of lightning.

"That's Barney's rain coming," Kathleen had to shout as a louder rumble interrupted her. "He's worth twenty of the 'casts'."

The Greens appeared in the gathering gloom and

rapidly ushered them back into the kitchen. Richard closed the door behind them.

"Just in time!" he announced thankfully.

"We were coming to see if we could be of any help," David offered.

"No, everything is done now. Luckily, we finished the harvest yesterday so all we had to do was to tidy up and put vulnerable things under cover. The forecast this morning said there might be thunderstorms in this area."

"Barney, who David told you about, knew it was coming three days ago," Kathleen tried not to sound smug.

"Did he indeed?" Richard raised his eyebrows. "Is he usually as accurate?"

Kathleen nodded. "I learned to rely on him anyway."

"I might have a word with George about him then. We don't want to waste a real countryman's skill if we can help it."

Kathleen felt a warm glow of satisfaction. If Barney was to be truly appreciated it would make her abandonment of him much easier to bear

Outside, the overladen clouds decided to empty themselves in a hurry. Hazel switched on the light to combat the increasing darkness and started fetching things out of the adjacent larder.

"Now, Miss, or is it Mrs Pierpoint, would you like to scrub these potatoes while I get a pan of mince organised."

"Miss I suppose," Kathleen replied. "Certainly not Mrs! But it sounds terribly formal, I'd prefer you to call me Kathy if you will."

"Kathy but not Kath!" David interposed with a smile, and she nodded in confirmatiomn.

"All right by me Kathy Pierpoint," Hazel agreed. "But I still want you to scrub these potatoes!"

Kathleen examined them as she tipped them into a bowl of water. She had previously known 'potatoes' only as a bag of uniform grey squares supplied by the NutriMart; these in front of her however,had traces of soil adhering to their reddish skins and they almost glowed as she rubbed at them with a small stiff brush.

"I didn't know potatoes looked like this," she said,

deciding to admit to her ignorance. "Where do you get them from?"

Hazel clucked disapprovingly, but it was Richard who answered.

"We grow them ourselves from our own seed. They are much better than what you'll be used to."

"I suppose you've only had that mass produced pap from the Mart," Hazel commiserated. "Well girl, I can tell you that you're in for a treat tonight.

"The Federation cares for the welfare of all its citizens," she went on, mockingly quoting the appropriate directive. "NutriMart will only supply foods that comply with the required nutritionary standards. Tosh!"

David came to the sink and watched what Kathleen was doing for a moment.

"I could help you with that if you like," he offered.

"A man that will offer to help in the kitchen!" Hazel glanced sharply at her husband then chuckled. "When I was young he would have been snapped up before he could blink!"

Kathleen concentrated on her work and Richard came to her rescue.

"Come and sit down, David. There are some things I would like to discuss with you and these women don't really want us to interfere!"

"George told me that you were some kind of computer expert," he continued once they were seated. "In what way exactly?"

David explained his role as a software designer, initially trying to keep it in layman's terms; he soon realised however, that Richard had considerable knowledge of the subject and was able to become more technical. As he finished he felt compelled to acknowledge his guilt for creating what had developed into a monster.

"You shouldn't be so hard on yourself," Richard suggested. "Lots of folk believed that the Federation would bring huge benefits to the population. Old Jack there worked in Admin for years before he realised what was happening. Now he is one of the strongest supporters of the Resistance movement."

"I wish I didn't feel so bad about it. Maybe if I can do something worthwhile to end it I will feel better." David gestured apologetically with his hands.

"You've still got that blocker over your persaCom!" Richard exclaimed. "I'm sorry, we should have taken it off as soon as you got here. We'll go down to the cellar now and get rid of it."

He led the way into the larder and lifted an almost imperceptible section of the floor, revealing a flight of stone steps. These took them down into a small room, the contents of which made David whistle with surprise. There were benches round the walls and these were loaded with tools and electronic equipment.

"Like it, do you?" Richard smiled. "Long ago this was a 'priest's hole' where they could hide from religious persecution. Now we have it totally screened from any kind of transmissions and use it to re-program persaComs and so on."

He quickly removed David's glove; after unlocking the persaCom with a key similar to those used by the Police he placed it into a small metal box and carefully closed the lid.

"Did you say that you can re-program them?" David asked.

"There are a couple of guys with us who can alter the transmitter section so that we can wear them again. As long as you have one on your wrist you will pass an inspection point; it's not very likely that there would be monitoring equipment capable of checking the output."

"I had no idea that you had that kind of expertise," David said admiringly.

"You might be surprised at what we can do. But that is what I wanted to discuss; can you really gain access to the core software?"

"I should be able to. I was a bit worried whether it would be possible without an official terminal but seeing what you have here makes me a lot more optimistic."

Excitement was apparent in Richard's voice as he said, "Would it be possible to break into a program with a short message occasionally? It would be a huge advantage if we could spread a little doubt in people's minds. And if we could do it how long would it take the Authorities to trace the source?"

"If I can get the necessary equipment it would be comparatively simple," David assured him. "But I might be able to do better than that. Most newscasts are recorded so that their content can be checked before they are transmitted, just in case some deviant manages to work his way into the Information section. It would be possible to delete sections and replace them with our own material so that it would appear to be part of the official broadcast. Because I would be operating through the core of the system, any attempt to trace the intrusion would lead back there and come up against the barriers I have installed."

"If what you say is true then I think that all my birthdays have come at once," Richard laughed. "It seems that we must make arrangements for you to meet some of our group as soon as we can. In the meantime, lets see if the girls have got dinner ready."

Thunder still rumbled outside as they closed the trapdoor behind them. The kitchen seemed more cosy than before with the warm glow of lamplight successfully overcoming the challenge of all but the brightest of lightning flashes. Kathleen was putting plates and cutlery on the table while Hazel added the finishing touches to her cooking. Both of them glanced an inquiry as the two men entered.

"That smells good," Richard exclaimed heartily. "Are we having a celebration meal to welcome our new members?"

"Mince and potatoes is not what I would call a celebration meal," Hazel retorted with a sniff. "And you needn't think soft soaping will get you men out of doing the washing-up! Now, call Jack for his supper will you."

Kathleen felt a sense of unreality as they sat round the table. The surface normality of five people enjoying a meal in comfort, while the grumbling storm outside subsided into occasional petulant muttering, could not obscure the fact that here were two fugitives from an oppressive regime being given shelter; shelter that, if discovered, would bring the direst punishment to their benefactors. She tried to acknowledge the gratitude she felt along with trepidation about the risks to their hosts but her words were instantly dismissed.

"We happen to consider that what we are doing is worthwhile," Richard assured her. "And at our age we know exactly what our future will be if CenCon stays in control so it's not really a difficult decision."

"You seem to believe that there is at least a possibility of striking a serious blow against the Federation?" David asked. "That means that you have some kind of plan made, a plan that you think would have a greater chance of success with the use of my knowledge. Do you trust us enough yet to tell us about it?"

Richard looked across the table at Jack before spreading his hands and smiling disarmingly. "It's not a matter of trust David. George and Nellie trusted you, otherwise you wouldn't be here. Hazel and I totally accept the truth of your story, you are far from the first to be crucified by this corrupt Administration. But there are quite a few people involved and we would like you to meet them, form your own opinion of the group before you or we commit ourselves to any specific action. We are going to arrange a sort of conference in a few days so until then I would ask you to be patient."

"Fair enough," David agreed, looking at Kathleen for confirmation. "We are in your hands after all, and happy to be so; I want you to know that we are both willing to help in any way you want."

"Point taken," Richard nodded.

"That's not a subject for mealtimes," Hazel chipped in firmly. "Now Kathy, how do you like the taste of real potatoes?"

"They're wonderful," Kathleen enthused. "They are so dry and crumbly and full of flavour compared with that soggy 'mass produced pap'."

For the rest of the meal they talked generally about farming and crops. When they had finished, Jack, who had said very little, returned to his room and Richard, in response to an unspoken command from his wife, gave a theatrical sigh and offered David the choice of washing or drying. Leaving the two of them busy at the sink, Hazel gathered sheets from an old-fashioned airing rack and took Kathleen up two flights of stairs to a little attic room.

"David can go in the other room up here. You'll be fine and quiet if you want to have a lie in in the morning" she promised while they made up the bed. "We don't stay up late ourselves but you two can watch the vids for a while if you like."

"I don't want to lie in," Kathleen protested. "If there is work to do surely we can give you a hand."

"There won't be much to do even if there's no more rain tonight. Just you come down when you fancy some breakfast, that'll be time enough."

Kathleen had no desire to watch vids but she was glad to be able to have a private word with David after the older couple had retired.

"Did you manage to find out anything when you went to take that glove-thing off?" she inquired. "You must know more than I do about what we're getting ourselves into."

David nodded. "I suppose I have learned a little but, understandably I suppose, they probably don't fully trust us yet; I can make a guess at some things, but it will only be a guess."

He told her about the equipment in the cellar and the probing with regard to patching messages into the official broadcasts.

"I wouldn't be surprised if there is a scheme for a big event that could provide the focus for a popular uprising so long as enough people were aware of the reason behind it. That could explain why he was so pleased with what I told him."

"But wouldn't that just be like the 'troubles' in the past? Wouldn't the Police and Urfor just stamp down on it?"

"You would have thought so. But remember what Jack told us, that world opinion has to be considered. Perhaps we'll get a chance to talk to him some more before we are on the move again."

Kathleen groaned. "My bottom says it's not ready for another ForTrak journey yet."

"Mine neither," David agreed. "But you must have felt it far worse than I did. How are your bruises coming along anyway, are you starting to feel a bit better?"

"I'm fine so long as I don't think about them," she assured him.

"That's good." He stretched and announced through a yawn. "I don't know about you but I'm ready for bed."

Kathleen could hear rain drumming on the roof above her as she snuggled between the fresh sheets; it must have acted as a lullaby for she only heard it for a little while.

CHAPTER SIX

The attic-room window was close enough for Kathleen to be able to part the curtains without getting out of bed. Habitually she rose as soon as she woke but this morning there was little encouragement in the lowering sky, the blustery wind and the drift of fine drizzle washing continually against the glass. She lay luxuriating in the unaccustomed leisure for a little while but eventually a feeling of guilt forced her to push back the covers.

Dressing hastily, she stopped in the bathroom long enough to splash some water on her face; after knocking on David's door until he called an acknowledgement she hurried down to the kitchen where she found Hazel preparing breakfast while Richard divested himself of his wet-weather gear.

"Up already?" Hazel inquired. "I thought you would have been glad to have a lie in, especially as it's such a miserable morning."

"I've been awake for a while," Kathleen assured her. "I'm used to doing the early chores so this is quite late for me really. I thought that perhaps there was something I could do to help."

"We won't be doing much work outside today," Richard commented. "That small rain creeps through everything in a few minutes, and there's nothing urgent enough to be worth getting soaked for anyway. We'll have an easy day and maybe make some plans for when and how you're going to move on."

"Eggs and bacon okay for you Kathy?" asked Hazel, lifting the frying pan lid to release a tantalising aroma into the kitchen.

"Eggs and bacon will be fine," Kathleen replied, attempting without much success to keep the eagerness out of her voice. "Is it a feast day every day here, or are you just trying to spoil us?"

Hazel clucked dismissively. "What's special about a proper farm breakfast? Surely you had the same where you come from."

"We managed to keep a few hens," Kathleen admitted. "But I can't remember when I last had a taste of bacon, I thought meat from pigs was banned because some people might be offended. I know you can't get any from the NutriMart."

Hazel shook her head scornfully and started to make a sarcastic retort but bit it off as David came into the room.

"Another one that doesn't want to rest! Is there something wrong with the beds in this house?"

"Nothing wrong with the bed," David said regretfully as he covered a yawn with his hand. "I would have stayed in it quite happily if some overactive person hadn't decided to bang on the door." He gave a mock glare at Kathleen who felt obliged to justify herself.

"Surely you don't want to sleep when there are all sorts of adventures waiting for us?" she reproved him gaily. "And you wouldn't want to miss the food that you're smelling would you?"

"I'll forgive you because of breakfast then," he admitted with a smile.

Kathleen found herself enjoying the leisurely atmosphere as they sat at the table; 'not surprising really,' she thought, 'the last couple of days have been pretty hectic.' She was dawdling over a second cup of tea before Richard mentioned any future action.

"I think it would be best if we get the two of you moved into an active group as soon as possible. It's pretty important that David gets to meet our electronics people so that we can discover how best to use his knowledge and it will also be safer for you to be out of the way as soon as possible. If you are happy with that I will make arrangements for you to leave tomorrow morning."

David raised his eyebrows at Kathleen and, after receiving her nod of assent, voiced his agreement.

"Whatever you decide is okay with us. As I said before, we are totally in your hands."

"How will we be travelling?" Kathleen asked, dreading the expected answer.

"By ForTrak over the fields I'm afraid," Richard smiled

apologetically at Kathleen's involuntary groan. "I would like to tell you that we could use the roads, but it would be too risky at the moment. There is always a chance of being stopped and you must remember that neither of you have a persaCom at the moment. That can be remedied at your destination, then you will have a lot more freedom to move about."

"I'll take you half way," he continued. "and someone will meet us to take you the rest of the distance. It will mean a full day unfortunately, but we'll try to find something to make it a bit less bone shaking for you. In the meantime I suggest that you take it easy; you will be comfortable enough in Jack's sitting room and you'll be out of sight if there are any visitors."

"He won't mind us being in there?" Kathleen asked.

"Not at all, he'll be glad of the company. He loves talking about the old days and when he gets tired he'll go off to his bedroom for a nap." Hazel assured them.

There was no sign of the old man in the concealed room; Kathleen was quite glad because it gave her a chance to ask David about a problem that had begun to bother her.

"It sounds as though this Resistance are eager to get you involved, that you can be a real help to them because of your expertise," she started. "But I am worried as to how I can be of any use; I want to be able to play a part in whatever scheme is being planned but I'm basically an outdoor person and really not good at anything apart from growing barley."

"Until we can learn more about what is going on I can't offer you any reassurance," David replied. "I have to admit that it is unlikely that barley could be a tool to use against the Federation but anything is possible. How well do you understand day-to-day use of the VidCom?"

"I haven't spent a lot of time at it, but I suppose that I understand the procedures well enough. I've never had any problem using it for farm business."

"Would you like to learn more about it? There is likely to be a lot of tedious work if we are to be successful and I could probably teach you enough for you to be of real assistance. It would be a bit of a challenge to keep your mind occupied and maybe stop you from worrying. I know it's not exactly the outdoor work that you are used to but it might not be too bad seeing that we will be moving into the winter months."

"I'll certainly give it a try," Kathleen decided. "When will you be able to start my lessons?"

"The first thing is to make an access terminal and link it so that it can't be traced, and that won't be until we see what facilities the Resistance have available. They can obviously alter the standard persaCom so I am reasonably hopeful......" he tailed off as Jack came into the room.

"Good morning to you," the old man greeted them.

"Good morning," they chorused politely in return.

"We missed you at breakfast," David added.

"I had something before you were up. I usually go outside for a bit of exercise before it gets light and then go back to bed for a while. I don't exist remember!"

"I suppose we don't either," David said ruefully. "It's going to be quite hard to adjust to having to hide all the time."

"You won't have to do that, it's only because of my age that I daren't be seen by strangers; once you have got your modified persaComs you will pass anything except for a major security check."

"I suppose a lot depends on how seriously the Authorities view our disappearance," David said thoughtfully.

"Yes, I do have some concern in that direction. I have suggested to Richard that we lay a false trail to indicate that you tried to escape by sea and perished in the attempt."

"How would you manage to do that?" David was astonished.

"It's not too difficult. People have got away in the past by using small inflatable boats; the dangerous part is finding a safe route through the energy stations in the dark, so if a wrecked dinghy were found by the patrols it could well be assumed that you were both drowned."

"It might look like an obvious plant," David demurred.

"Our big advantage is that most of those in Authority are basically lazy. So long as an investigation is carried out and all the right boxes are ticked it will end up in limbo with millions of other files."

"You seem to have thought of everything," David said admiringly.

"We do try." The old man sighed wearily. "Sometimes I get depressed and think that we are fooling ourselves with our brave ideas; your coming along has given me the first real encouragement for quite a while."

"I hope that we can live up to your expectations then." David took care to include Kathleen in his remark.

They spent the rest of the day in sporadic conversation with Jack, interspersed with watching 'tapes' of non-Federation transmissions. Kathleen grew to understand a lot more of the complex system of regulations and controls which governed their lives but as the afternoon drew on she started to chafe at the enforced inactivity.

"Don't tell me that you are eager to get into the ForTrak again," David teased when she voiced her discontent.

"Not really," she admitted. "But I would love to go outside to get some fresh air."

"Let's see what the others are doing," suggested Jack. After checking that the coast was clear, he led the way into the kitchen.

They found Richard sitting at the table totting up figures scribbled on a scrap of paper.

"Just making sure that everything checks out before I load it into the VidCom," he explained. "The last thing we need at the moment is a visit to investigate any anomaly."

"These two youngsters have had enough of my company and want to get a breath of fresh air," Jack told him. "Will it be safe enough outside now?"

"It's too misty for the choppers to be out, so if you keep to the back fields it should be all right. The road patrols don't like getting wet so even if there is one in the area they won't want to see anything that would mean getting out of their vehicles. There are waterproofs at the back door, help yourselves."

Hazel's gumboots were too small for Kathleen so she had to settle for a spare pair of Richard's that were on the large side. However she was happy to clump along in the sodden fields with her coat hood pushed back, letting the fine rain tickle at her face and creep into her hair. The fact that it would soon be trickling down her neck didn't perturb her at all.

It was quite different from 'The Beeches' she decided. She had noticed yesterday that the scenery gradually changed as they travelled north but actually treading the ground gave a greater impact; the big almost lazy trees she was used to had changed to smaller and rather more rugged varieties; the land itself undulated incessantly with busy little streams, leftovers from the night's downpour, hurrying through the hollows; the fields of rough stubble which spoke of a recently gathered harvest were interspersed with uncultivated patches where lank grass and weeds gathered around the occasional outcrop of rock. It was different, she acknowledged, but she was content to be walking in the open air with at least the illusion of freedom.

"It's lovely, isn't it," she smiled at David who was plodding silently beside her.

"That's not precisely the way I would describe it," he grumbled. "I'm getting wet through, my feet are squelching in these boots, it's so slippery I have to watch every step or I'll end up on my arse in the mud! No, lovely isn't the first word that springs to my mind."

"You didn't have to come with me," she retorted.

"I would only sit and worry that you'd be snatched by a patrol or something. Not that I could do much to prevent it but I feel responsible for your situation so, in spite of being wet and miserable I prefer to be with you instead of sitting indoors fretting."

"Charming!" she sniffed. "But seriously, do you have to be so concerned about me now? You must admit that this is heaven compared with my fate if you hadn't got me out of that cell."

"If I had acted differently in the past you might never have been in a cell," he replied sadly.

"Oh David, stop being silly! You can't take the blame on your shoulders for all the evils in the world; I'm going to start kicking you if you keep going on like that."

"I'll try not to mention it in future then," he promised with a faint smile.

"You'd better," Kathleen warned him. "Now, since you're not enjoying our walk we'll head back to the house; we could even try running if you are in a hurry to get out of the rain!"

"Walking will be quite all right," he assured her hastily.

"Kathy, I've put some of those old things of mine into a bag and left it in your room," Hazel announced as they stripped off their coats at the door. "You look wet enough to need a change so you might as well use them now."

"I think I will," Kathleen agreed, realising that the trickles down her neck had permeated most of her clothing. "How about you David, have you got something else to wear?"

"Yes, I brought a change of clothes in my bag," he assured her.

Once in her room, Kathleen couldn't resist inspecting the garments which Hazel had left for her; on the top were sensible shirts and trousers along with chunky sweaters but underneath them she found smart slacks and a couple of dressy skirts with matching blouses. She shook her head ruefully as she lifted them; she had never had the occasion to wear pretty clothes and didn't think it likely that she ever would. As she went to put them back she saw, at the very bottom of the bag, the green dress which she had admired the previous day.

'Strange woman', she smiled to herself. 'Whenever does she think a farm worker like me would have the opportunity to dress herself up like a vid artiste?' It would be churlish to refuse the gift however so she carefully replaced everything before going downstairs.

"I believe it's going to be dry tomorrow," Richard announced after the evening meal. "So your journey should be a bit more pleasant."

"What time are we leaving?" David enquired.

"As soon as it's light. I'll be taking you all the way to the coast and Jenny will pick you up there for the second leg of your journey."

The coast! Kathleen could not imagine what it would be like where the land came to an end and was replaced by ocean. She was certainly going to broaden her experience more than she would have in her previous life!

"I've found an old cot mattress that you can use to sit on," Hazel informed them. "And I'll make you up a bit of snack to eat on the way, a picnic lunch we used to call it when we could go for a day's outing without having to fill in a form to explain ourselves!"

"That sounds like luxury to me," David laughed. "Perhaps this time I won't have to listen to someone grumbling beside me all the way!"

Kathleen pulled a face at him but couldn't think of a suitable riposte.

It was still dark when Richard roused them though, by the time they had eaten a hasty breakfast, the eastern sky was showing enough light for their journey to commence. There was a sharp autumnal feel to the morning and a brisk breeze tugged at the topmost branches of the trees, freeing an occasional leaf which swirled and tumbled its way to the ground. Kathleen and David huddled together on the mattress, thankful that the plastic canopy provided some shelter from the chill air.

Richard drove cautiously at first until a watery sun, finding a gap between horizon and the patterned layers of cloud above, gave enough light for him to properly see the ground ahead. As on their trip with George they followed tracks bordering the fields and nosed through rough gaps in hedges which gradually gave way to more or less crumbling stone walls. Occasionally, when their transport crested a rise Kathleen spotted on her right a line of high peaks forming a distant horizon and wondered fleetingly about their eventual destination. Well, she would know soon enough she told herself, and it would certainly be different from anything she was accustomed to.

No longer did the terrain run unchanged with only hedges to break it into separate fields; here and there the land now rose at times to hills and ridges, the majority of which were scarred with ugly concrete pillars in varying stages of dilapidation.

"They're the remains of the old wind farms," David told her. "At the beginning of the century it was thought they would provide cheap power for everyone but on land they turned out to be hopelessly uneconomic. Then bio-fuels became the new craze so when these things broke down they weren't repaired; the mechanical parts were taken for re-cycling and the rest abandoned, one more monument to grandiose ideas."

It so happened that the ForTrak was heading towards a ridge boasting a cluster of half-a-dozen of the pillars and as Richard drove past Kathleen got a closer look, able to note the crumbling concrete, the smashed access door revealing a dark hole into the interior.

"They don't exactly enhance the landscape, do they?" Kathleen commented with a shudder. For some reason the dark maw evoked memories of a childhood storybook full of incarceration and torture by witches.

"Trees would be prettier I suppose," David conceded with cheerful misunderstanding.

"Not too long now," Richard interrupted them. "From the top of that hill ahead we should be able to see the sea!"

A short while later, he halted the ForTrak on the crest and all three of them jumped down, glad of the chance to stretch their legs. Kathleen forgot the ache from her bruises as she gazed in fascination at the view.

The land fell away gradually from where she stood, before levelling off into a plain which ran unbroken except for a few small lumpy hills until it reached what must be the distant shoreline. Beyond that, if she strained her eyes she could see a line of white surf and beyond that again a featureless expanse of grey that could only be the sea itself. Where it met the similarily coloured sky she could not be sure but after a while she thought she could make out a line of regular structures where the horizon might be.

"Is there a line of ships out there?" she asked Richard.

"Those are the energy farms you're seeing. They stand all round the coast now, generating electricity from wind, wave and tide power and feeding it into the main Federation network."

"What happens when there is no wind and the sea is calm?"

"Power cuts! There are generators that run on Ectol but they are only used sparingly because of the limited supplies."

Kathleen knew about power cuts of course. It was common enough for the VidCom to have a list of times in each area when electricity would be available and it was second nature to plan the work accordingly but she had never realised that the fluctuations were subject to the vagaries of the weather.

"We'd better be getting along," Richard told them. "It's further than it looks and we want to be on time ....." His voice tailed off and then he muttered an imprecation under his breath.

"What's wrong?" David's query was sharp, urgent.

"There are helicopters spread out in a search pattern." Richard's voice was quiet but full of anxiety. "Look, you can just see them as they move against the lighter coloured fields."

Kathleen strained her eyes, her chest tight and her breath catching in her throat. 'Don't let it end here,' she prayed silently. 'Please, please don't let us be caught and dragged off to such a terrible fate!"

Noticing her look of anguish, David put a comforting arm round her shoulders.

"They haven't got us yet, Kathy. I'm sure Richard will have a plan."

"There is only one option I'm afraid," their companion told them grimly. "You will have to hide and I will have to go back the way we've come as fast as I can. If they are being thorough they will land and check on the ForTrak and if I'm too far from home they will ask awkward questions."

"Will you be able to come back when they've gone," Kathleen asked, hoping for the comfort of an affirmative answer.

"I'll try, but I can't promise. If they seem in any way

suspicious I will have to be careful of my movements for a few days. The best thing for you is to hide inside one of the old windmills until you are sure that they have moved on. If I don't get back this afternoon you must try to get to the coast yourselves. Head for the gap between those two little hills, then go on all the way to the shore; look out for Jenny in a souped-up ForTrak; she's blonde and cheeky and she's also my daughter!"

Less than five minutes later, Kathleen and David were left beside one of the decaying structures and the ForTrak was rapidly disappearing into the distance.

"Well," David commented as the last rumbles of its engine finally faded into slence. "I suppose we'd better explore.

Lifting their two bags and a rolled-up plastic sheet which Richard had given them to use as a thermal shield he turned towards the black and uninviting doorway; after carefully examining the condition of the overhead lintel, he gave her a wry smile.

"I don't think it's going to fall down for a day or two. Do you want to go first with the light or would you rather I did?"

If it hadn't been for the searching helicopters and the consequent prospect of spending the rest of her life as an Impy Kathleen would have refused to consider entering the old windmill. But she had to go in! She couldn't allow David to perceive her as a frightened wimp!

An irrational but nonetheless pervasive dread of what might lurk in the black depths spread like a black cloud in the instinctive part of her mind as she cranked the handle of the wind-up torch Richard had given them. Forcing her legs to move, she stepped warily into a blackness full of the stench of stale lubricants and ancient rusting machinery which grew in intensity the deeper they went. With a sharp turn in the passage they lost the last trace of daylight and a moment later she stumbled, put out a hand to save herself and dropped the torch. It apparently fell on to something soft as there was no clatter but of course the bulb dimmed, reddened and went out as the generator stopped turning.

Anger at her own clumsiness momentarily replaced her fear and she crouched down to search. It couldn't be far away; desperately she groped among the soft and rubbery things which covered the floor.

Her knuckles bumped against something hard and she seized the torch triumphantly, winding it into life before getting to her feet. As the light spread though, she almost cried out in disgust; only inches from her face, the things she had been feeling were revealed as pale, slimy almost phallic growths rooted in whatever obscene mess covered the ancient concrete. Some of them still wobbled vaguely from her touch and even as she recoiled the top of one of them split open to discharge puffs of yellow unhealthy looking spores. Swallowing against an attack of nausea, she stood up in a hurry and allowed her instincts to speak for her.

"I don't want to hide in here David," she said as calmly as she could. "It feels all wrong to be trapped among all this rotten stench. I'd sooner take a chance of finding somewhere outside."

The reflected torchlight was sufficient to see the surprise on David's face. He opened his mouth to protest but she forestalled him by immediately heading back towards the entrance; unless he wanted to be left in the dark he would have to follow her!

Outside in the daylight, a few deep breaths soon restored her to normality. Making a quick survey of their immediate surroundings, she noted a hillock topped by a craggy looking clump of grey weathered rocks.

"Let's try up there," she suggested, before he had a chance to speak.

"I don't see why," he grumbled. "It may not be very nice in there but its got to be a lot safer than out in the open!"

"It feels wrong," she repeated. "At least let's take a look, we'll hear them in time to hide."

"If you say so." His response lacked enthusiasm but it was agreement of a sort! Taking her bag from him, she hurried off before he had time to change his mind.

There were various nooks and crannies among the

rocks, though most of them were uncomfortably open to surveillance from above. Kathleen, had reached the stage of trying to persuade herself that her fears of the old ruins were illogical when she tripped, caught at the rock to steady herself and discovered a crevice below an overhanging ledge. It was big enough for them both to crawl into and as a bonus the floor was of fairly dry sand. Hopefully she called to David and he came to inspect her find.

"It's no more than a rabbit burrow!" His protest died away as the first sound of rotor blades intruded into the afternoon silence. Urgently, just like rabbits, they scuttled under the rock, wriggling as far back as they possibly could before they arranged the plastic cover to block most of the entrance.

Kathleen could move just enough to be able to press her hands over her ears, shutting out a small part of the noise as the squad of machines came nearer and nearer to their refuge. Her lips moved as she begged any God who might be listening to allow them to remain undiscovered, to avoid capture and the subsequent appalling but inevitable fate.

One of the helicopters must have crossed directly above them for the sheltering rock vibrated briefly in harmony with the clattering blades. Sandy dust fell over them and she wondered fleetingly if their protection was stable, or might it collapse and crush them into oblivion? Dismissing the fear, she decided that it would be preferable to being an Impy anyway!

Gradually she became aware that above the noise which swelled and faded continually there was an intermittent detonation. Puzzled, she lifted the cover a fraction and peered under it; by moving slightly she was able to spot one of the machines, slowing its passage to hover momentarily alongside one of the ruins. A shiver of fear ran through her body as she saw the trail of a missile flash across into the entrance, followed by a small puff of smoke and the detonation she had heard earlier. Knowing that David was also watching she turned towards him with an unvoiced question.

"Gas grenade!" he mouthed against her ear, making the meaning clear by grasping his throat and pretending to choke. His eyes were dark with the horror that could so easily have been their fate; when he found and squeezed her hand it was an apology for his previous protests. Kathleen returned the pressure in silent acknowledgement.

They couldn't see the whole area but they had to assume that every one of the old windmills was treated in similar fashion. It seemed to take forever but as the searchers moved gradually away from the immediate area their fear of discovery ebbed and they became inevitably more aware of the discomfort of their position. When eventually the last trace of sound had faded into the distance they dropped the cover and moved out into the open, gratefully stretching and massaging their cramped muscles.

"I think you just saved our lives!" David's admission was accompanied by a rueful smile. "Whatever they were firing into the windmills probably wasn't particularly healthy!"

"Did they mean to kill us, do you think? Mightn't the gas just have been to knock us out?

David shook his head slowly.

"In that case they would have landed and checked each one out afterwards. No, Kathy, if it is us they're looking for I'm afraid they've decided that dead is the quickest and surest way to stop us causing any trouble!"

"Why are they searching here?" she wondered. "Do you think they have trailed us somehow?"

"I don't think so. Probably there are squads out covering all the likely routes we might have taken, or it may be that they have decided to work inland from the coast."

"There's a fair chance that we will be OK for a while then." Kathleen smiled as she felt a measure of encouragment.

"Depends what you mean by OK." David didn't smile in return. "The afternoon is well on and there is no sign of Richard coming back. I do hope that he's all right."

He surveyed the empty landscape disconsolately. "I

would rather give myself up than have him come to harm on my account," he muttered, almost to himself.

"Our account," Kathleen corrected him firmly. "And if he is okay, surrendering would lead the police straight to him, so we have to do what he told us and stay put!"

David gave her a fleeting smile.

"You're right, as usual. But even if he arrives now, there is no way he can get us to our destination tonight. The ForTrak lights would draw attention to something unusual going on so it looks as though we will have to spend the night out here!"

Kathleen curled up her hand to make a peephole and painstakingly scanned in the direction which Richard had disappeared but her enhanced vision revealed no movement of any kind. With a sigh, she accepted the logic of David's assessment.

"I suppose we'd be safer under cover," David reasoned aloud. "It's always possible that they might come back with searchlights and infra-red in the hope of finding us in the open."

"It would be warmer," Kathleen admitted with a slight shiver. An autumnal chill accompanied the disappearance of the sun and her sweat-dampened clothes accentuated the fact.

"It would be warmer," she repeated. "But I don't think I want to go back into one of the wind things. Even with the sun shining outside it gave me the shivers!"

"That gas might still be lingering in them." David's ready concurrence made her heart leap with relief. "I suppose we could go back under that ledge," he continued. "It was pretty dry in there and we could use Richard's sheet to shelter us from the wind."

Gratefully, she agreed with his suggestion. After making a frugal meal from the 'picnic' Hazel had provided, they made themselves as comfortable as they could while sufficient light remained to see what they were doing. A couple of sticks broken off a bush enabled them to prop up the cover yet leave a small gap for air circulation. Kathleen wriggled unsuccessfully in an attempt to find a softer position for her shoulders; it was going to be a long night!

Less than half-an-hour had passed before she started to shiver, slightly at first, then with increasing tempo as the enervating chill seeped irresistibly into her bones.

"Are you cold Kathy." David's solicitous enquiry could not be denied.

"I'm f...freezing," she admitted, unable to control the chatter of her teeth, and he rolled onto his side to face her.

"Please don't take this the wrong way, but we would be better cuddling together." He made the suggestion cautiously, still fearful that after her recent experiences she would be reluctant to endure any kind of close contact with a man.

"If I can't trust even you David, there's a very lonely future ahead of me," she declared firmly, though her body tensed involuntarily as he gently drew her against him. Gradually, their combined warmth drove the shivers away, but unfortunately she became aware of a different discomfort caused by lying on her side.

"I could do with a pillow," she grumbled, lifting her head off the hard earth to ease the muscles in her neck. She had her bag of clothes of course but it was of rigid plastic, too hard to be of any use

"Try this." David groped behind him to find the small kit-bag he had brought. "It's pretty soft, it should be reasonably comfortable."

"That's better." She let her head rest on it and sighed with satisfaction. Then, struck by a pang of conscience, raised herself off it again.

"What about you?" she demanded. "It's not big enough for both of us."

"I'm fine," he insisted, but she knew he was lying.

"I can't use it while you have nothing!" She was adamant, and she felt him shake his head in reproof.

"Try this then." Placing his arm so that her head could rest on the pad of his biceps, he tucked the makeshift pillow under his own head. "Is that better?"

"Much!" she agreed, snuggling against him to regain the warmth which had dissipated as soon as they moved. Grateful for the security of his other arm over her, she dared to place her own around him.

Drowsiness crept over her as she relaxed in as much comfort as the hard earth and her residual bruising would allow. Her trousers, damp in patches with slime from the fungus, were clinging unpleasantly to her calves and she wished briefly, that she could take them off and feel freshly laundered cotton sheets against her skin.

It was still dark when she awoke, though the shred of sky showing above the cover was not totally black. David was breathing steadily, she couldn't tell whether or not he was sleeping, so she lay without moving, watching the growing light which heralded dawn proper. She must have dozed off again, suddenly it was full daylight and she could see David's eyes fixed on her face.

"Good morning! Did you sleep well?" His greeting came with an amused look.

"I must have done," she allowed, stretching as much as she could in the confined space. "What about you?"

"I'm fine thank you." He didn't answer her question directly, just smiled at her as he pushed the cover to one side. "Do you want to get up and have some breakfast?"

Kathleen glanced out of the opening; the sun was not yet over the horizon and the night-time chill would still be in evidence.

"Not yet. I'm lovely and warm and I don't want to go out and get cold again; so long as you don't mind?"

David gave her a brief nod to convey his agreement and they lay for another half-an-hour before dragging cramped muscles outside and exercising them into a semblance of normality. The remains of yesterday's sandwiches weren't so palatable now, but it was that or nothing; Kathleen thought longingly of Hazel's version of breakfast!

Their hunger temporarily assuaged, they turned their attention to the hoped-for arrival of Richard. David copied her trick, making a telescope with his hand and painstakingly scanning every inch of the way they had come. Nothing moved however, and a deep feeling of unease settled on them as the morning wore on interminably.

"I think we have to face up to the fact that he's not coming." David finally voiced their unspoken fears. "He said to make for the coast ourselves if that happened."

Kathleen had to agree, though her heart sank at the prospect. If Richard's movements had brought him under any kind of suspicion there was no way he could take the risk of coming after them again. They were on their own it seemed, with only a tenuous chance of making contact with whatever Resistance organisation existed.

"Yes, I think we should make a start." She tried to make her voice as cheerful as possible. "It didn't look too far from a ForTrak but legs are an awful lot slower!"

"Will you be allright?" David didn't have to explain the reason for his query; she was still reminded of her beating by Stephen Lock whenever she moved.

"I'll be fine," she assured him with her fingers firmly crossed. Picking up her bag, she led the way to the top of the hill from where they had first seen the searching helicopters.

"Between those two hills was what he said wasn't it?" She made a line with her arm to indicate the direction. "Then we're to make straight for the shore."

"Downhill all the way!" David commented hopefully. "Perhaps it'll be easy enough."

Kathleen, knowing rather more about the land than her companion was well aware that what looked like even terrain from a distance could prove rough and arduous going at close quarters. She said nothing however and smiled in response.

"Shall we go?" she invited.

Legs are indeed much slower than wheels on a roadway but on rough ground it was almost worse. A ditch or a bank that the ForTrak's large soft tyres would bounce over without affecting its speed were still big enough for legs to have to clamber down and then back up again. Their progress was disappointingly slow but once Kathleen's injuries had settled into a dull ache they got no worse and for this at least she was thankful. Most of the time she led the way and David plodded along a few paces behind her.

Neither of them had any means of telling the time but they could make a fairly good guess as to when midday had passed. During the afternoon however, the cloud cover thickened, lowered to touch the hilltops then relentlessly descended until they were occasionally enveloped in a light mist.

Beads of moisture gathered on their clothes but Kathleen was more concerned about the reduction in visibility. It was becoming difficult to be sure they were going in the right direction. It was only when she turned to voice her fears to David that she realised how thoroughly miserable he looked.

"I know you don't like the rain David," she tried to be cheerful. "But it's not really wet yet!"

"Yet!" he responded bleakly. "But we will get wet and we will get cold to-night; we don't know where we're going and we won't know if we ever get there; we won't die of thirst but we could well starve if we don't die of exposure. I'm afraid I'm not making much of a start at this Resistance business and I'm letting you down too!"

Kathleen cursed under her breath; he was blaming himself for everything again, descending too easily into the depression that seemed to afflict him. She had to lift his spirits but how could she do that.

"Don't be silly," she scolded. "Its not your fault and remember we are supposed to be in this together. People can go a long time without food you know so long as they have water and we're not going to get wet and cold just yet so cheer up will you!"

"I'm sorry, but it all seems so hopeless." He shook himself vigorously in an attempt to dispel his mental gloom. "And we are going to get wet unless you have a tent tucked away in that bag of yours!"

"No tent, but something nearly as good!" She started to retrace her steps to where, a couple of minutes earlier, she had caught a glimpse of something through the mist. There it was, an obviously abandoned ForTrak; both of its back wheels were missing so that it sat with its nose in the air but the canopy, though scratched and battered was still in one piece.

"You want lodgings? You've got lodgings!" Kathleen waved casually as though she had created it herself. "And as it is going to rain soon we might as well stop now before we get wet. It's getting hard to see where we're heading anyway."

David bowed his head in acknowledgement.

"Does it have central heating?" At least the question now came with the ghost of a smile.

"No, but we have! That thermal sheet that you've been lugging along, if we put it round the two of us like a cocoon we should be as warm as toast. Mind you, we'd better go behind a hedge and do what we have to first 'cos it won't be easy to get out once we're wrapped up!"

The tilted-back bench of the ForTrak was actually not too uncomfortable. Half-sitting, half-lying, huddled as close as possible inside the plastic sheet, they were surprisingly warm. Neither of them could move very much which made for some discomfort but as darkness fell and rain started pattering on the ancient plastic canopy, Kathleen knew that their situation could have been very much worse.

CHAPTER SEVEN

Both of them managed some sleep, but never for longer than half-an-hour at any one time. At last Kathleen was able to watch the sky lighten and as soon as she could discern details on the ground she started to wriggle herself out of their cocoon. Gritty eyed and with her belly sending plaintive messages of hunger, she found enough of a trickle in a ditch to not only have a drink but also to splash water over her dirty and crumpled-feeling face.

The rain had stopped soon after midnight and the air looked washed and clean; already she could make out the two hills which they were aiming for, surely no more than a couple of hours away she told herself. David, who had been folding up their protective covering, made his own ablutions before coming to stand beside her.

"The bed was acceptable under the circumstances," he allowed solemnly. "But next time could you arrange for there to be a bit of breakfast as well?"

"I hope there isn't going to be a next time," she retorted. "We should be at those hills in a couple of hours and I reckon that will be at least two thirds of the distance to the coast."

"And when we get there?" He shook his head doubtfully. "Kathy, I know you think I'm a pessimist but surely we have to be realistic. It's likely that the searches will have scared off any Resistance people who might have been looking for us; they would hardly risk their whole organisation for a couple of runaways. And even if we do see someone how can we dare to approach them when they could just as easily be spies for the Authorities?"

"I know all that," she agreed. "But I'm not going to think about it until I have to and you should do the same. What alternative do we have anyway? Look for a Police Station and offer our brains for an electronic supplement!"

To her great relief his face broke into a smile.

"You're right of course. It's a good thing you're here to

tell me not to be an ass. Lead the way Captain, and I'll follow."

When the sun appeared over the horizon behind them they could feel the warmth on their backs but after an hour or so it vanished behind rapidly-moving clouds with only an occasional glimpse to cheer them on their way. It took them nearer three hours than two to reach the hills but after that the going became easier and they made better progress. As they neared the coast a brisk breeze encouraged them not to dawdle; though it wasn't exactly cold the lack of food and sleep left them sensitive to the least chill in the air.

An hour after midday found them carefully negotiating the rough ledges of a flood gully which led through the cliffs down to the beach itself.

"Well, we're here," David announced a little superfluously as they reached the bottom.

Kathleen nodded in acknowledgement, almost spellbound by the immensity of the scene so suddenly revealed. Where she stood was near the centre of a long curved stretch of wet sand, both ends of which terminated in bluff and rocky headlands; the sea itself was not the uniform grey she had imagined from the hilltop but was scattered with white streaks which, she soon realised were the tops of breaking waves; a line of surf where these met the shore was patrolled by various seabirds which swooped occasionally, squawking angrily at each other as they disputed whatever morsels the incoming tide provided. With a stiff wind fretting at the water and carrying a distinct smell of rotting seaweed the whole scene seemed somewhat unwelcoming. She looked further into the distance and could clearly discern the line of gaunt towers with slowly rotating blades, looking for all the world like alien invaders signalling to each other, discussing perhaps their intention to enslave the feeble inhabitants of this minor planet. Icy fingers crept up her spine and she gave an involuntary shiver.

"It is a bit cold," David allowed, coming to stand beside her.

"It's not that," she replied. "Those things out there look

so menacing, almost as though they were alive."

"They're only machines, Kathy," he assured her with a shrug. "If they hadn't been built our existence would be a lot harsher."

"What did we use for energy before them?"

"We still had electricity, made by using a fuel like Ectol but it came from under the ground. It only came from certain areas and the Federation adopted a policy that all energy must be from renewable sources. That is why there has to be maximum yield from the food producing areas because vast tracts of land are given over to the crops from which Ectol can be made."

"Do non-Federation countries still use the stuff from under the ground?" Kathleen wondered.

"I'm not sure," David admitted. "I got the impression from those recordings of Jack's that they do, but I could be wrong."

The wind sighing over the cliffs, the noise of the surf and the screeching birds emphasised the emptiness of their surroundings and indeed their own solitude. Scanning hopefully for any sign of human presence, Kathleen suddenly gripped David's arm.

"Look there!" She pointed at a patch of drier sand to their left. "Tyre tracks, ForTrak tracks!"

Though faint, the tracks were unmistakeable; disappearing in the wet sand then re-appearing on another dry patch. Kathleen and David, straining their eyes towards the distant headland spotted a small dot on the beach; moments later they knew that it was heading in their direction.

"Crunch time!" David murmured nervously. "Friend or foe? We'll have to hide until we can be sure."

He was right of course; urgently they sought cover, finding boulders at the base of the gully big enough to hide behind and with cracks to peer through but hardly adequate defence against a determined search.

The approaching ForTrak seemed to move in fits and starts. As it came nearer they could see that every time it stopped the driver alighted and walked about on the sand for a while before re-boarding and continuing along the beach. Closer still and Kathleen was sure she was seeing a female, and a blonde female at that.

"I think that she's looking for us," she whispered excitedly.

"Yes, but for what reason?" David's caution momentarily dampened her enthusiasm but it resurfaced moments later.

"I'm going out into the open," she stated firmly. David shook his head but her mind was made up.

"What if it's a trick? What if she arrests you?"

"Then you'll have to think of a way to rescue me!" Her response sounded more nonchalant than she felt.

Waiting until the ForTrak driver's back was turned, she slipped out from behind the boulder and strolled casually a little way towards the water. Watching the birds as though absorbed by their antics, her nerves jangling with apprehension at the roar of the approaching engine, she only turned to look when it stopped a few yards away from her.

The curly-haired girl who leapt lightly down from the cab looked rather more nervous than threatening.

"Might you be Kathy, who doesn't like to be called Kath?" she enquired, cautiously keeping her distance.

Kathleen nodded, tears of relief stinging at the back of her eyes.

"You must be Jenny, blonde and cheeky with a souped-up ForTrak?" she responded.

The smile she received in return answered all her questions. The girl ran to her and grasped both of her hands in welcome.

"We've been so worried about you," she cried. "But here you are at last. Where's David, you haven't lost him have you?"

Kathleen waved joyfully and David appeared from their hiding place. Jenny welcomed him in similar fashion, enquiring about their adventures since her father had left them on their own. Kathleen had to interrupt with an important question of her own to ask.

"You wouldn't have anything to eat with you by any chance?" she enquired hopefully.

"Of course, you must be starving!" Jenny ran to the ForTrak and returned offering a small parcel.

"It's only emergency rations I'm afraid, wodges of bread and cheese."

Kathleen, her mouth already full, waved her hands to indicate that bread and cheese was equivalent to nectar and ambrosia at this moment. Maybe through politeness, David hesitated, but only for a second or two before emulating her.

"I'm afraid that will have to do you until we get back to base," Jenny apologised as Kathy investigated the wrapper for any remaining crumbs. "And the sooner we start the sooner that will be. Shall we get going?"

David lifted their worldly possessions to stow in the ForTrak; about to follow him, Kathleen turned for a last look at the sea just as a sunbeam, finding a crack in the clouds, leapt joyfully to the earth below; she gasped in astonishment at the transformation.

The water was no longer grey and forbidding, instantaneously it had become blue with laughing little splashes of white water sparkling on the surface; the distant sinister figures were now just fabrications, ugly certainly but not any more so than those she had seen on the land; the sunlight shining on the wet sand was an invitation to come and play and Kathleen laughed with sheer delight.

"It's magical," she tried to explain in response to David's quizzical look. "How it can change so dramatically in just a few seconds. It makes me want to stay to see more of it!"

"But we have to go now," David's response was totally unromantic, and as the clouds hastily repaired the temporary breach he pointed out. "Look, it's gone dull again already."

Kathleen nodded and obediently boarded the ForTrak but her heart was still singing in response to the unexpected revelation of beauty. Some chord in her subconscious had been struck and she knew that she would never now be content with a future that did not include a chance to improve her acquaintance with the sea.

She was rapidly recalled to her immediate surroundings as Jenny started the engine and simultaneously stamped on the go-pedal. The ForTrak leapt forward and was soon racing towards the northerly headland with a plume of sand remarking its passage. Within minutes they passed by two high parallel fences which climbed the cliff and then disappeared inland.

"What are they for?" Kathleen asked David as she settled herself firmly on the surprisingly adequate cushions.

"That must be the border between food production and Ectol crops. The gap between them is supposed to ensure there is no cross contamination."

"So we are going to be in the Ectol producing area from now on?"

"It certainly looks like it," David agreed. "So far as I know, the only crossing points are on the main thoroughfares and we're not likely to be going through any of them."

"Oh well!" Kathleen commented wryly. "I didn't really think that the Resistance wanted me because I could grow barley!"

Jenny slowed the ForTrak to a crawl as she turned off the sand and on to the start of a stony track which led up off the beach. Her two passengers hung on grimly as the cab tilted and swayed alarmingly but they reached the top without mishap.

"That was the worst bit," Jenny assured them, accelerating again as she spoke. "From now on the going is mostly not too bad; I'll let you know when we come to any more bumpy bits."

"You seem to be able to get a lot of speed out of this machine," David was curious. "It doesn't sound quite like a standard ForTrak either."

"It isn't! Andy is a wizard mechanic and he's tweaked this one specially for me. And of course I am a top notch driver," Jenny concluded with unshakeable aplomb.

This part of the journey was certainly proving to be more comfortable than the earlier stage; Kathleen didn't know how much was due to the terrain and how much to the driver's skill but Jenny seemed able to anticipate the roughness of the ground ahead and to swing the heavy vehicle around the worst of the bumps. Certainly the cab swayed from side to side frequently but the rigid seat below Kathleen's bottom rarely bounced enough to lift her off the cushions. Grateful for the comparative pleasure of the ride she allowed herself to assess her immediate surroundings with professional interest.

The fields through which they passed varied in size but were predominately covered with a knee-high leafy crop characterised by yellow flowers in differing stages of development. The areas which were bare of vegetation bore a scatter of mangled stalks, mute evidence of recent harvesting. Occasionally they passed another ForTrak at work and, if close enough, exchanged waves of acknowledgement. Mostly however, their journey was monotonous and Kathleen lapsed into an idle reverie, re-living the simple satisfaction of tending to the land, nurturing it to produce the best possible return.

She woke from her daydreams as the ForTrak came to a halt.

"We are making good enough time so you can have five minutes to stretch your legs," Jenny announced, jumping down and waving her arms above her head to dispel the stiffness. Both of them quickly joined her, glad to avail themselves of the opportunity to exercise muscles cramped from sitting for so long.

Kathleen stooped to examine the vegetation which grew beside the track, noticing the multitude of long pods which hung among the leaves.

"These plants are what Ectol is made from?" she asked in surprise.

"This is one of them," Jenny replied. "There are other varieties modified to suit the soil and the climate in different places and also to get a spread of ripening times. The infrastructure couldn't handle the harvest and the oil extraction if the whole area was ready at one time."

"Do you actually make the Ectol locally?" David wanted to know.

Jenny shook her head. "Not officially, no. The rough

product of extraction goes away to central refineries in the rail wagons but," she added with one of her cheeky smiles, "we do manage to divert enough to our own little operation to ensure that we don't have to rely on our allotted rations."

"I'm impressed," David said with a laugh. "There is obviously an underground economy going on that CenCon isn't aware of."

"You'd better believe it," Jenny affirmed as she settled herself into the driving seat. "All aboard? Right, off we go again."

Many enervating miles later Jenny steered the ForTrak on to a proper road; switching on headlights to combat the gathering dusk she accelerated to an almost frightening speed.

"Last stretch now," she assured them. "I hope there's some supper left for us."

When they finally came to a halt it was too dark for Kathleen to detect more than the outline of a few low roofs against the sky. She wasn't particularly interested at the moment, any excitement at the prospect of new beginnings almost totally numbed by lack of sleep added to the fatigue of incessant motion and engine noise. Wearily she traipsed after Jenny and David to the nearest building, through a doorway and into a roughly furnished hallway.

"This is the bunkhouse," Jenny announced. "It's an old cowshed from the days when this region was mostly given over to livestock. There are rooms on either side of the central corridor where the stalls used to be, nothing fancy but they are reasonably comfortable. Bathrooms at this end if you want to freshen up; now, is it one room or two?"

Kathleen took a moment to get the drift of the question; she opened her mouth to make an indignant reply but David forestalled her.

"Two rooms please," he said with the merest trace of a smile.

"Sorree!" Jenny apologised looking at the expression on Kathleen's face. "Well, I didn't know, did I?"

She flicked a light switch and led them along the passageway; stopping to unlock one of the doors, she pushed it open.

"You can go in here David and we'll put Kathleen at the far end on the other side. I'll go over to the kitchen and see what cookie has left for us. Just come over as soon as you are ready, you'll see the light across the yard."

"You'll probably prefer this one," she confided as she ushered Kathleen into another room. "It's on the corner so it has two windows; some of the others are a bit on the pokey side. See you shortly."

Left on her own, Kathleen took a moment to examine her new abode. It was far from luxurious with painted plaster walls and a floor of plain wooden boards but a couple of scatter rugs made it look more homely. It possessed all the basics for reasonable comfort with a bed, wardrobe, and drawers and she was pleasantly surprised to see a washstand in the corner.

Realising how hungry she was, she gave herself a quick splash in the basin, changed into a clean shirt and, after a brief assessment of the temperature, topped it with a warm sweater. She made her way back to the entrance lobby and settled into a rather battered looking couch to wait for David.

Her stomach grumbled at her a couple of times before he eventually appeared and she jumped thankfully to her feet.

"You were quick," he said. "I thought women were supposed to take for ever getting ready."

"I'm starving," she explained. "You'd be amazed how fast I can move when hunger is the driving force. Let's see if we can find our way to the kitchen."

It was full dark outside, the cloud cover barring the least trace of light from the sky; they paused in the doorway until their eyes grew accustomed to it before carefully crossing the yard towards a welcoming gleam from a window.

"I can smell food!" Kathleen whispered delightedly as they found the entrance.

"You've got a one track mind," David accused lightly,

and she nodded in complete agreement.

Food indeed there was! The kitchen extended through a wide archway into another area, where Jenny sat at a big round table which was graced by a pastry-covered pie, a crusty loaf that bore little resemblance to the pale plastic-wrapped things supplied by the AgriMart, a dish of soft yellow butter and a tall jug of milk.

"I couldn't wait for you," Jenny apologised indistinctly through a full mouth as she slathered butter on to a thick wedge of bread.

"I'm not surprised," Kathleen said appreciatively, settling into a chair and grabbing a plate. "This lot would tempt a stone statue to eat, let alone a poor deprived waif like me!"

"Some waif," David commented drily, managing however to reach the pie before her. She almost drooled as, tantalisingly slowly, he cut a large portion for himself.

"Are you sure you want a piece of this?" he inquired with mock concern, hovering over the dish.

"If you want to see tomorrow morning you'd better pass it over right now," Kathleen snapped back and was rewarded with an amused chuckle from Jenny.

Nothing further was said for a while but stomachs do have a finite capacity and eventually the three of them sat back in repletion, not however, before the best part of what was on the table had disappeared.

"That was marvellous," Kathleen sighed turning to Jenny. "Who does the cooking here?"

"Mary does it all. She loves cooking and you'll find that it's very much her kitchen.

"Kathleen will be happy to stay here in that case," David said sardonically. "And I must admit that the meal we've just had outclasses the canteen fare that I'm accustomed to so I guess that means both of us."

"I'm glad it meets with your approval," Jenny returned. "Now, Alex is in the workshop waiting to fit you with a persaCom apiece so I'll take you there. The sooner you are semi-legit the better."

She led them along a corridor and into something resembling a broom cupboard; lifting a flap in the floor she revealed a sturdy ladder leading down into what appeared to be a well lit cellar.

"They're ready for you Alex," she called.

"Send them on down," came a distant reply.

"Off you go then," Jenny told them briskly. "I'll love you and leave you 'cos I'm needing my bed and you will probably be ready for yours once you are finished here. Breakfast is at sunrise so I'll see you about then."

Kathleen allowed David to precede her down the ladder; reaching the bottom she turned to see him already being greeted by a short wiry man with thinning ginger hair.

"And you must be Kathleen," He turned towards her with a smile of welcome. "I think you've been told that I am Alex. Glad to have you both aboard."

"Let's get down to business," he continued. "You have come a long way and you must be tired but this won't take too long."

Leading them to a bench against one of the walls he picked up what appeared to be a perfectly standard persaCom.

"These have been modified," he explained. "The ID chip now has a non-existent number which is transmitted in a 'fuzzy' manner so as to make identification uncertain as can happen in areas with less than perfect coverage. It is slightly risky in that a specific search would reveal an anomaly but to be honest, there are so many millions of persaComs that we regard it as an acceptable risk. There is also the facility to switch off the transmitter if you are on a journey that might require explanation, I'll give you the code for that in a moment. The lock has been altered too so you can take it off whenever you want."

"That's marvellous," David enthused. "But would it not be even better if a false identity file could be inserted into the database."

Alex looked at him sharply.

"Indeed it would be better," he agreed. "But I am afraid that is quite beyond our capabilities. Are you going to tell me that you could do such a thing?"

"Given the right equipment, yes. How much I can

achieve depends on getting the hardware to break into the system; without that I'll hardly be of any help at all."

"What would you need." Kathleen could hear excitement ringing in Alex's question. The two men moved into a conversation of which she could understand next to nothing so she allowed her attention to wander to her surroundings.

Cellar it may have been but it was huge; where they stood was like a normal sized room but an archway at the end revealed another room and though it was dimly lit she could see the outline of another opening beyond that. Looking above her, the shape of massive beams seemed to be sheathed with the same kind of shiny, reflective material with which the walls were covered. Idly, she wondered for what purpose it had originally been built and caught herself using a hand to stifle a yawn.

Alex noticed her movement.

"I'm sorry," he apologised. "I'm getting a bit carried away here. Let's get these things on your wrists and get you off to bed."

"I don't mind carrying on if you want," David told him.

"Better not," Alex gave a regretful shake of his head. "We'll get some of the others down tomorrow, then you won't have to explain things twice."

After being fitted with the modified persaComs they re-ascended the ladder and Alex followed them into the kitchen.

"You can find your way to the bunkhouse all right," he enquired.

"No bother," they assured him and after wishing him goodnight retraced their steps across the yard.

"Goodnight David," Kathleen managed through another yawn.

"Goodnight Kathy, sleep well." He smiled at her.

"I don't think that'll be a problem," she muttered as she headed for her room. She had intended to have a bath but was now too tired to bother; hastily she dragged off her clothes and crawled gratefully under the covers.

CHAPTER EIGHT

It took the first rays of the newly risen sun to rouse Kathleen from her slumber and she hesitated for a moment, wondering if the desirability of having a shower outweighed the possibility of missing breakfast. Deciding that the shower was imperative she made the best haste that she could but the sun was more than a finger above the horizon as she hurried across the yard. She was glad to see that Jenny was still in the kitchen, along with another girl.

"Here you are, better late than never," Jenny joked as Kathleen hesitated in the doorway. "Don't be shy, come and sit down."

"I'm sorry," Kathleen apologised. "I don't usually have any trouble waking up in the morning."

"It's a funny thing but most people who have spent a day with me in a ForTrak seem to be tired afterwards," Jenny excused her with more than a hint of amusement.

"Mary, this is Kathleen," Jenny continued. "She is going to be one of your best customers, she had three helpings of that pie you left out for us!"

Kathleen found herself shaking hands with a small slip of a girl who looked to be scarcely out of her 'teens. So much for stereotypes, she thought ruefully.

"I love cooking," Mary confided shyly. "And I love it even more when people enjoy what I've made."

"If last night was anything to go by, I can promise to please you a lot," Kathleen assured her.

"David was up early," Jenny informed her. "He's gone off with the rest of the electronic geeks; the others have gone to work so you are the last to be fed."

Mary disappeared before Kathleen had finished her breakfast leaving only Jenny and herself in the kitchen.

"I hope I'm not keeping you back from anything," she asked with a feeling of guilt.

"Not at all," Jenny assured her. "I've set aside a few hours to show you round our unit, W19 of N/Seven officially, and explain what we do here: You haven't got wellies I suppose?"

Kathleen admitted her lack of outdoor clothing.

"There should be some in the store that will fit you. Some of our crowd move around quite a bit so there is always spare gear lying about."

Shortly afterwards Kathleen, suitably equipped, was following her new acquaintance to the ForTrak.

"We'll take this but it'll only be for a short run," Jenny assured her. "I just want to get to some of the outlying fields to check the condition of the crop."

Up till now, Kathleen had been in too much of a hurry to pay any attention to her new surroundings; perched on the ForTrak however, she was at last free to look around.

The two-storey building which housed the kitchen, and the bunkhouse, was not the only one adjacent to the yard. There were a number of others, mostly single storied but an open sided high shed might have been a feed store at one time. As they sped along a track she saw at once that the distant hills she had spotted yesterday were indeed much closer, so close in fact that the cultivated area spread on to their lower slopes; above that, rough ground scattered with gorse and bracken sloped steeply upwards to craggy tops where tendrils of mist formed and reformed in response to the dictates of the stiff breeze. The brightness of the morning sun was frequently broken by patches of fast-moving cloud and Kathleen was grateful for the warmth of the sweater below her jacket. Trying to reckon on her fingers the number of days since she had sweated in just a shirt she concluded that they must have travelled far enough North for there to be a noticeable difference in the temperature.

"Here we are," Jenny announced, stopping the ForTrak in a field where the yellow flowers of the crop had faded into a dull brown.

She picked a couple of the fat pods, cracked them open to reveal the seeds within and showed Kathleen how to crush them with a stone. A smear of oil was discernible and Jenny rubbed it between her fingers before pronouncing that it was ready for harvest.

"I assume that you have driven a ForTrak?" she enquired. Kathleen nodded her assent.

"With harvesting equipment?"

"Our harvest was done with big machines from a central Depot," Kathleen admitted. "But I've used the gear for ground preparation and seeding."

"Some of the smaller Units work through a Depot but we are big enough to do our own harvesting; we also use a small rig for testing and for some of the more awkward fields. We might as well let you have a go now." Jenny grinned and added, "I'm sure that you would prefer an audience of one rather than a dozen for your first attempt."

Kathleen agreed wholeheartedly that if she was to make a fool of herself she would indeed prefer spectators to be kept to a minimum.

They drove to where various pieces of machinery were parked and Jenny reversed up to a complicated looking rig surmounted by a large hopper; she demonstrated how to connect its umbilicals to the ForTrak.

"Right!" she announced. "I'll do a cut to demonstrate then you can have a go."

Kathleen watched anxiously as Jenny drove expertly alongside the crop; the extended boom of the reaper, munching and thrashing, left a swathe of bare stalks behind it while a continuous stream of vegetation poured into the hopper. After turning the vehicle at the end of the field and swinging the boom to the other side she vacated the driving seat.

"Your turn!"

It didn't look too difficult but Kathleen was desperate to prove her ability; her palms were sweating as she gingerly operated the controls but by the time she had reached their starting point a measure of confidence had returned.

"Not bad at all," Jenny complimented after looking critically at the result. "You might as well do a bit more until the hopper is full."

Cautiously, Kathleen swung the ForTrak round and set off on another cut; she was no more than a third of the way however when a rapid bleep sounded in her ears.

"That's it," Jenny told her. Taking over the controls she released the rig, detached the hopper and secured it into clamps on the back of the ForTrak.

"This has to go to the crusher now, but I'll take a roundabout route so that you can see the extent of our Unit."

Kathleen was impressed by the size of the area for which this team were responsible. Far bigger than 'The Beeches', it extended all the way to the base of the hills. She saw one other vehicle at work and though they exchanged waves they didn't stop until they reached a complex where large storage tanks were grouped alongside an industrial type of building. Jenny backed up and transferred the hopper to a device which tipped it into the maw of what Kathleen assumed was the previously mentioned crusher.

"There are a couple of our gang working in here on a repair job today so you might as well come and meet them," Jenny declared, hurrying towards an open doorway. Wondering briefly at her guide's obvious urgency Kathleen followed to where two men were working on a piece of machinery.

"This is Andy, the wizard mechanic I told you about, and this is Peter who is nearly as good but not quite so special. Don't shake hands with them 'cos they're both usually covered with oil!"

Andy was tall with curly black hair surmounting a swarthy complexion and he was lean enough to make the muscles on his arms and shoulders seem almost out of proportion; the glow on Jenny's face made it pretty obvious in what way she regarded him as special. Peter was stocky with a craggy face that lit up in a pleased smile as he saw Kathleen. She guessed that they were both in their middle twenties.

"Please call me Kathy," she murmured in response to their greetings.

"Glad to meet you Kathy," Peter responded ardently while his eyes made a rapid but detailed assessment of her figure. "It's nice to see a pretty girl joining our company, I hope we'll get to know each other really well!"

"Watch him!" Jenny warned, her light tone not entirely masking a note of seriousness. " 'Randy' Peter thinks he's irresistible to women. He'll tell you anything if he thinks it will help him get into your pants."

Kathleen face reddened at the bluntness of the remark but Peter didn't seem unduly concerned.

"Would I do that," he protested, trying unsuccessfully to look innocent.

"Yes!" Andy retorted. "The only reason you shave your head is because you think it makes you look sexy!"

"It's not my fault that I know how to please a woman," Peter pleaded with a soulful look. "Don't listen to them Kathy, I'll talk to you again when these so-called friends of mine aren't about."

Kathleen shook her head in bewildered amusement. This lewd and light-hearted banter was something which she would obviously have to learn to accept. They were young, she reminded herself and the thought made her turn to Jenny with a question.

"I got the impression from George that the Resistance was made up of older people but everyone I've met here is comparatively young. Is that true of the rest of you?"

"George is an old fuddy-duddy like Dad! Don't get me wrong, I love them all to bits and we need them to help with planning but when it comes to action they are out of their depth."

Andy nodded in vigorous assent before giving Peter, who was still gazing admiringly at Kathleen, a sharp nudge.

"Come on," he urged. "We've got this bearing to fit and you've got to have your mind on the job."

Peter turned away with a loud sigh, muttering under his breath something that sounded suspiciously like 'it is'! Kathleen chose to think she had misheard him and was relieved when Jenny pointed out a panel on the wall.

"These are the test results of our sample," she said, busily transferring the figures to her persaCom. "We'd better go now and let the boys get on with their work."

"Is Peter like that all the time," Kathleen asked as they strolled back to the ForTrak.

"He's all right really. He comes on strong to every new girl he meets even if she is obviously paired but if you make it clear that you are not interested he only flirts a bit. He tried it on with me as soon as he arrived but now he treats me the same as one of the boys."

She stopped and stared seriously at Kathleen for a moment.

"You can do what you like about him but it's 'hands off' as far as Andy is concerned, understand."

Kathleen couldn't help but burst into laughter.

"Jenny, Jenny," she chided. "I'm an old woman compared with you lot. For goodness sake, I'm nearly thirty-five!"

"Never," Jenny exclaimed and when Kathleen assured her that it was true, went on. "Well, all I can say is that I hope I wear as well as you. What's your secret?"

"None that I know of," Kathleen shrugged. "As far as I am aware I'm just an ordinary woman for my age."

"That you're not," Jenny averred. "You have the kind of looks that men notice. "Oh yes," she continued with a flash of her grey eyes, "Andy noticed you too though he wasn't as obvious as Peter. I'll be having a little talk with him later."

Kathleen laughed and pulled the younger woman into a hug.

"If I promise that I won't trespass will you help me to put a damper on Peter?"

"Leave him to me. I'll tell him that I'll stop his beer ration if he so much as says one word out of turn!"

"Beer ration? I thought you could only get beer in designated taverns."

"You've got a lot to learn about us Kathy. And I'd like to hear something of your history if you don't mind telling me. All I know is that you were in a bit of trouble with the Police."

Jenny let the ForTrak meander slowly back to the base as Kathleen, struggling a little at first, gave a resume of her previous life and the circumstances which had led to her flight. Her voice caught briefly when she came to the crop inspection but Jenny reached for her hand with a comforting squeeze and she was able to carry on. She was surprised to discover that talking about her experiences made her feel a great deal better.

Jenny halted the ForTrak and turned to her with a look of genuine distress.

"I'm so sorry Kathy," she almost cried. "I never would have let Peter talk to you like that if I had known."

"It's all right really," Kathleen assured her. "It seems that in some ways I have had a sheltered life and it will do me the world of good to mix with normal people."

Jenny shook her head and her mouth formed into a angry line.

"Well," she uttered grimly. "If I ever had any doubts about the rightness of what we are doing you've put paid to them for good. God, you were lucky that David managed to get you out when he did."

"I am," Kathleen agreed with a shudder. "I suppose if it hadn't been for him I would be wearing a blue uniform now and chanting that odious anthem."

"He seems nice enough. Do you like him." Jenny changed the subject with a rapid reversion to her usual mischievous self.

"I'll be eternally grateful to him," Kathleen replied firmly. "I think he regards me as a wounded puppy that he's saved from being put down and that's fine with me. Does that answer your question?"

"Not really." Jenny tossed her head. "But it doesn't matter. On a lighter note she added, "it's past midday, can I interest you in a snack."

Kathleen's affirmative nod terminated abruptly; she had to grab for support as the ForTrak leapt forward and raced the rest of the way to the yard.

David and Alex were in the kitchen putting hunks of bread and cheese together; with them was a young couple whom Jenny introduced as Jason and Sonya.

"Eggheads both!" she declared with apparent scorn. "They might be brilliant with chips and bytes but take them outside and they are like lost bunny rabbits."

"Each to his own," Sonya retorted spiritedly. "Where would you be if you had to program your own persaCom next time you go gadding off round the country."

Kathleen left them to their banter; helping herself to some food she sat down beside David.

"How was your morning," he inquired with a warm smile. "I thought about giving you a knock but decided it would be too cruel."

"You should have done," Kathleen told him. "I only just made breakfast!"

She sketched an outline of her activities then enquired as to what he had been doing.

"Making good progress," he assured her happily. "I think that there is everything here to make the terminal we talked about, it is really now just a matter of time to get one assembled and checked out."

"And how long will that take?"

"Weeks anyway. Mass production can turn one out in seconds but doing everything by hand is a laborious and painstaking process. It would take a lot longer but Sonya and Jason there are brilliant at this kind of work."

"I wonder how they manage to be on an Agunit in that case. You would think that the Authorities would have wanted to make use of their skills."

"They are illegals like us," David told her in a low voice. "They escaped from a Produnit in the middle of winter and tried to get to the coast hoping they could find a boat and get away. God knows what would have happened to them if Richard hadn't found them sheltering under a hedge, half dead from cold and starvation."

Kathleen was intrigued but decided to put off any questions until she had David on his own. The snack break was quickly over anyway, those present disappearing back to their tasks; it wasn't long before herself and Jenny were the only two remaining.

"I'll show you round the base when you are ready," Jenny suggested. "Then I'll print some stuff off the VidCom so that you can get a better insight into what we'll be doing on the unit for the next few days. Normally you could access what you want on your persaCom but you'll understand that yours isn't, and can't be, linked."

"How many are here altogether?" Kathleen asked. "I

seem to have met quite a few already."

"Six supposedly but it can vary according to the season. Alex and I have AgriCerts, we are officially in charge but because of the size of the unit and also because we have to maintain and operate the crushing plant we are allowed a certain number of helpers. Then there are the illegals, four now counting yourself and David."

"It must be difficult getting enough credits to cover food and clothing for the non-persons. How do you manage?"

"Food isn't a problem, we get a lot of stuff locally," Jenny assured her. "Clothes are a bit more difficult but we get by. How are you fixed in that department?"

"I'm okay for most things, your mother kitted me out from her store, but I'm kind of desperate for underwear," Kathleen admitted.

"I'll find something for you after we've finished our tour," Jenny promised. "Shall we go?"

The main house containing the kitchen was the centre of a group of buildings which were clustered around it. Although at one time they had been used to house stock and feedstuffs, some of them were now converted into living accommodation and others into workshops and storage for equipment.

"This is where Andy and I hang out, and Sonya and Jason have the other half," Jenny explained outside one similar in size to the bunkhouse. "Mary is paired with Alex and they live upstairs in the 'big' house. Peter is in the next building so at the moment you and David are the only ones in the bunkhouse."

"Mary looks very young," Kathleen commented. "Young enough to have had to be in one of the training establishments."

"Don't let her appearance fool you, she's older than me and as tough as old boots; when she's not on kitchen duty she'll do as much outside as any of us."

"I more or less manage the unit," she resumed, "Alex spends a lot of his time in the workshop, perhaps a bit less since Sonya and Jason arrived. I suppose that David will be in there with them so what do you think you want to do yourself?"

Kathleen told her about David's suggestion that she should learn about the CenCon programme and possibly how to manipulate it.

"I won't be able to start until they have built a terminal and hooked it into the network though. I hope you can find me work outside till that happens and even then I wouldn't want to spend all my time indoors."

"Nobody does," Jenny shook her head. "At the busy times everybody has to muck in, boffins and all. Even Peter and Andy help whenever they are not involved with the machinery. We can ask for extra staff from some of the adjacent units with staggered harvest arrangements but I prefer not to unless it's absolutely necessary. I like to think that if we manage on our own we get brownie points that make our holding of this unit more secure.

"We have a number of harvested fields that need preparing for the next sowing," she continued. "You can take one of the ForTraks out tomorrow if you like, but first you need to familiarise yourself with the layout of the place."

"I'll certainly need to do that," Kathleen agreed. "It's much bigger than what I was used to."

Leaving Kathleen in the kitchen, Jenny went into the 'office', returning shortly with a few sheets of printout which she placed on the table.

"This one is a plan of the unit with all the field numbers and this is the same thing but with the cultivation schedule superimposed. If you look at 22 for example, you will see that it is coloured black; refer to the side panel and black indicates harvest has been completed and it is ready for tilling and fertilising prior to re-seeding."

Kathleen studied the charts for a moment before admitting that it seemed pretty straightforward.

"This last one gives the numbers of the various equipments that are kept in the park where we were this morning and details of how to attach them to the ForTrak. If I said to you to work on 22 tomorrow, these should contain all the information you need to get on with it," Jenny concluded confidently.

"I imagine so," Kathleen agreed. "It certainly makes it easier to have everything laid out like this. On my own place I did it all out of my head but of course my unit was much smaller with only one planting and one harvest each year."

"You have to go by the book at AgriCol or you won't get a Certificate; I carry it all in my head too but this way does avoid confusion if there are changes in personnel even if it is a bit of a chore putting the details into the VidCom.

"That's what I've got to do now," Jenny continued, "so I suggest that you take the plans with you and amuse yourself till feeding time. You can take one of the ForTraks and familiarise yourself with the access routes if you want."

"That would be great!" Kathleen enthused, accepting a key from the rack on the wall and, a short while later, she drove happily out of the yard. For the first time since the Police knocked on her bedroom door she was, if only for a brief period, master of her own destiny.

Controlling the vehicle took little of her attention, leaving her free to reflect on the tumultuous events of the last few days. The transposition from an acceptable if humdrum existence, through fear, total despair, rage and finally a glimmer of hope to a future that promised uncertainty with a measure of danger should have left her reeling. The Unit manager who had inhabited her body a week ago would have been close to panic yet here she was, in unknown territory, surrounded by strangers, and her prevailing emotion was of eagerness to meet the challenges that lay ahead. 'It's me that's changed,' she thought, 'I've seen and learnt so much in such a short time that I'm a different person now. If I was offered the chance to go back to 'The Beeches' I don't know if I would take it, I'm not sure if I could be content there any more. I feel as though I'm alive for the first time in my life'.

How had such a rapid transformation come about? After her traumatic experience at the hands of Stephen Lock - she found she could be more dispassionate about it since her talk with Jenny - she had dumbly accepted

David's unexpected intervention. George and Nellie had been kind to her as had Richard and Hazel, probably the first to do so since she had said goodbye to her parents. Her new acquaintances seemed genuinely friendly and she was already aware of a sense of empathy with Jenny. Somehow this had instilled in her a sense of purpose, an urgent desire to play an important part in whatever attempt was made to overthrow the intolerable system which governed their lives.

She braked the ForTrak to a halt as her aimless progress brought her to a high fence which separated the cultivated area from the scrubby hillside. Letting her eyes drift upwards past small clumps of bushes scattered amongst rocky outcrops, she observed that there was no discipline in the land rising behind the barrier; it was wild and beautiful, obviously free of official regulation. Gazing still higher she noticed little dots like white stones; it was only when one of them moved that she realised that they must be animals, maybe the sheep she vaguely recollected reading about in her past life.

'Is that what has made me different?' she asked herself. 'The boundaries of the farm used to be my whole world but for the first time I have looked beyond them; I have marvelled at the vast expanse of the sea and now I am seeing hills, no, mountains with their heads among the clouds disappearing into the far distance'. She could almost feel her spirit rising in response to the limitless grandeur before her, chafing a little at the presence of the fence that prevented further exploration.

Glancing at her wrist, she sighed regretfully, forced her thoughts back to reality and set the ForTrak into motion. She needed to memorise as much as possible of the maps she had been given and knew that the required concentration would not be forthcoming out here. Taking a roundabout route delayed her return to the yard a little but all too soon she replaced the key in the kitchen and settled down in her room to study. Even there she found distraction as the fitful sunshine alternately lightened and darkened the south-facing window so, after catching herself gazing pensively at the view for the umpteenth time, she moved to the couch in the entrance lobby; she was still there when David came in through the door.

"I was wondering where you had got to," he greeted her cheerfully. "Have you been enjoying yourself?"

"I have actually," she smiled in return. "Jenny let me take a ForTrak to explore our new domain and I would be out there yet if I didn't have these maps to study. How was your day?"

David stretched wearily and rubbed his eyes before glancing at her papers; he groaned as he sat down beside her.

"I'm shattered," he complained. "I haven't concentrated so hard in years trying to keep a step ahead of Sonya and Jason, they pick things up that fast. They make me feel old!"

"Me too," she admitted, telling him about her encounter with Peter, expecting him to laugh with her but he frowned instead.

"Talk like that is common enough in certain places but he should have been more careful, he could have upset you badly."

Kathleen shrugged her shoulders. "I was surprised, not upset. I can't expect to be wrapped in cotton wool because of what has happened in the past and that is where it is now. I had a long talk with Jenny and told her everything and it seems to have helped me to come to terms with it. I'm more concerned with the future now, in fact I'm quite excited about what it may hold."

"I'm glad that you're feeling more positive," David said with a relieved smile. "I must admit that I am quite excited myself about the potential of what we are working on, I can't wait until we get this terminal built. Do you still want to join in when we get it operational?"

"More than ever. Jenny can keep me busy with outside work and I'll be glad to do it but that isn't going to be enough for me now. I realised today that my horizons have extended dramatically since you got me out of that cell and I want to expand my capabilities to match. You'll have a very eager pupil as soon as you are ready."

"That's what I like to hear." He pushed himself up of

the couch. "Now I'm going to throw some water at my face to help me to stay awake until we go for supper!"

She put a hand on his arm to delay him. "I wanted to ask you about Jason and Sonya; you said they escaped from a Produnit but I thought that everyone there would be brainwashed?"

"Obviously not," he paused for a moment then went on. "They didn't say very much but it must have taken a great deal of courage to leave as they did without the least idea of where they were going. It could be that there are a lot more who would jump at the chance of a better life, even try to get away but not many would have Jason's expertise and be able to disable a persaCom."

"That's true." Kathleen had forgotten about the pernicious signal from the communicator. "And if others had tried and been caught it would never be publicised."

"Am I excused now, Miss?" he asked meekly as he stood up.

She tried to put a stern look on her face. "Well..., I was about to ask you to test my memory on these papers but seeing that you've been good I'll let you off this time! See you at supper."

The table was only just big enough to accommodate the group gathered around it. Kathleen slid gratefully into a vacant chair beside Jenny and studied the circle of faces. 'Alex, Jason, Sonya, Peter,' she ticked them off mentally. 'Andy, Jenny, me and David'. Mary, busy at the cooker, completed the group.

"Now that you are all here," Alex raised his voice for a moment to quell the buzz of conversation. "There will be a meeting tomorrow night to discuss the avenues opened up by our new arrivals, David here and Kathy. I believe that there are profound implications which could considerably improve our chances of success. Richard and Hazel will be coming," he paused to smile at Jenny, "and the other group leaders so we had better eat in shifts before we assemble in the crypt. Any comments?... Right then piggies, noses in the trough time!"

Mary came to sit down with her own laden plate and the rest of them took it in turns to help themselves from the array of pots. Apart from the clatter of cutlery and occasional requests to pass salt or pepper there was silence until everyone had finished when, without a word, Peter and Jason rose from the table and set about washing dishes.

"Rota!" Jenny explained in response to Kathleen's look of enquiry. Indicating a card on the wall she went on. "One to wash, one to dry. You and David are on the day after tomorrow."

Kathleen nodded comprehension then, as Jenny turned to talk to Alex, noticed that Sonya had moved to sit beside her.

"How are you coping, Kathy?" she asked a little nervously, pushing her long fair hair over her shoulder. "David told us a little of how you came to be here, it must have been terrible for you; I wanted to be sympathetic but am afraid of saying the wrong thing."

Kathleen gave the girl a reassuring smile. "I'm okay, really I am. It may sound strange but although it was bad at the time I'm almost thankful to have been forced to abandon my previous life. I realise now that I was living in a strait-jacket and after just a few days of new experiences I don't think I'd ever want to go back to it."

"That's great!" Sonya's normally serious face was transformed into a smile of such genuine pleasure that Kathleen warmed to her immediately.

"I'd love to hear your story," she ventured, "If you don't mind talking about it. I don't know much about Produnits but I've heard that they are dreadful places, it's almost miraculous that you managed to get away."

"They are bad," Sonya agreed with a momentary shudder. "Most people seem to accept the life there without complaint, but Jason and I felt as though we were being strangled. Old Jack told us that there is sedative medication added to the water supply in the Produnits but for some reason it didn't seem to work on us. Can you imagine what it was like to have a fixed period for sleep, for work, for your compulsory exercise program, for entertainment, even for 'conjugal activity', all along with hundreds of others, not to mention having to eat the food rations prescribed according to your dietary requirements? Once we found that there was a chance of getting away we knew we had to take it even though we had no idea of what to do afterwards; we both would prefer to die in freedom rather than exist any longer in such a place."

"It must have taken tremendous courage to head out into the absolute unknown," Kathleen marvelled. "In comparison to you I was just a piece of flotsam swept away by the current."

"I had to persuade Jason," Sonya admitted with an unexpected hint of steel in her voice. "We weren't even sure that our persaComs were disabled to start with so we stayed by the side of a river for a while; if the Police came for us we were going to jump into the water and try to drown ourselves."

Kathleen was too shocked at the matter-of-fact manner in which the girl mentioned suicide to make an immediate response and after a pause, Sonya continued.

"When no-one appeared we thought that if we headed west we would come to the coast where we might be able to steal a boat. We walked for days but without food we got very weak, so weak that when Richard found us we couldn't do anything to stop him from taking us wherever he wanted. It was a couple of days later before we were sure we had found safety."

Sympathy at the thought of two poor souls driven to such desperation brought a prickling feeling to the back of Kathleen's eyes; reaching for Sonya's hand she held it between her own, trying to convey comfort.

"And you were feeling sorry for me!" she said eventually.

Sonya shook her head as if to banish unwanted memories before she spoke.

"It turned out to be worth while. We never dreamed that an organisation working against the Federation existed or that we would get a chance to fight for a better future but here we are. And in a way, it was easier for us than for you because we had each other; we are really strong together as a result of what we did."

"From what you say, there could be others in the

Produnit who might be prepared to rebel," Kathleen suggested.

"There is certainly dissatisfaction but it's only in whispers, very low key. The threat of becoming an Impy is enough to scare most people into submission." Sonya caught Jason's eye and rose from the table. "We agreed to do another couple of hours in the workshop before bedtime so I'll have to go now."

As the two of them departed along with David and Alex, Kathleen found herself alone in the kitchen. Deciding that a bit of revision, followed by an early night, wouldn't do her any harm she retired to her own room where she got into bed with the papers spread on the covers; when she lay back to see how much of them she could remember however, it hardly seemed worthwhile sitting up again and it wasn't long before she switched off the light.

CHAPTER NINE

Gulls outnumbered crows among the flock of birds which followed the steady progress of the ForTrak across the field, squawking and squabbling as the trail of freshly turned earth revealed a bounty of worms and other tasty denizens of the soil. Glancing at her wrist, Kathleen decided that they would have to wait for their next instalment until she'd had something to eat herself; pulling into a sheltered corner, she thankfully switched off the engine.

She had made sure to be up bright and early this morning, and had been one of the first to partake of breakfast; as soon as Jenny appeared she had enquired as to her allotted task and been given field 22, mentioned yesterday as an example, to till. Intending to achieve as much as possible, she had put together a sandwich and Mary, seeing what she was about, had produced a flask of coffee to accompany it; now, with about a third of the field completed, she was more than ready for sustenance.

The continual effort of handling the machinery had warmed her enough to make her strip to her shirt, but now, although there was real heat from the sun it was tempered by brisk eddies of wind that crept down from the nearby hills. She debated for a moment whether it would be advisable to put her jacket on again but decided against it. Moving the seat to its rearmost position, she rested her feet on the steering bar and leant back to enjoy a moment of relaxation.

'This is not much different from what I would have been doing if I was still at home', she mused idly. 'I'd be ploughing in the left-over stubble and making sure that Albert had done his part properly'. Her face took on a bleak expression as associated memories threatened to spoil her mood but she resolutely pushed them away into a distant corner of her mind.

'I never really looked very far ahead,' she reflected. 'I didn't expect anything else, didn't imagine there was anything other than the next week's work and then the week after that! I just plodded away and let myself be used like a slave through ignorance.'

The sound of an engine intruded into her wool-gathering; seeing a ForTrak approaching, she hastily grabbed her lunch pack and was busy eating by the time Jenny stopped alongside.

"Slacking already!" The accompanying smile robbed the accusation of any offence as Kathleen waved a sandwich by way of explanation.

"You've done well though," Jenny said approvingly, dismounting and kicking her boot through the fresh soil.

"Glad you think so boss." Kathleen copied the lightness of tone. "I won't get it finished today though."

"I didn't expect you to," Jenny retorted. "I just came to tell you that you can carry on up to field 26 if you like. That should keep you out of my hair for a few days."

Rubbing a hand over her forehead she came to stand beside the ForTrak; Kathleen finished pouring a cup from her flask and held it out to her. Jenny accepted it gratefully and took a hasty mouthful.

"I've been running about like a blue-arsed fly all morning," she confessed. "Alex is deep into the clever stuff with your David and the other two so I don't want to ask him to leave it even for a moment but it does get a bit hectic occasionally."

"I don't suppose I can do anything to help," Kathleen offered, feeling guilty about the time taken yesterday to show her around.

"You're already doing it," Jenny assured her warmly. "Knowing I can leave you to do a proper job out here takes a load off my mind." Climbing back into her vehicle she added, "Don't be late coming in, remember the conference tonight!"

Though Kathleen lost no time in getting back to work, it seemed to be only shortly afterwards that an increasing chill in the air caused her to stop to don her jacket. Startled to see how low the sun had dropped, she checked her wrist and decided that two more passes would be all that she would manage today.

The last vestige of the sun dipped below the horizon as she arrived back at the yard, tired, but with an undeniable feeling of satisfaction. A quick shower and a brush-up dispelled most of her fatigue however, and she felt ready to face the enlarged company.

Noticing a light under David's door, she knocked and enquired if he was ready.

"Nearly," he called. "You can come in if you want."

The room, though a little smaller than her own, had much the same furnishings; David was standing in front of the mirror pushing a comb through his hair, and as he turned to smile at her she was surprised to notice that he was wearing dress jeans topped by a smart shirt.

"Will I do," he quipped, noticing her stare.

"You look very spruce," she complimented him. "But...why? Is it that much of an occasion?"

"Not really, but Sonya told me that Jenny's mother likes to see her looking nice, so they both agreed to dress up and then it just sort of spread."

"And I suppose I look scruffy?" Kathleen glanced at herself in the mirror to confirm her fears.

"Never scruffy Kathy," he assured her hastily. "But if you have something a bit smarter..."

"Wait for me for five minutes," she begged, heading for the door.

"Only five," he taunted.

"Only five," she flung back at him from half way down the corridor.

Deciding that her legs weren't ready for a skirt yet, she grabbed a pair of slacks and hesitated briefly before selecting a blouse that she hoped would match. That took about three minutes, so she was able to spend one on her hair before sauntering slowly back to David's room, trying to look as if she had been ready for ages.

"You amaze me," he congratulated her without irony. "You look marvellous. May I offer you my arm madam?"

Suppressing a desire to giggle, Kathleen took the proffered arm with as much dignity as she could muster, but when she caught the amused gleam in his eye she could control herself no longer and her ensuing burst of laughter set him off as well.

"Dear oh dear," David sighed eventually with mock gravity. "We make a fine pair of revolutionaries don't we."

"I think we'll be a hungry pair of revolutionaries if we don't get moving," she replied, giving his arm a squeeze. "Come on!"

A hum of conversation greeted them as they entered the kitchen; after spotting an immaculately turned out Jenny standing with her parents, Kathleen was thankful she had followed David's advice and changed her attire. Jenny waved but it was Hazel who left the group and bustled over; gripping both of Kathleen's hands she gave her a searching look.

"You look well Kathy," she announced. "None the worse for your adventures after you left us it seems."

"We were worried about Richard more than anything." Kathleen responded. "Did he have any problem with the searchers?"

"They asked him a few questions, but he had prepared an excuse for being off the Unit. They told him that they were hunting for dangerous escaped criminals and that he should stay close to home for safety. That was why he couldn't come back, but it seems you managed very well by yourselves."

"We were pretty tired and hungry by the time we met up with Jenny," Kathleen admitted. "But good food and a couple of nights sleep have worked wonders!"

"They must have done, for you are a different girl to the one I met just a few days ago."

"I feel different," Kathleen agreed with conviction. "Mostly thanks to you and Richard and Jenny."

"Tosh!" Hazel retorted, adding enigmatically, "Nobody can make a racehorse out of a donkey." Turning to David she gave him the same scrutiny. "You look better too, you're only carrying half the world on your shoulders now instead of all of it."

"I do feel a bit lighter," David acknowledged, "And like Kathy I am grateful for the help all of you have given us."

Hazel led them to join the others and Richard greeted

them both warmly.

"Obviously you didn't get scrambled on your journey here," he remarked drily, with a sideways glance at his daughter. "Is it possible that she's growing up a little bit at last?"

"Now Dad!" Jenny threatened. "You can be thrown off the Unit without any supper if you don't treat the manager with proper respect. I can quote the appropriate Regulation if you want!"

Pretending he hadn't heard her, Richard addressed David and Kathleen.

"I'd better introduce you to the other group leaders before it's our turn to eat."

They dutifully shook hands with James, Ewan and Margaret, who she guessed were all well into their forties. They were apparently the managers of three other units allied to the cause. Uncomfortably conscious of being the subject of unspoken scrutiny, Kathleen hung back and let David do most of the talking; as far as the one called James was concerned that wasn't difficult because he virtually ignored her existence. She was thankful when a call to the table put an end to the conversation.

Later, they all trooped down into the crypt where a circle of chairs had been set out. There seemed to be no particular order in which people took their places and Kathleen, feeling a little vulnerable, was thankful to secure a position between Jenny and David.

Richard cleared his throat for attention.

"This conference tonight is to bring you all up to date with the latest developments, especially those arising from our new recruits, David and Kathleen here. They are not yet aware of the substance of our plan so, with your approval, I will do a resume of it prior to exploring the new opportunities available to us." He looked round the circle for any sign of dissent before continuing.

"Our intention has been to bring about an event of sufficient impact that news of it will reach the world outside the Federation. We believe that using our present resources in conjunction with the standard transport of raw oil to the Ectol refinery, we have the capability to create an explosion of sufficient magnitude to achieve our purpose, especially if, as we intend, that explosion takes place in the middle of the tunnel which links this island group of regions with the rest of Federation territory. If we succeed in blocking the tunnel for a time, Urfor will be hampered in any attempt to subdue the surge of unrest which we hope will follow, and we would intend to use that time to send out appeals for outside assistance."

He looked enquiringly at Kathleen and David.

"Without going into detail, that is the basis of our plan at the moment. Do you have any questions at the moment?"

Kathleen was too amazed to speak; how could he discuss such a enormous operation as calmly as if he were planning a grain harvest; looking round the circle of faces she realised that the astonishment was confined to herself and possibly David.

"Would you anticipate a lot of casualties as a result of the explosion?" he asked hesitantly. "I'm sorry if I sound a wimp but it does bother me a bit."

"We would expect some," Richard admitted. "But depending on the success of the work you are doing, which we are about to come to, there may be an opportunity to minimise the numbers. Anything else?"

David shook his head and Richard addressed the group again.

"What has changed the picture is that David here is an expert in computer programming, so expert in fact that he was instrumental in designing the software that enables CenCon to control the Federation!"

Now there was open astonishment on a number of faces, astonishment mingled with more than a trace of hostility. Kathleen reached for David's hand and gave it a comforting squeeze.

"I know that some of you may have feelings of resentment, but he is far from being the only one to have supported the Federation at the outset. Before he had finished creating the programme he had doubts himself, and he inserted codes known only to him which allow untraceable access to the core software, with the ability to change it, even to wipe it out completely. He has offered to place his entire knowledge at our disposal."

Richard paused as excited comment ran round the circle.

"Why didn't you shut it down long ago?" one of the Unit managers demanded.

"I was afraid of the consequences," David admitted frankly. He went on to explain how so many functions of their lives depended on the system that a total shutdown could bring about unacceptable levels of deprivation and even death.

His accuser nodded understanding and Alex, after a glance at Richard took over as spokesman.

"I can tell you that I am astounded by the opportunities which confront us. Where we had previously only been able to hope that some kind of uprising would occur, we will now be able to insert our own messages into the VidCom bulletins. And if that weren't enough, David tells me that given time and sufficient assistance, he could replace sections of software with others created by himself, while leaving those parts essential to the wellbeing of the public to remain in operation. Imagine if, when our event happens, simultaneously the persaCom location facility is disabled along with the Impy control network and possibly all communications from CenCon to the regions. I personally doubt that the Authorities could respond effectively to such a situation."

He paused to let everyone consider the implications of what he had said before continuing.

"If, as we hope, enough people are sick of the way we are governed and are prepared to show their resentment, we should be able to co-ordinate demonstrations appealing for change; James and Margaret here, whose Units maintain discreet contact with non-Federation countries can then appeal to them to insist that internationally supervised elections take place. What we had envisaged as the first shot in a campaign suddenly takes on the potential to achieve our desires at a stroke."

There could be no doubt about the impact of this information on the assembled group, as David and Alex did their best to satisfy the torrent of questions which followed. Some enquired about the specifics of what could be achieved; others suggested programmes that could usefully be altered; they all wanted to know how long it would be before they could access the CenCon system.

"We are looking at maybe two weeks to get a terminal put together," Alex told them. "Then, if it works okay we will build a couple more to speed things up; David will have to teach the operatives what to do so realistically it will be something in the region of six months before we are ready."

"As you all know, our biggest shipments of oil are usually about the end of July." Richard took over. "I recommend that we make that our target and try to have everything in place by then."

The general agreement which followed his suggestion seemed to end the formal part of the meeting; Kathleen turned to David with an enquiring look.

"Well! Now that we know what we've got ourselves into, what do you think?"

"I have to confess to being quite excited," he admitted. "I've drifted along for so long and suddenly there is a goal to work for. A lot of hard work to be sure but it'll be good to stretch myself again. What about you?"

"I can't wait for you to start teaching me what to do! I just hope that I'm not too stupid to be able to help."

"You don't need to worry on that score," he patted her hand reassuringly. "You're anything but stupid."

There were so many people waiting with questions that she had to let him go, relieved in a way that she was not considered important enough to warrant a lengthy inquisition. Making polite conversation, she circulated among the group, thankful when Richard's announcment that the meeting was over precipitated a general withdrawal to the various transports. It was late enough anyway, and after a hasty drink of tea the remainder of the company drifted off to their beds.

The days were noticeably shorter by the time the new terminal was ready; outside work had to finish earlier, and most evenings Kathleen accompanied David down to the crypt to start her training. It took a while for her to learn all the procedures well enough to be allowed to operate without supervision; once she had accessed the software by using David's secret codes her work had to be meticulous, for any carelessness could result in revealing the source of the breach. More than once she declared that he was wasting his time, that she would never be able to master the complexities required, but whenever this happened he patiently coaxed her to persevere. She felt less guilty once another couple of work stations had been linked into the system, though still of the opinion that David should have more important things to do than concern himself with her.

Unknowingly, she was making progress however, and the day came when, after dutifully seeking out and tabulating files from a list that had appeared to be nothing more than another exercise, Sonya immediately took the results to her station.

"You actually wanted them," Kathleen exclaimed in surprise.

It was David who answered.

"Yes Kathy. That's your first contribution to our operation. Well done!"

Feeling a warm glow of satisfaction she demanded - and received - another task. Suddenly, what she was doing was comparatively simple and a few days later, when she was asked to try making simple alterations herself, she agreed willingly.

As her capability increased, she spent more and more time in the crypt, although the inevitable curtailment of her time out in the open made her chafe occasionally. While she rapidly became conversant with the Com system, she also came to understand much more of what had been achieved prior to her and David's arrival. Something however, still puzzled her and one evening as they finished their session, she took the opportunity to ask David about it.

"You remember when you took me and Barney to George and Nellie's place? George must have sent a message to Richard because he was expecting us, and someone had to do the same to arrange for Jenny to meet us by the sea. The different units can obviously talk to each other but how do they manage it?"

"They don't exactly talk, but they do communicate." David assured her. "Have you ever tuned into the Chatter Channel?"

Kathleen pulled a face. Long ago she had discovered Albert engrossed in it and had been less than impressed by his choice of viewing. Basically an outlet for suppressed desires, Chatter Channel carried offerings ranging from pathetic efforts of lovesick poets to very detailed and frequently embarrassing fantasies from the anonymous senders.

"Once," she admitted reluctantly. "Once was enough!"

"I don't blame you," David grinned in sympathy. "But in among all that dross, a simple code is all that you need to be able to send messages in perfect safety."

"I suppose it's a good idea," she agreed, adding with a shudder. "I wouldn't like the job of sorting through all that stuff to find the right one though!"

"You don't have to. There are pre-arranged headings for each day so the search facility usually cuts it down to a handful. Even then, some of them can be pretty unpleasant to read!"

Kathleen wondered how long this Resistance group had been in operation; they had communications, could modify persaComs, had a network established with all the essential safeguards; to reach this level of organisation before herself and David arrived must have taken some time, probably years. It could be that Jenny's description of the older members as 'fuddy-duddies' was a little inaccurate.

"I don't know when they started," David responded when she put her thoughts into words. "But as you say, it must have been quite a while ago. We may be lucky in that we're coming into it when there's a real prospect of something happening."

"I feel a bit bewildered at times," she confessed. "Learning about Ectol crops and this Com stuff and also living with people who have a totally different outlook makes me see my old life as almost being in a time warp."

"I know you'll be allright Kathy." He put his arms round her for a brief hug and she leaned against him for a moment, enjoying the sensation of comfort.

The final crop of the year gave her a welcome respite from the crypt. For a few days she drove the harvester up and down, filling hoppers for transport to the crushing station, watching occasionally as the raw oil was pumped into the waiting tanks. All too soon however, the clanking train departed and she resigned herself to being indoors for another spell.

The year's final shipment of oil heralded a collective sigh of relief among the group; the target had been achieved with a modest surplus, not counting the amount which had been diverted to their own secret refinery. There was still some work to do in the fields, but there was no pressure to get it done immediately. Jenny spent a couple of days completing paperwork, while Andy and Peter pottered around the crushing plant, preparing it for a period of inaction. Mary decided to give the kitchen a birthday and while this was happening, their meals were frequently taken in whatever corner they could find.

There was no let-up in the crypt however. Though David declared himself satisfied with their progress so far, he wanted to be well ahead of schedule in case unforseen problems arose. He sat at one terminal while Kathleen and Sonya worked at the other two, feeding him with information. Jason beavered away on the benches assembling the fourth which Kathleen's participation had made necessary.

The days went by in a blur; get up, breakfast, crypt, lunch, crypt, supper, crypt, bed. As often as she dared, Kathleen excused herself for half a day, feeling that her continuing sanity required the therapy of physical effort.

Even these periods of relief were denied her when the weather turned foul, with almost incessant wind and rain for a couple of weeks; the fields became too soggy for the heavy ForTraks and Kathleen spent practically every waking hour in the crypt.

Her pleasure when she finally woke up to a dry

morning was reduced a little as soon as she stepped outside, a sharp drop in the temperature making a return to her room in search of warm clothing imperative. She joined Jenny to watch the weather 'cast, childishly delighted when the announcer spoke of a 'northerly airstream with snow falls on high ground'.

"Are these hills high enough to get snow," she asked.

"Certainly!" Jenny replied. "In fact there's probably some already on the tops."

Kathleen decided that the crypt could wait for her a little while; throwing on boots and a coat she hurried to where the buildings no longer obstructed the view.

There was a clarity in the cold air, the northmost peaks clearly visible yet somehow unfamiliar with their white mantles glinting in the pale sunlight. She stood enthralled, drinking in the spectacle until a pang of conscience made her return to her duties.

"Have you seen the snow on the hills this morning?" she greeted David.

"Is that where you've been to get such cold cheeks," he teased, holding his warm hands against her face for a moment.

"I went out to look at them," she admitted. "Oh David, they're so lovely. I don't think I've seen snow since I was a little girl, when we all went out and played in it and built snowmen and threw lumps of it at each other."

He looked at her fondly then reached for his jacket.

"Come on then," he invited. "The Revolution can spare me for ten minutes. Shall we go and inspect them together?"

She thought at first he was teasing, but he accompanied her outside without demur; the view had changed in her brief absence, the altered angle of the sun's rays highlighting different facets and losing others into shadow, and the wind had increased; feeling the chill, she snuggled against him to share their warmth.

"I see what you mean," he murmured into her hair. "Thank you for opening my eyes for me."

"Back to work unfortunately," he continued regretfully.

"Work isn't going to last for ever David," she assured

him as they returned to the house.

CHAPTER TEN

The bitter and relentless northerly had been blowing for days now, and though in theory the Unit was sheltered by the nearby hills, their snow-covered tops added an extra chill that was sharp enough to bring tears to Kathleen's eyes. She was well wrapped up and had pulled a scarf over the lower half of her face before getting out of the ForTrak, but the wind paid little heed, sneaking into her clothing as insidiously as an expert seducer intent on taking possession of her warm body with its icy fingers.

'I asked for this', she reminded herself, giving the posts and wire a cursory examination, her boots ringing on the frozen ground as she strode briskly along the perimeter fence. 'I begged Jenny for an outside task so that I could get away from that dammed screen for a few hours, so I'd better make the most of it.'

She could of course have checked the fence just by driving alongside, but she knew that her desire, need, for fresh air would not be satisfied inside the admittedly draughty plastic canopy. If the air out here was rather more fresh than she would have preferred, well, it would be doing her that much more good wouldn't it!

"It's not really necessary," Jenny had told her. "There isn't a lot we can do out there until the ground softens a bit, but if you are determined to be a masochist, a routine security inspection always looks good on the report."

David had declined an invitation to accompany her with a mock shudder.

"I still remember that walk you took me on at Richard's place," he quipped. "I don't want to be suffering from frostbite at the Christmas party tomorrow!"

Kathleen could recall celebrating Christmas with her parents, not with a party as such, but she had received gifts of new clothes or shoes and her mother had always tried to make a special meal; eventually, these attempts at festivity had petered out in the face of increasing hardship, and Federation disapproval of Christian religious symbolism or indeed anything else that might interfere with production. Jenny however, had decreed that they would have two whole days of holiday.

"One day to get ready for the party and one to recover from it!" she promised with a wicked look.

"The Authorities might be upset!" Alex warned, with mock seriousness.

"That for the Authorities," Jenny declared, making an inelegant gesture with her finger. "It's three weeks till the next Inspection and what they don't know won't upset them.

"I hope you've got a drinkable brew ready from that infernal machine of yours," she continued, turning to Peter.

"Don't insult me Jenny," he fired back. "Have I ever made a bad one?"

"Yes!" came a chorus of half-a-dozen voices.

"Nobody round here appreciates genius," Peter said with pretended chagrin. "It would serve you right if I drank it all myself."

"You've had plenty of practice," Jenny's final comment had been unanswerable.

A stronger gust, carrying a dusting of fine snow particles brought Kathleen to a halt, and a quick look at the rapidly darkening sky was sufficient to persuade her that it would be foolish to stay out any longer. By the time she got back to the ForTrak, the insistent fingers of cold had made themselves familiar with enough of her body to make her grateful for the partial shelter provided by the cab, and even for the oily smelling heat from the engine. Though taking the most direct route back to the yard, she still had to switch on the headlights before reaching it; hurrying into the hallway, she quickly divested herself of her outdoor clothing and entered the welcoming warmth of the kitchen.

"Here you are," Jenny looked up from the game she and Andy were playing. "We were nearly ready to send out a search party. What's it like out there?"

"C-c-cold!" Kathleen assured her as she held her hands

above the stove. "I think it is trying to snow. Maybe we're going to get a white Christmas."

"Don't think so. 'Cast says that a warm front will cross overnight followed by south-west wind and rain." Jenny didn't sound disappointed. "Just as well, 'cos a pretty frock doesn't look the same with long woolly socks and a thermal vest!"

"We are expected to dress up for this party then, are we?" Kathleen enquired.

Jenny raised her eyebrows. "But of course. We're going to be tarted up like the women in the old vids, you see if we're not."

"I suppose I'll have to give some thought to what I'm going to wear then," Kathleen laughed.

"I think I'd better decide that for you," Jenny told her firmly. "Left to yourself you'll probably come in your working shirt and trousers! Tomorrow afternoon, Andy's being banished next door with Jason while Sonya and I get ready; you must come too so that we can make sure that you are properly turned out."

'They seem to have me all organised,' Kathleen thought with amusement as she made her way to the crypt for another couple of hours of 'key bashing', though she couldn't deny that she was looking forward to the occasion with pleasurable anticipation.

David looked up and smiled as she came towards him.

"You are really getting into the spirit of things," he commented. "Your face is lit up like a set of Christmas lights!"

Kathleen, detouring to inspect herself in a mirror, saw that he spoke the truth. The blood coursing through her body in response to the transition from cold to warmth certainly was imparting a glow to her cheeks; unfortunately, the wind had played havoc with her hair which now resembled nothing more than a long disused birds nest.

"Oh dear," she sighed. "I do look a mess."

"You could never look a mess Kathy," he assured her gravely, and as she couldn't think of anything to say in reply she sat down at her desk to resume the task she had abandoned earlier.

That evening, they dawdled over their meal, discussing arrangements for the following day. Mary had completed a marathon of cooking to give herself an equal opportunity to relax; for the next couple of days it was to be a 'get it yourself and tidy up after you' routine. David had gone back to the crypt to 'tie up a couple of loose ends' as he put it, and there was still no sign of him by the time Kathleen decided to head for her bed.

It was still bitterly cold as she crossed the yard, but the wind had died away completely; above her the sky was now clear of cloud, and a million twinkling stars begged individually for her attention; she lingered for a little while, gazing upwards until the pervading chill drove her to move.

The following morning, it was after eight-o-clock before the dawn reluctantly admitted that it had a duty to perform, grudgingly allowing a grey parody of itself to creep through the curtains. The sound of rain lashing at the windows was sufficient reason for Kathleen to snuggle down into the covers and she lay for a while, half dozing, half awake, enjoying the unaccustomed lack of activity. Eventually however, increasing pangs of hunger forced her to get out of bed so, after a 'lick and a promise' at the washbasin, she hung a waterproof over her head and hurried across the yard to look for breakfast.

Finding no-one there, she quickly decided that a dish of scrambled eggs would be worth the chore of scrubbing the pot afterwards. She was on her second round of toast when Peter stumbled into the room, his face an unhealthy shade of grey.

"I'm not well," he moaned, holding his head in his hands.

"What's the matter Peter?" She felt some concern, but had a sneaking suspicion as to the cause of his ailment.

"I was tasting the new brew to make sure it's all right," he muttered almost inaudibly.

"And is it?"

"It's fine! It's so good that I tasted a bit too much."

Kathleen managed to contain her amusement; she had

heard comments before about Peter's tendency to overindulge in his product.

"Poor soul!" She injected sympathy into her voice. "What you need is a bit of breakfast to settle your stomach. How about some nice greasy bacon with a couple of fried eggs swimming in fat!"

Peter gulped and went to stand by the sink. "Don't Kathy!" he pleaded after taking a few deep breaths. "Don't kick a man when he's down."

He was so palpably miserable that she hadn't the heart to tease him any more; she made him eat some dry toast and swallow a cup of strong coffee and his colour gradually improved.

"I'm going back to bed for a while," he said as he got up from the table, obviously feeling better for he blew her a kiss from the doorway.

"Remember to save a dance for me tonight," he called as he went out.

A dance! Would she be expected to dance? She had jumped and swayed to music as a child but since then her only acquaintance with dancing was watching the elaborate routines shown on the VidCom. She had as much chance of doing anything like that as of making a ForTrak sit up and beg.

'You're going to be on a sharp learning curve Kathy Pierpoint,' she told herself firmly. 'Again!'

She was washing her dishes when Sonya and Jason appeared.

"Early bird!" they greeted her cheerfully. "We thought we would be the first."

"Peter was here for a while," Kathleen told them. "He said he was going back to bed."

"Uh oh!" Jason's face creased into a smile. "Was he bad?"

"He looked dreadful. I can't imagine he'll be fit for the party."

"He'll be fine," Jason said confidently. "He's got a constitution like reinforced concrete. I've seen him under the weather before, I guarantee that he'll dance the rest of us off our feet tonight."

Kathleen seized the moment to make her enquiry.

"Talking of dancing, I'm a bit worried because I've never danced in my life. I don't want to make a fool of myself in front of you all."

"There's nothing difficult about what we'll be doing," Sonya exuded confidence. "You'll be okay. You are coming over to Jenny's this afternoon to get ready aren't you?" Kathleen nodded assent, and Sonya continued. "Well then, we can run through a few steps together so that you get the feel of it."

"It's easier for a woman," Jason put in. "As long as her partner knows what he's at she just has to follow his lead."

"That doesn't always apply with you," Sonya told him without malice. "You can be a bit wooden at times."

"I'm afraid you're right," he admitted frankly. "Sometimes I wish I could move like Andy and Peter."

"Never mind darling," Sonya comforted him with an arch look. "You have your own special talents."

Kathleen made her excuses and left the kitchen. Wondering how to occupy this unwonted period of idleness, and noticing that the rain had stopped, she decided that some exercise wouldn't go amiss; after donning wellingtons and a jacket, she left the circle of buildings and splashed through the puddles into the adjoining fields.

She found it necessary to tread carefully, for the going was treacherous; the rain had softened a top layer of soil which now slid easily over the still frozen ground below. She took her time, force of habit making her stop to examine the battered looking growth which had been sown in the autumn, hoping that these young plants weren't susceptible to frost damage. She felt invigorated though, the fresh moisture-laden air coursing into her lungs and soothing her skin, a pleasant contrast to the debilitating chill of the previous day; nearly two hours had passed before she felt ready to return.

"Walkies again!" Jenny accused, coming in as Kathleen kicked off her wellingtons. "What are we going to do with you? Why can't you just slop out like the rest of us?"

"I like to be doing something," Kathleen excused herself. "I've not much experience of having time on my hands."

Jenny shook her head then laughingly threw a towel at her.

"You're soaking. You look like a dog that's been running through wet grass!"

Kathleen smoothed her hands over her hair, shivering as cold water trickled down her neck. Grabbing the towel she gave herself a quick scrub before following Jenny into the kitchen, where she found most of the company sitting about in various postures of idleness. Peter was absent though, and there was no sign of David.

Accepting the offer of a cup of tea, she sat down with Sonya and Jenny.

"So what's the grand plan for this afternoon?" she enquired.

Jenny yawned and stretched lazily before replying.

"There you go again Miss Hustle-Bustle. First, we're going to sit here and drink tea; then we will have a leisurely lunch; then we will sit for a while longer; then I will inspect your wardrobe and decide what you're going to wear; then you will bathe; then you will come to my place bringing your stuff; then we'll have a taste of Peter's hooch while we help each other get ready. Does that sound busy enough for you?"

"Sounds all right to me," Kathleen smiled her acceptance and tried to look relaxed; she was glad to see David arrive, obviously fresh from a bath and wearing smart casuals.

"You certainly like your sleep," she greeted him. "I was all prepared to make breakfast for you as a treat but nobody appeared apart from Peter."

"I would be surprised if he wanted food this morning." Jenny commented drily.

"He didn't. When I offered him a nice greasy fry-up he wasn't at all appreciative!" Kathleen tried to sound mournful.

David gave a short laugh. "It looks like I needn't come to you expecting sympathy if I ever have a hangover."

"Absolutely not!" Kathleen agreed lightly.

She managed to get involved in setting out lunch, and the ensuing tidying-up, so the time passed relatively quickly until Jenny rose to accompany her to the bunkhouse.

"That's perfect!" she declared as, after riffling through Kathleen's wardrobe, she made her hold up the green dress.

"Are you sure," Kathleen demurred. "I'm not really used to skirts and I've certainly never worn anything like this; it seems...well...a little bit skimpy."

"You don't know what skimpy is!" Jenny was adamant. "Anyway, you promised that you would let me decide. I'll take it with me now and we'll see you in about half an hour."

Kathleen subdued her misgivings and agreed to defer to the younger woman's judgement. Later, as she crossed the yard, she was glad to see that a watery looking sun had managed to significantly dry the atmosphere.

'At least it shouldn't be tippling down on us tonight,' she thought, as she knocked on the door of Jenny's dwelling and obeyed the call to come in.

She found the two girls discussing the merits of various articles of clothing which were spread about the room. Jenny immediately filled three glasses from a jug of amber liquid.

"We were waiting for you," she said, thrusting one of them into Kathleen's hand. "Now we can try 'Peter's Punch'. I propose a toast to us."

Kathleen, not knowing what to expect, took a cautious sip and let the liquid roll across her tongue. Long ago Albert had brought bottles of the standard blue-and-yellow labelled Federation beer back to the house and insisted she try it; she had found the taste sour and unpleasant but this 'Punch' of Peter's was quite different. Much sweeter for a start, it had a complex of flavours which were redolent of wild flowers Taking a swallow, she was pleasantly surprised by the feeling of warmth in her throat.

"Downfall to the Federation!" They drank enthusiastically to Sonya's proposal, then the other two looked expectantly at Kathleen. She took a moment to come up with an idea.

"Here's to tonight's party!" she suggested.

"Now you're getting the idea," Jenny applauded as they raised their glasses again.

"Right, to business," she continued, offering Kathleen a small jar of ointment. "You rub this into your arms and legs, it helps to make your skin smooth and it smells nice too."

Kathleen dutifully did as she was told. The ointment did indeed have an attractive aroma and she was gratified by the silky feeling it imparted to her skin. She felt more relaxed now, her earlier concerns about being 'tarted up' fading by the minute; Jenny and Sonya must have been feeling the same for by the time they were finished with the ointment all three of them were as merry as monkeys.

"We'll get you dressed first Kathy," they announced, fussing round her like mother hens in dispute over a solitary chicken. She submitted patiently as they debated what to do with her hair, slipped the green dress over her head and turned her this way and that; then she had to keep her face straight while Jenny dabbed and brushed with items produced from a small box and finally pronounced herself satisfied. Then, though not before, she was allowed to look at herself in the mirror.

Unaccustomed to taking a great deal of care with her appearance, she was astonished by the transformation. She had allowed her hair to grow longer than the short crop she had previously favoured and in response to intense brushing it now fell in a natural wave around her face and on to her shoulders; her eyebrows and lips were subtly enhanced with some preparation from Jenny's box and there was an indubitable trace of a blush on her cheeks. Her shoulders were bare apart from the spangled dress straps and the dress itself, though loose fitting, clung to the curves of her body all the way from the low neckline until it ended a few inches above her knees; experimentally she swung from side to side, the soft fabric sliding against her skin so delicately that it felt like a caress.

Jenny and Sonya were watching her intently. "Well,"

they chorused. "What do you think?"

"It feels wonderful," Kathleen admitted, and laughed. "It's a beautiful dress but... there seems to be an awful lot of me outside it!"

"There's supposed to be a lot of you outside it, silly!" Jenny said dismissively. "That's what party dresses are all about!"

Kathleen still wasn't sure. "I almost feel that I should be wearing something else with it," she suggested.

"My dear! You don't mean a 'brassiere'!" Jenny pretended horror mixed with mockery. "The only reason you strap your boobs up in those things is when they get too saggy and that's one problem you certainly don't have to worry about. Have you ever worn one, do you know how uncomfortable they are?"

"My mother made me wear a bra when I was young," Kathleen admitted. "I hated it, but she said only loose women went without them and when I eventually rebelled she said I was shameful!"

" You've no cause to be ashamed of what you've got Kathy." Jenny was forthright. "Here!" she waved the jug. "have some more 'PP' and we'll drink to shameful women."

Kathleen recalled her mother's attitude to the scanty costumes sometimes seen on the VidCom. 'Tarts and trollops' she would snap, with a glance at her husband to prompt him to change channels immediately. 'No decent woman would flaunt herself like that'. Yet these two obviously decent girls regarded the display of a bit, well actually quite a lot of flesh as a normal part of being 'dressed up'.

'Who am I to say that they are wrong?' she told herself firmly. 'I'm in a different world now.'

Whether it was the effect of the drink or seeing the clothes the others had chosen, any qualms about herself soon disappeared. Sonya had opted for what she told Kathleen was a 'crop top' which left a large expanse of her midriff uncovered, and the accompanying skirt hardly reached half-way from her waist to her knees; Jenny's skirt was similar and with it she wore a buttonless blouse which tied in a knot above her waist.

"I feel quite decent compared with you two," she commented as they stood admiring themselves. "I would never dare wear anything like that!"

"This is nothing," Sonya retorted, raising the hem of her top until it almost exposed the bottom of her breasts. "Now that is what I would call revealing! And I've been known to wear skirts that would make this one look positively ankle-length!"

"Bit much for this occasion my dear," Jenny drawled. Mischief crept into her tone as she added. "Though it would almost be worth it to see Peter's reaction!"

"He asked me this morning to keep a dance for him," Kathleen remembered.

"You should. He's so good that it's a pleasure to be on the floor with him. Just make sure his hands stay where they belong, that's all! Now, try these on will you, I think they're about your size."

Jenny held out a pair of soft black almost slipper-like shoes and watched as Kathleen slipped them onto her feet.

"Comfortable?" she queried.

"Yes, they are," Kathleen stood up and took a few tentative steps. "They are lovely. Wherever do you get all this stuff from?"

"Deals!" said Jenny mysteriously, holding a finger to the side of her nose. "High-ups in Admin can get all sorts of fancy things and sometimes they want something we can provide so..." she shrugged expressively.

"Time to get some food into us I think," she continued. "'PP' packs quite a punch and we don't want to be staggering in front of the men!"

As they trooped across the yard Kathleen reflected briefly on the insouciance of her two companions and compared it with her own somewhat spartan attitude. Even under the stern rule of the Federation these two girls' upbringing had obviously let them see more, do more, have more fun than she would have dreamed possible. It wasn't her parents fault she hastily assured herself, they worked so hard and never looked beyond the farm gate so she had naturally grown up in an enclosed and sheltered environment. But perhaps Albert's accusations that 'you're nothing but a bloody prude' might have have held an element of truth.

A chorus of cheers greeted them as they entered the kitchen.

"Here you are! We were just about to start supper without you" Alex called cheerfully. "But you're forgiven; the way you all look it was worth the wait."

David came towards Kathleen with an expression of wonder on his face. Taking both of her hands in his he studied her for a moment.

"I can hardly believe it's the same girl I saw earlier," he said quietly. "Kathy, you look absolutely lovely!"

Normally she would have been flustered by such a compliment, compelled to dismiss it as a joke; now, perhaps due to Peter's Punch she was able to accept it gracefully.

"Thank you David." The old Kathleen was thankful that his eyes were fixed on her face, but a newly liberated devilish imp in her head wouldn't have minded if they had strayed more obviously to admire the rest of her.

"You look pretty smart yourself," she told him, and indeed he did in a silky black shirt over dark blue trousers.

"Thank you Kathy," he returned formally. "May I escort you to the table?"

They ate until everyone declared themselves replete, then played parlour games, the main purpose of which seemed to be to reduce everybody to a state of helpless laughter. Later, after their meal had settled a bit, Alex found a music channel on the VidCom and switched it through to an extension speaker.

"Come on!" Mary urged, jumping to her feet and going into a complicated series of movements in the middle of the floor. She was quickly followed by Sonya and Jenny; Kathleen watched with amusement as they stepped and swung but soon found herself swaying in time to the insistent beat; she obeyed Jenny's command to join in with only a modicum of reluctance.

"Let yourself go with the music," they instructed her. "Just do your own thing. It's easy!"

And indeed, after a couple of minutes she was enjoying herself thoroughly, no longer afraid of looking foolish as she copied her partners extravagant gestures. It was only exhaustion that made her drop out; fanning herself vigourously she gratefully accepted a glass of 'PP'. Jenny and Sonya were next to retire; Mary, left on her own pouted at the assembled company.

"What's wrong with you, are you all getting old?" she goaded.

It was Andy who responded first to the challenge, then Peter and Kathleen was astonished to see the way they moved. 'Talk about double-jointed, they must be made of rubber' she giggled to herself as the two men competed to fling themselves about in wild abandon. She turned to David who was watching with equal fascination.

"Can you dance like that," she enquired mischievously.

"Never in a hundred years," he admitted cheerfully. "The only time I ventured onto a dance floor my partner suggested that I must have been carved out of a block of stone."

"That wasn't very nice of her. I assume it was a 'her'," she probed lightly.

"It was a 'her'," he kept his eyes fixed on the dancers. "And you're right, she wasn't very nice."

His tone suggested that he had no desire to elaborate further. The moment of awkwardness was broken as the music changed to a slower tempo and Peter joined them.

"How's my guardian angel," he greeted her and turning to David continued. "Did she tell you that I was at death's door this morning and she saved my life!"

"I did hear something about greasy bacon," David teased.

"Ah, she was only being cruel to be kind," Peter defended her. "And you promised me a dance remember."

"You'll have to show me what to do," she pleaded as he led her to the floor where Alex and Mary were gyrating slowly; she tried to respond to the pressure of his hands on her waist as they took a few cautious steps but stumbled more than once.

"We're supposed to move as one," he told her, stopping to guide her arms around his neck. "Just relax and follow me, let me do the work."

She had to admit that it was easier as he held her tightly against him; she could feel him start each movement and allow her body to respond in harmony; she was soon enjoying the sensation of floating around the floor, indeed it was so pleasant that she took a little while to realise that the way he held her was becoming rather more intimate. Then of course her body started to react and she was glad to escape as soon as the music came to an end.

"I see what Jenny meant," she muttered to herself, feeling stupidly annoyed with herself as she sought the safety of David's company.

"What was that you said," he asked as she sat down beside him.

"Nothing," she assured him hastily. "But if Peter comes and asks for another dance you must say that I've already promised you."

"You might regret it," he warned, glancing at her feet. "Those shoes won't give your toes much protection when I stand on them."

"I'll stand on yours then and you can carry me about," she suggested. "We can be two blocks of wood together."

"If you insist then." He smiled at her and took a folded slip of paper out of his pocket.

"Christmas is a time for presents," he continued, holding it out to her. "I wanted to give you something and thought this might please you. That's why I went back to the crypt last night."

She stared at him for a moment. A gift for her. What kind of gift could he produce in the crypt.

"What is it," she demanded.

"Open it and see."

Intrigued now, she took the proffered paper, astonishment coursing through her as she absorbed the contents.

'Kathleen Pierpoint,' it was headed and went on with a list of the personal information which the authorities required to be held. She skimmed through it, noticing that a good deal seemed to be missing.

"What have you done?" she asked, puzzled.

"I called up your persaFile Kathy and altered it. There is no record of your arrest or charges against you any more, nothing to connect you with Stephen Lock or harbouring an illegal or any kind of misbehaviour. You have an unblemished record as manager of Unit D/356 on temporary secondment to Ectol production so whatever happens now you are safe, you could go back to 'The Beeches' if you wanted. I even chased your old file down into limbo and filled that section with so much rubbish that it's gone for good."

She gazed at him open-mouthed as she realised the implications of the document.

"David, I don't know how to thank you. It must have taken you ages to do this."

"It did take a while," he admitted. "There were a lot of cross-references that had to be deleted in other files. That's why I was so late getting up this morning."

Kathleen wanted to express her gratitude somehow; she wanted to give him a hug and tell him how much she appreciated his consideration; she was about to do so when she was interrupted by a shout from Mary.

"Come on you slackers! Everybody on the floor for this one."

They were made to join in a procession which slowly wove around the room in time to the music, surmounting challenges of increasing difficulty with a swallow of 'PP' as the penalty for failure until they all collapsed in a mixture of laughter and exhaustion. After they recovered, the music slowed and Kathleen was claimed for a dance by Alex and then by Andy while the other girls took turns to drag David onto the floor. When, finally, they were together again he looked at her with a fatalistic expression.

"Are you going to risk your feet with me," he asked humbly.

It wasn't as bad as he'd threatened but he was too afraid of hurting her to allow himself to relax and after a few circuits she gratefully accepted his suggestion that they sit down.

"I'm afraid I'm going to make my apologies and call it a night," David covered a yawn with his hand. "I must be getting old!"

Kathleen, looking around noticed that Sonya and Jason, Mary and Alex and Jenny and Andy were still on the floor, but obviously totally absorbed in each other; she felt rather than saw Peter's glance in her direction.

"I'm not staying without protection," she said firmly. "If you're going, I'm going with you."

David gave her an amused smile as she tilted her head towards Peter; they managed to catch Jenny's eye and wave goodnight before they went, holding hands as they negotiated the darkened way to their quarters.

Kathleen stopped David in the hallway of the bunkhouse.

"I never thanked you for my present," she apologised. "I was about to when we were interrupted. I only wish I could give you something in return."

"You already have Kathy. You've filled a place in my life that has always been empty. If you're really determined though, I'll accept a goodnight kiss in payment!"

"A kiss isn't much of a reward," she murmured, reaching for him, holding her face up to his so that their lips met. From the way he kissed her she thought that he hoped for something more, something that she would dearly like to give him. She hugged him as tightly as she could, welcoming the sudden strength of his return embrace, the feel of his caress but only for a moment. Just as in the past, her body tensed and then froze until she stood rigid and unfeeling; a moment later he dropped his arms from around her and moved away.

"Goodnight Kathy," was all he said as he went to his room.

CHAPTER ELEVEN

Jenny's allocation of a 'day to recover' proved to have been a wise move; it was past midday by the time a very subdued company, thirsting for tea or coffee, gathered in the kitchen. Kathleen had to admit to herself that, although not suffering from the headaches which seemed to be prevalent, she did feel jaded with none of her normal desire for activity.

Earlier, she had reflected for a while on her mixed feelings of the previous night. She had been quite happy to kiss David, indeed it had been so enjoyable that, welcoming the increasing sensation of being loved and wanted, she had felt a momentary impulse for something more. But as soon as her body had slammed its deep-rooted barrier down he had gone cold and distant, hadn't tried to overcome her resistance in any way.

'Maybe he doesn't fancy you enough Kathy girl' she told herself ruefully. Whatever the reason, she would have to tread warily for the next few days until she could assess whether his attitude towards her had changed.

She need not have worried however. Once the holiday was over he treated her exactly as he had done previously; they worked and talked and laughed together, though perhaps he was less inclined to touch her hand or put his arm round her shoulders than he had been before. It certainly wasn't difficult to push the memories of that night into the back of her mind for there was plenty of work to keep everyone busy; the official activity on the unit increased sharply as the days slowly lengthened and Kathleen frequently found herself on a ForTrak preparing ground for planting or fertilising from first light and when it became too dark to work in the fields she went straight to the 'crypt'. She was skilled enough now to operate a terminal without supervision and there was always a list of files to be accessed, checked, sometimes copied to where David painstakingly reproduced them with the appropriate alterations. Luckily, Sonya had quickly acquired the ability to write basic programmes and, although David always checked what she had done, she was able to take a lot of the more mundane work off his shoulders. They had set themselves so much to do however, that it became commonplace to return to it after a hasty supper, only calling a halt when increasing tiredness brought the risk of making mistakes.

Kathleen enjoyed the mental challenge of what she was doing; she certainly broadened her knowledge of the ramifications of CenCon's reach while working with it but she was grateful that the demands of the Unit ensured that a lot of her time was spent outside. 'This is where I really belong,' she told herself as she tended to the rapidly ripening crop, checking growth rates, taking small samples for analysis, trimming ever encroaching weeds. Whenever possible she met up with Jenny to share their midday break for their initial rapport had developed into a close and enduring friendship. Their discussions ranged from politics and the running of the unit to life in general and men in particular.

"I sometimes wonder why you and David aren't a pair," Jenny announced frankly on a day that they had stolen a few minutes to bask in the sun. "You fit together so well in every other way. You are fond of him aren't you?"

Kathleen took her time before replying, gathering her thoughts, wondering how much she wanted to reveal.

"Yes, of course I'm fond of him," she allowed cautiously.

"Very fond?" The question was insistent.

"I suppose I am really. Oh Jenny, I might as well admit that I don't know what I want. There's some kind of barrier with me and I think there's the same with him. Maybe we're just not meant to get together."

Jenny turned to face her with a look of sympathy.

"It's obvious he thinks the world of you and I'm positive he's not gay. Maybe he's just so involved in what he's doing that he doesn't want any distractions at the moment."

"So I'm a distraction now, am I?" Kathleen tried to

make a joke of it. "Seriously though, he used to have this hang-up about being responsible for the CenCom program, being unworthy and wanting to make a sacrifice of himself. He hasn't mentioned it for a while but maybe that's because I threatened to kick him if he did."

"That's plain silly," Jenny protested. "Surely what he's doing now more than makes up for any imagined error in the past."

"I know. I'd just like to be sure he realises that himself."

"It's going to be all right for you Kathy, it has to, you deserve a bit of happiness," Jenny comforted as she rose to her feet. "Ah well, duty calls, we'd better get back to work."

As the time for the main harvest approached, an unmistakeable air of tension surfaced among the group, often expressed as spats or sharp words in response to behaviour that would normally have resulted in, at the most, mild remonstration. Alex and Jenny seemed to spend most of the day checking and rechecking every aspect of the preparations and David finally demurred when it was suggested that he go over his programs for the third time.

"I know they are okay," he protested. "If I check them again I'll start to see errors where there aren't any. It would do us all good to chill out a bit or we'll explode before D-day."

"I suppose you're right," Alex admitted wearily. "If I'd spent as long as you have looking at lines of symbols I think I'd be asking someone to put an implant in my head!"

"I'll tell you what," he continued. "You and Kathy aren't familiar with what is going to happen when the oil is collected. Why don't we go to the depot and I'll explain things? The fresh air will do you good."

Kathleen wanted to retort that she was still working plenty of hours in the open but managed to hold her tongue. Poor David certainly could do with a change, he had seen so little of the summer sunshine that his skin looked pasty white compared with her own healthy tan.

Anyway, it would be interesting to see exactly how the plan was to be put into operation.

She made sure she was first to the ForTrak, taking the controls and leaving the two men no choice but to suffer the bench seat in the rear, though she did her best to make the trip to the depot as smooth as possible. Alex led them round the building to where rusty iron rails ran under an overhanging gantry and started his explanation.

"You already know, don't you, that the transport comes in on this branch that is connected to the main north-south line? Well, whenever our holding tanks are full there is a collection but during the main harvest we also run the plant at maximum capacity so the shipment is much bigger. It takes a little bit longer to fill them but it saves having to stop whenever we run out of storage.

"Each container is stopped under the pipe and when it is full an alarm sounds; the Inspector and someone from the Unit verify the quantity, then the cap is closed and an official seal put over it. All we have to do is to halt the filling of one container for long enough to introduce our special package!"

"How will you stop the Inspector seeing what is going on?" David asked.

"Easily I hope." Alex smiled at them. "He's not a bad sort and he happens to be partial to Peter's brew; often enough he leaves us to carry on with the work while he goes inside to sample the latest batch. The only other problem could be the driver but usually the train has picked up at a few other depots first so it is pretty long and the cab should be out of sight of the loading bay."

"Driver?" David questioned. "I thought the rail network was fully automated."

"There has always been a driver for loading, but what happens after that I don't know," Alex confessed.

"This one tank will be filled with a more volatile mixture that Andy and Peter have produced so it should detonate with sufficient force to set the others off in a sort of chain reaction," he continued. "The outcome is a bit uncertain but at the least there will be a major conflagration. Hopefully the intense heat in a confined area will cause a series of explosions along the line which should make the tunnel unusable for quite a while."

"How long do you think it will be before CenCon manage to trace the sabotage back to here?" Kathleen asked.

"No idea," Alex shrugged. "We will have to keep a constant watch on their communications and if it looks dangerous we will all have to disappear."

"We can interfere with those communications until they realise that they can't rely on the network," David pointed out. "At a guess, they will then be running about like headless chickens!"

They went into the crushing plant where Peter demonstrated how he intended to introduce the special fuel into the filling process. David seemed impatient for their tour to be over.

"I think we should have a look at how the transport system operates," he explained as, after returning to the house, he led them into the crypt. "If we start from different angles it shouldn't take too long."

Kathleen found herself wearily accessing files, tracing the route back from the central refinery; it was relatively straightforward and she only had to make a few notes of the procedure until she came to the tunnel itself. There it became slightly more complicated when she discovered that there was a recently imposed restriction on speed over one section. Why, she wondered, expanding her search to seek out the reason for this precaution; a feeling of excitement spread through her as she found what she was looking for.

"David, Alex," she said urgently. "I think you should have a look at this."

She moved back to let them see the displayed report of the routine structural survey. Marked 'Restricted Viewing Only' it referred to the evidence of a number of surface cracks in one section of the tunnel roof and recommended immediate closure until a more detailed study could be carried out.

"Damn!" Alex muttered. "If they close it now all our plans are in the air."

David's fingers flew over the keyboard and soon he had the results of the Safety Committee's deliberations.

'Deferred for further consideration,' he read out. 'Temporary speed limit for heavy traffic.' "They're not going to do anything that will affect us but if there is a weakness in that area we could exploit it."

"Timing is the problem," Alex warned. "All we have allowed for is that the explosion will happen somewhere in the tunnel. How could we be precise enough to make sure it is in that exact spot?"

"Go with it," David declared. "Although the main route is all automatically controlled, the regulations I've been looking at stipulate that there must be a driver on board at all times. I could go instead, bail out at the entrance and set the timer as it actually enters the tunnel."

"No," Kathleen protested. "You'd be taking too big a risk of getting caught."

"There isn't a great deal of risk," David insisted. "I would be wearing the driver's persaCom and leave it in the cab when I get out. All I would have to do then is to find my way back here."

"We could kidnap the driver I suppose," Alex said thoughtfully. "Though he would have to be kept out of circulation at least until we knew what was happening."

"I'll leave you to deal with that," David gave a wry smile. "Being confined has got to be preferable to being blown up!"

"So it's settled then that this is the best way forward?" he continued eagerly.

Kathleen wasn't very happy about it but she had to admit that David seemed excited by the prospect of action; unable to think of a valid objection, she added her grudging assent to Alex's considered endorsement.

"Right!" David turned enthusiastically back to the monitor. "I've only got a couple of days to learn how to be a 'transport attendant' so I'd better get busy."

Kathleen left him to his research and went to discuss the revised plan with Jenny and the others. Their almost casual acceptance of it did nothing to dispel her feeling of unease, but luckily there was sufficient pressure of work to allow her to push any doubts to the back of her mind.

The arrival of the train of tanks heralded a bout of frenzied activity with every bit of machinery operating at maximum capacity. As soon as loading started Kathleen worked non-stop with one of the reapers, pausing only long enough to exchange her full hopper for an empty one, snatching her midday snack on the straight sections where she could control the ForTrak with one hand. The pumps were insatiable, drawing from storage whenever the fresh supply couldn't keep pace so even after loading stopped for the day the harvest continued until the Unit's tanks were topped up ready for the morning. At last, weary but with a sense of achievment, she entered the kitchen to find a furious debate going on.

"What's the matter?" Kathleen demanded as she gratefully sank into a chair.

Alex swiftly lifted his hand as they all tried to answer at once.

"It's a different Inspector," he said grimly. "Our usual man is off sick or something and this one is an officious prat. He'll stand there following the rules all day so there's no way we'll get an opportunity to put the package into the tank."

"Can't we do it at night, after he's gone," she suggested.

Alex shook his head. "The full tanks are sealed and the empties are sealed too until the pipe connects. Any damage to a seal is picked up by the monitors."

"I think there might be a way to distract the Inspector," Jenny's remark was scarcely audible and she appeared to be distressed. "If it's the only way we'll have to consider it!"

"What's way's that," they all demanded at once.

"When we were going through the formalities this morning he never stopped undressing me with his eyes!" Jenny flushed as she spoke. "He even hinted that he could get me a job in Admin if I was co-operative. I think if I flaunted myself I might be able to tempt him into the pumphouse for a few minutes!"

"The lecherous bastard!" Andy burst out angrily. "I'll

put his head in the crusher before I let you do that!"

"No you won't Andy!" Jenny's voice became stubborn but Kathleen could see that she was close to tears. "You'd only get us all into trouble. No, I'll have to try if it's the only way"

Kathleen's heart went out to the younger girl who had done so much to help her and who was now prepared to sacrifice herself; in a wave of love and sympathy she spoke without pausing for thought.

"No Jenny, you're not going to do anything of the sort," she said briskly. "If anyone is to get this man out of the way I'll do it!"

A shocked silence greeted her statement and she continued.

"You told me yourself that I had a figure that men notice and I'm sure that I can manage to do a bit of flaunting. Much better that I try because I'm older than you and more experienced in that kind of situation. About how long will it take you to do the job?"

"No more than five minutes I hope," Alex advised.

"It's too big a risk," David started to protest but she cut him short.

"That's what I said when you decided to go off on the train," she reminded him briskly. "It didn't change *your* mind, did it?"

He couldn't find an answer for her; turning away he headed for the crypt while Jenny came and embraced her.

"Are you sure about this Kathy," she whispered. "I was trying to put on a brave face but I don't know if could really go through with it; I don't want you to be hurt though."

"I'll be all right," Kathleen's reassuring tone was as much for her own benefit as for anyone else. Long suppressed recollections of the past were clamouring for attention; the effort of forcing them back into quietude lent a touch of bitterness as she added."I've had plenty of practice."

While she had a bite to eat she enquired about the other problem, that of the train driver. Alex was able to smile as he satisfied her curiosity.

"I don't think we'll have any difficulty on that score. The driver's name is Terisa and she accepted an invitation to eat with us; she seemed to be quite taken with Peter and they have gone to his room to sample some 'Peter's Punch'. Before they went he assured me that he'd be able to take care of her!"

"I'm sure he will!" Kathleen laughed, thinking just how capable Peter's 'care' could probably be. Yawning to make an excuse, she retired to her room to consider just what she had volunteered for. She was going to show off her body in front of this Inspector, to encourage his lust until it overcame his sense of duty. Then she would lure him into the pumphouse and keep him occupied until such time as her friends had achieved their purpose!

'It will only be for five minutes,' she assured herself, resolutely dismissing any misgivings as to how long five minutes could acually be. 'It's a chance to repay Jenny and the others for everything they have done for me so I'm not going to let them down.'

The words gave her some comfort, but did not totally suppress the trepidation she felt and she had to force her thoughts elswhere until eventually the toll of the day's labour demanded she surrender to sleep.

She spent the morning hard at work in the fields then took a few moments to prepare for her task; wondering what to wear, she eventually selected an old pair of dress jeans, low waisted, which would display her navel and the top of her belly, along with a shirt which had shrunk in the wash so that she could hardly get the buttons closed. Heading for the loading depot at the arranged time, the heat of the sun gave sufficient reason to open some of the buttons, although the resultant exposure made her feel uncomfortably like a tart.

'That's just what you have to be this afternoon,' she told herself firmly.

The Inspector, big but a little flabby and with a rather florid countenance, scowled when, having ostensibly relayed a message, she took over the recorder and Alex departed.

"He's had to go on an errand," Kathleen explained.

"I'm to fill in until he gets back, so long as you have no objection."

"It's not proper procedure," he grumbled, then, after giving her a quick appraisal continued hastily. "But I'll make an exception this time so long as you do what I tell you."

She congratulated herself on successfully passing the first hurdle; as the hum of the pumps indicated the resumption of tank filling, she watched the readout change with the increasing level, hoping that he would take the opportunity for a more detailed assessment of her figure.

The hooter sounded as the filling hose retracted and after checking that the totals corresponded, they both pressed the OK tab on their recorders; the Inspector climbed up to close the cap and affix the official seals. Praying that he was watching, she took the opportunity to stretch her arms behind her head as though in lazy contentment; the shirt strained over her breasts until she felt another button give up the unequal struggle but she pretended not to notice. The Inspector gave an audible gasp and nearly fell off the ladder as he descended.

"Can you have a look to make sure that it's set properly for the next tank?" she asked, giving what she hoped was a deferential smile, leaning towards him so that he could see the recorder in her hand. He glanced at it for less than a second but his subsequent gaze into her cleavage was so intense she could almost feel it creeping salaciously over her flesh.

"Everything looks fine to me," he assured her, wetting his lips. "You must be pretty bright to have picked it up so quickly. Don't you think you're wasting your talents working in a primitive place like this."?

'Here we go,' Kathleen thought, amusement mingling with relief at her initial success; she gave a deprecatory shrug.

"I've no qualifications so it's the best I can hope for. I have to do something after all."

"Oh, you've already shown me that you have qualifications which would get you a cushy number in Admin. If you could persuade someone with influence to give you a recommendation you'd have a foot in the door; after that it would be entirely up to you how far you wanted to go!"

"There's not much chance of getting a recommendation when I'm stuck out in this wilderness." She managed to sound despondent.

"That's where you're wrong. You're looking at a man right now who's words carry a lot of weight and who knows the right ears to speak to." His boast carried a trace of condescension.

Kathleen managed to look suitably impressed.

"That would be like a dream come true," she enthused and then adopted a disconsolate attitude.

"But how could I possibly get an important person like you to put in a good word for me?" She treated him to a look of sadness and resignation.

"I always say that a favour given deserves a favour in return," he suggested, ogling all of her body with such lecherous intensity that she had to re-assure herself that her clothes hadn't suddenly disappeared. It was abundantly clear as to which particular favour he hoped to receive!

"I'm not sure what you mean," she teased with a pretence of innocence.

"If we could meet up after I've finished here, I would enjoy explaining it to you," he ventured hopefully.

'This isn't getting me anywhere," Kathleen thought dismally. 'I've got to tempt him out of sight of the tanks but if the suggestion comes from me he might well be suspicious.

"I'll have to work on the harvest until late tonight," she countered. "And by then I'll be too tired to do anything but sleep!" Feeling desperate, she tilted her head to look at the sky, putting her hands up as though for shade, arching her shoulders back, well aware that as she did so, her already inadequately covered breasts were close to escaping altogether from their confinement.

"It's scorching out here," she complained, feeling like a whore but still holding the pose long enough for him to make a thorough inspection. "How I wish I could get into the shade for a little while."

"It is rather warm," he agreed, his voice a little hoarse. "Tell you what, while the next tank is filling we could grab a few minutes in there if you like." He nodded in the direction of the pumphouse.

"Could we? That would be marvellous." The smile she gave him did not have to be feigned this time. "I'm sweating so much that my clothes are sticking to my skin!"

She had to suppress a desire to laugh as his eyes took on a gleam of lust.

"I should be able to help you with that problem," he assured her, swallowing as he spoke and glancing impatiently at the recorder's read-out. The moment he descended from sealing the full tank, he nodded again towards the pumphouse.

"Shall we go?" he invited with a show of gallantry.

Kathleen complied willingly, letting her hips sway erotically for his benefit as he followed close behind her; she thought she could feel his eyes burning on her backside.

"Hurry up," he begged eagerly.

"You know it's no good being too quick." She wondered fleetingly at how being in the company of Jenny and the others had increased her fluency with double meanings, but her amusement quickly evaporated when she reached the shade inside the building.

"Don't worry yourself on that score," he growled, urging her into the little office and closing the door. "Just get your piCode entered here and I'll show you how long I can last."

She hadn't expected him to be quite so explicit.

"Don't you want to get me in the mood first?" she invited, with an attempt at archness.

"You won't catch me out like that," he told her. "I'm not laying one finger on you until I've got your Consent."

"What will happen if I agree?" she tried to sound teasing.

"I'll get you a post in Admin, I promise." His tone was business like, direct. "It won't be difficult, you've got a body that more than one of my superiors would be glad to get his hands on. The deal is that I get to enjoy it for a while first! If you don't want to do business, okay, we'll get back to our duties."

Kathleen considered her options, realising that she really didn't have any. She had promised to get the Inspector out of sight and in that she had succeeded but the others would be relying on her now to keep him in the pumphouse until they gave the all clear signal; if she refused Consent he might just go straight back outside where he would probably catch them in the act of sabotage and that would spell disaster for the entire group. Whatever it cost her, she had to protect her friends and though she pretended to consider, dragging out the moments until a sense of his mounting impatience made action imperative, she finally nodded in agreement.

The problem with the Consent regulations was that they included no half measures. If you agreed to physical relations, this covered every possible form it could take and there was no facility for a change of mind. Kathleen took as long as she dared with the keys, but all too soon the gadget gave a satisfied bleep and he grasped her shoulders, pulling her to him.

"Mine too," she insisted. "You know it's supposed to be mutual."

"You don't think I'm going to accuse you of rape?" he sounded incredulous.

"You don't trust me, I don't trust you," she replied, attempting a smile as she carefully called up her persaFile. Impatiently, he grabbed her wrist and stabbed at the keys. This time however there was no bleep of acceptance.

"What the Hell!" he shouted angrily, almost spitting with frustration.

"I told you not to be too quick," she quipped, taking her time to recall the file, making him wait before offering him her wrist.

Suspicious now, he checked that the readout was correct before entering his number, but there was still no rewarding bleep.

"Sod it!" he declared, "I'm not waiting any longer."

Grabbing her again, his mouth found hers and, remembering the role she had assumed, Kathleen responded with a show of enthusiasm. Almost immediately however, his tongue was probing and his hands were grasping her bottom, pulling her belly hard against his crotch.

"Not so fast, big man," she protested archly. "Aren't you even going to tell me your name?"

"Names.....don't.......matter," he muttered distractedly. With one arm around her waist holding her captive his free hand roamed over the bold curves of her bosom with eager anticipation. Mindful of the part she must play, Kathleen offered no resistance as he opened her shirt; nor while both of his hands explored her exposed breasts, teasing and caressing; when his mouth joined in the onslaught, licking, nibbling and sucking, she even managed a moan of apparent pleasure.

"The only thing that matters now," he lifted his head, giving her a momentary respite. "Is that I'm going to fuck you until you don't know if you're coming or going!"

"Don't be in such a hurry!" she pleaded, trying to push him away, to slow him down. Her attempt at showing arousal was doomed to failure she knew; she could already feel the tension, her body stiffening, becoming rigid in anticipation of what was to come. But he had her trapped against the desk and she couldn't escape him even if she wished.

"There's no need to wait," he contradicted. "You're such a hot piece I bet you're about ready for me now!"

Giving up any hope of delay, she let her arms fall to her sides in weary resignation. She had given her Consent as an necessary expediency; and if her body was now to be used for this man's pleasure, that was a price she must pay! She had experienced a like situation in the past and although she had no desire for recollection, the similarities were too great. Breaching the mental barriers she had so carefully constructed, the black and hateful images came storming relentlessly from their enclosure, making her relive those times as vividly as if they were happening at this very moment.

It had been only a couple of weeks after her parents had left for their supposed retirement; one evening she had offered mild criticism of the standard of Albert's work and he had taken it badly.

"Madam High and Mighty herself is it? It's about time I took you down to your proper level."

"And what do you consider my proper level?" she snapped back.

"Lying on your back with a man between your legs, that's what!"he declared coarsely. "A good fuck is what you're needing, and I reckon I'm the man to give you one!"

"Never while I'm breathing." She laughed to express her contempt.

"Is that so? He leered at her confidently and she felt a qualm of discomfort.

"Is that so," he reiterated. "When they come to put an Implant in your head you'll wish you'd been nice to Albert while you had the chance!"

"Have you gone out of your mind?" She was genuinely puzzled.

"It's you that's out of your mind harbouring an illegal on this Unit. I've only just found out and it's my duty to report it. I'll even be in line for a reward!"

If the farmhouse had fallen down at that moment, she couldn't have been more shocked. Stunned and horrified, she hastily ran through the implications of his threat.

"Oh yes," he gloated. "Your precious Barney will get an Implant and end up in a gang, sweeping the streets; you'll probably get an Implant too but if the stories are right the gangmasters will find another use for your body for a while! You'll be fucked in every way and I'll be the Boss-man here!"

"Please Albert."She knew immediately that not only was she at his mercy but that Barney was vulnerable too. Poor dear Barney who was like a child to her, how could she allow him to suffer such a fate. "Please Albert, don't do that to us, I'm begging you!"

"It's my duty as a good citizen," he responded with odious self-righteousness. "But I suppose there is a way you could persuade me to let you off!"

Dismayed as she was by his threat, she fell helplessly into a bottomless pit as she realised the real purpose of his scheme.

"I want your Consent to Physical Relations, Madam High and Mighty!" He swaggered forward until he was near enough to touch her, offering his PersaCom for agreement

"If I won't?" She had to ask although she already knew the answer.

"I'll just call the Authorities then." He turned away, pressing keys on his PersaCom.

"No Albert, No, don't do that." She had to stop him, there was no time to prevaricate. "I'll give you my Consent!"

"I knew you would," he gloated. "Get your Code in here and prepare yourself for the thrill of your life.

There was no finesse, no foreplay; as soon as the formalities were completed he stripped off sufficient of her clothes for his purpose, pushed her into a suitable position and used her body with no thought for anything other than his own gratification. Though her ordeal was short-lived, less than a minute in fact, she felt pain and revulsion enough to last for a thousand years until at last he grunted with satisfaction.

Breathing heavily, he stood back and looked at her with an expression of triumph.

"Not so High and Mighty now are we," he chuckled. "I'll give you one like that every day until you learn to like it!"

She couldn't speak, couldn't overcome her mortification at what she had let herself in for. In her haste to protect Barney she had neglected to consider that the blackmail would inevitably continue. And of course it did, the very next morning in fact, and rarely missing a day thereafter. She soon learned to avoid the least trace of criticism for that seemed to inflame him and inevitably led to her further degradation.

If it hadn't been for Barney she would probably have done away with herself but continuing responsibility meant it was out of the question. And although Albert's demands on weekdays had at least the mercy of brevity the weekends came to hold a special dread! Confident of his position, her tormentor started going to the local Citizens Tavern on Saturdays and after these sessions not only did he inevitably demand Consent but took much longer about it. With hot beer-smelling breath he would slobber and grope and fumble interminably; convinced that she was enjoying his attentions while in reality she recoiled from every move in a state of absolute wretchedness.

For nearly six weeks she existed in the utter depths of misery but in the end it was the drunken Saturdays that gave her an idea.

As usual, he came unsteadily through the door and paused to give her an ingratiating grin.

"You're a lucky girl," he slurred, indicating his crotch. "I've brought you a big present to make you smile!"

"That's a joke," she retorted with a show of contempt. "A bit of boiled spaghetti would be as much use to a woman as what you've got hanging there!"

He stared at her in momentary amazement before his face took on an angry flush.

"You fucking smart bitch!" He moved towards her, staggering a little but still exuding menace. "Just for that I'm going to fuck you into the middle of next week!"

"Oh yes!" she taunted. "That'll be longer than the usual ten seconds then!"

Forgetting caution, he grabbed the neck of her shirt. Buttons popped as he dragged it down over her shoulders and, while her arms were trapped in the sleeves, he slammed her down onto the table. Moments later he had hauled her trousers off and was forcing her legs apart with his own.

"Say you're sorry, bitch," he demanded.

"Sorry you're not more of a man," she flung back at him, steeling herself as he swung a hand and slapped her face in vicious retaliation.

That was enough! She fled to her mental sanctuary, hiding while he used her with deliberate and sustained brutishness, only forcing herself back to reality when a series of grunts announced that he was finished.

"There!" he panted confidently. "There's no way you can still be sassy after that!"

"No," she agreed coldly, sitting up and gathering her clothes together. "I hope you think it was worth it when you get your Implant!"

The import of her words took a moment to register, then his euphoric expression changed into one of dismay; he swayed unsteadily and stumbled to a chair.

"Kath....." he protested but she didn't let him continue.

"I gave no Consent so that was rape, Albert Arden, violent rape into the bargain." She indicated the marks on her face. "I've got the bruises to prove it, so you haven't a scrap of defence. There'll be no need for a trial, you'll be an Impy by this time tomorrow!"

"I can still shop you and Barney," he threatened feebly.

She shrugged expressively. "If they even give you time to talk, it's my word against an Impy's?" Actually he was still dangerous but she had to bluff him into submission.

Sobering rapidly, he snivelled, whimpered, begged until she offered a lifeline.

"A signed confession to rape with violence," she told him. "Never look at me again without remembering that I have it. Never a word to the Authorities about Barney or anything else on this Unit. Do what you are told without arguing. And if ever again you come near enough to touch me ....!"

He blustered and wheedled but she gave him no choice, even as he had done to her just a few weeks ago.

"You're a frigid bitch anyway," he sneered in attempted bravado as he signed his confession. "You're not really worth the bother of fucking!"

She let the remark pass without comment. Maybe it was true, but it was immaterial now for she had managed to escape from the trap in which she had been held for six horrible and horrifying weeks. The recollections of shame and humiliation might well stay with her for ever, but at least they could be banished, fenced off behind a mental barrier.There indeed they had remained until her present situation brought them, clamouring and insistent, to the forefront of her mind.

Even as the long-suppressed memories made her cringe she was uncomfortably aware of her trousers being opened, of a hand exploring inside them with uncompromising purpose. Building new defences against the moment when her body would become nothing more than a receptacle for this man's fulfillment, she only slowly became aware of the strident rasp of the hooter.

"We have to go!" she cried out, struggling and managing to sit up during the temporary cessation of his attentions. "The tank is full!"

"There's no hurry," he told her casually, with what he probably thought was welcome reassurance. "It's all automatic, I can easily check more than one tank after I've finished filling yours!

Kathleen fought her way back from detachment and forced herself to think rationally. She had promised to keep the Inspector occupied and she had done so. Her accomplices had completed their task, so there was no longer any need to continue her ordeal but it was now evident that she was not free to make the decision. The Inspector had no intention of letting her go until he was satisfied, and if she tried to oppose him physically she was sure that he could, and would, use whatever force was necessary to achieve his purpose.

The easy option would be to submit to him, to deaden herself and then bury the whole episode along with the others. But Kathy Pierpoint was a different woman now, stronger, more confident; she had at least to try something!

He reached for her again but she caught his hand in her own, moving it on to the unmistakeable bulge in the front of his trousers. His eyes widened with surprise.

"If you're going to fill my tank," she teased with coy

pretention. "You'll need a hosepipe to put into it. Is that what you've got hidden in here?"

The surprise on his face was rapidly replaced by a delighted smirk as she unbuckled the old-fashioned belt. Growing impatient, he took over, yanking his trousers down and letting his erection, big and imposingly rampant, spring into view.

"I've got a hosepipe all right!" The boast was uttered in a voice thick with lust.. "Now show me where you want me to put it!"

Kathleen smiled and nodded in agreement. Reaching inside his half-open shirt she ran her hands sensually over his hairy chest then, carefully bracing herself, gave a sharp push with every ounce of strength she could muster. Taken completely unawares he staggered backwards until, impeded by the trousers round his ankles, he fell heavily to the floor.

"What the fuck...!" He looked up at her in bewilderment for a moment, then started to swear viciously while struggling to get to his feet. Kathleen, dreading what he would do if he got a hold of her again, dodged round him, making sure she reached the office doorway before stopping to fasten her her clothes.

Realising that he couldn't prevent her escape, he slumped back against the desk.

"What about me?" He groaned in evident frustration.

""Sorry about that, big boy," she consoled, almost giddy with relief. "Better luck next time!"

She hurried outside, laughter bordering on the hysterical bubbling within her as a cry of 'Cock teasing bitch' followed her through the door.

A swift glance located Alex, watching for her and giving a discreet thumbs-up. She smiled as she reached him.

"Are you all right Kathy," he asked, full of concern.

"I'm fine," she assured him, her mirth breaking into a giggle.

"It took a bit longer than we expected and I was worried that......." His voice tailed off in embarrassment.

"You were worried that I might need rescuing!

Honestly, it's all right! I was saved by the bell!" She was anxious to convince him.

"You seem to be finding it very funny though?" he accused.

"It is." She giggled uncontrollably, trying to stop herself, knowing that she could burst into tears at any moment. Alex looked even more worried and she managed to bring her emotions under control.

"He's still a bit excited so it might be a few minutes before he comes out," she explained weakly.

Alex gave her a shocked look that broke into a smile.

"You'd better keep out of his way I think." He spoke seriously and added. "I'll take over here, you can have the rest of the afternoon off if you want."

"No way! I'd prefer to be busy so I'll go back to the ForTrak." she told him adamantly.

Between sweeps with the reaper, she found time to reflect on her reaction. Her body had been violated to a certain extent, but she had been prepared ultimately for worse so she couldn't really complain about the outcome. Her over-riding emotion turned to one of satisfaction that her ruse had been successful, and that her own efforts had enabled her to escape.

There was an almost tangible feeling of excitement among the group as, with the loading finished, they took their evening meal together. The train was scheduled to leave at first light, and Peter was obviously busy entertaining Terisa again. Some time tonight he would remove her persaCom, so that David could wear it when he took her place in the cab, then keep her locked up for as long as necessary. Things had gone well so far, but they all realised that the final part of the operation could still be critical. Kathleen was congratulated for her part in overcoming the obstacle of the Inspector; she still felt a little lightheaded, and didn't immediately notice David's absence. It was Sonya who answered her question.

"He said he wasn't hungry and went to his room. He was very quiet all day too, but that may be because he's going over his plans for tomorrow."

On reflection, Kathleen had to admit that he had

seemed rather withdrawn that morning. Maybe he was more concerned about the next stage than he was prepared to admit, she allowed, but doubted if there was anything that she could do to help him.

After supper, she indulged in the luxury of a long soak in the bath, before wrapping herself in a robe and heading for her room with the intention of having an early night. Her route took her past David's, and a sudden impulse made her stop and tap gently on the door; hearing a mumbled response, she cautiously pushed it open.

It was pleasantly warm, the rays of the setting sun streaming through the westward facing window. David was in bed, lying with his hands behind his head, staring at the ceiling. He didn't turn to look at her.

"What's wrong David," she asked gently. "Why weren't you there for supper? Do you think there might be problems with your journey?"

He shook his head. "Not particularly," he muttered.

"What is it then?"

"I couldn't face you," he whispered, so softly that she had to lean forward to catch his words.

"Why ever not?"

"I can't bear to think of you alone with that monster Kathy. We should never have asked you to do it."

"No-one asked me, I volunteered if you remember. And the Inspector had to be got out of the way or everything we've been working for would be wasted."

"We could have found another way, or waited for a bit," he mumbled stubbornly.

"No we couldn't. You know very well that this was the ideal opportunity; we might never get the same chance again."

"I don't care," he burst out angrily. "the thought of that brute getting his hands on you makes me want to kill him."

"David, I only got squeezed and groped a bit; it wasn't much worse than being pawed by Peter at the dance and at least there was a good reason. If I couldn't put up with that to ensure the success of our plan, I would be ashamed of myself."

"Anything could have happened to you," he grumbled, only slightly mollified.

"I suppose it could," she admitted. "And that would have been horrible for me and for everybody else as well. But nothing did happen." She gave him an edited version of the afternoon's events, hoping vainly that he would laugh at the business with the piCode. "So you see, there's no need for you to be concerned."

"Concerned!" He almost shouted the words at her. "Kathy, how can I not be concerned when I love you!"

Shock and anguish filled his face as he realised what he had said and he looked away from her as though in shame.

Kathleen was staggered by the forced admission; she had no idea what to say but he was obviously hurting so much that she had to think of something.

"Why have you never told me that before?" she asked, making her voice as gentle as possible.

Her heart went out to him as he turned towards her again, the haunted look in his eyes speaking of inner torment.

"How could I?" His sad gaze was fixed on her face as he continued. "I think I fell in love with you that first night in my office but obviously I couldn't say anything just then; when you offered to be my sister I knew you were starting to trust me; when we were hiding from the helicopters that night, lying in each other's arms, I never slept because every moment was so precious. All I wanted was to be with you and feel that you needed me, I was happy with that until the night of the Christmas party."

He swallowed, obviously finding it difficult to continue.

"Tell me," she insisted.

"You were wearing that green dress." He was dragging the words from somewhere deep inside of him. "You danced with me and I held you in my arms. When we got back to the bunkhouse..." he stopped again.

"When we got back to the bunkhouse and you kissed me, I didn't want you to stop; I wanted you to go on loving me. But you just said goodnight and went to your room." She was trying to make it easy for him.

"God! How I wanted to go on kissing you." The floodgate opened and words were pouring out in a torrent. "I wanted to kiss you and kiss you, but I also wanted to tear that dress off and make love to you! But I must have been too eager because you suddenly froze and I knew I'd frightened you, that you were convinced I was just another man who would hurt you; I was afraid you would never trust me again and I would lose you altogether."

It was out now; he had bared his soul and was waiting only for the expected confirmation of rejection, the pain in his eyes replaced by something akin to despair.

Kathleen stared at him in wonder. Apart from that one night he had never given any indication of feelings other than tenderness towards her; he had been her saviour, her friend, her companion but, since being rebuffed she had tried not to consider him as anything other than a companion. Now she realised why! Self doubt, along with an over-protective attitude had combined to put him in a mental strait-jacket. He was about to go into the most important part of the operation tormented with self-guilt and expecting his admission of desire to drive her away.

'Dear silly David,' she thought fondly, wondering if she could perhaps do something to help him.

"You've no reason to feel ashamed," she said, shaking her head in mock reproof. "I told you already, that night I wanted you to do more than kiss me, and I thought you did too."

"But....." He looked at her with a puzzled expression. ".......you switched off as though I had done something wrong. I thought you were seeing me the same as that......apology for a man who beat you up?"

She shook her head again, exasperated at herself this time. He was blaming himself and would almost certainly go on doing so unless she explained the real reason for her behaviour. Could she bring herself to tell him? If there was to be any chance of helping him to carry out his mission without torturing himself with his own failings, she would have to, and risk the consequences.

"I wasn't frightened of anything you did David," she

started bravely enough. "I know how I reacted but it wasn't your fault. It's something inside myself."

It wasn't going to be easy to bring her long-repressed secret into the open, to make her confession and watch the hurt and rejection come into his face. Dropping to her knees, she rested her arms on the bed to steady herself, took a deep breath, and painfully dragged the whole miserable story from behind its protective barrier.

"Kathy...!" Overwrought, her confession had stumbled hesitantly to a close before she noticed how his arms were round her, how he was rocking her gently, how his wet cheek was pressed against her own. "Kathy......My dear......My love...." he was murmuring again and again. "How could anyone.....? I'm so sorry........ I never dreamed! Please let me help you?"

"I feel so ashamed, so guilty for letting it happen!" She was determined to abase herself but he gripped her shoulders and stared into her face.

"Ashamed! Guilty! Never in a thousand years," he almost shouted. "What choice did he give you? You sacrificed yourself to protect poor Barney who couldn't help himself! That's about the bravest thing I've ever heard of in my life. Oh, my dear, I'm so proud of you!"

Totally drained, empty, she couldn't really understand what he meant but was content for the moment to be held, to be comforted, to be loved. Outside, the sun slipped below the horizon leaving a welter of gold and crimson clouds to mourn its passing. In the room the light gradually faded into dusk and David switched on a lamp before he spoke.

"Will you let me love you Kathy?" The question came so softly that it was hardly more than a whisper. "Will you let me care for you as much as I can? I promise not to make demands, not to touch you in any way that might upset you."

"No David!" After the catharsis and David's welcome reaction she had been able to think fairly sensibly. Seeing the instant distress on his face she hurriedly reassured him.

"I don't mean no like that. I want you to love me and care for me, I want to be able to love you in return. But I want to be like other women David, not a 'frigid bitch' like Albert called me!"

"I don't understand....." He was trying, she knew but he needed a little more.

"Help me David!" she pleaded. "Show me how to relax, teach me how to love you, how to really want you in the way a woman wants a man! Don't let me be alone for ever!"

She was leaning over him now, looking down into his face, seeing the mixture of hope and wonder and joy in his eyes. Her robe had fallen open but she made no move to cover herself; he obviously had to want her first if he was going to be able to help her.

He looked at her steadily for what seemed like half a lifetime as though he needed to be certain. Then he lifted a corner of the bedcover.

"I don't want you to be out there on your knees getting cold," he told her firmly. "You'll be warmer and more comfortable in here."

Gathering her courage, she complied and lay beside him, not sure what to expect. But he only pushed her hair to one side before ever so tenderly trailing his lips over her forehead and her eyelids; he kissed her fingers, one-by-one and the palms of her hands, her arms, the soft skin inside her elbows.Little by little she relaxed as tiny sensations of pleasure thrilled along her nerves. Determined that she would allow him anything, everything so long as it would make him happy, she wriggled out of the robe and threw it to the floor.

"S'too warm," she excused her action and he answered with a smile.

Slowly and with infinite tenderness, the caresses became more intimate, but never demanding, softening whenever her body began to tense until she was able to relax again. Somewhere, hidden in the wreckage of her emotions he found a tiny spark and nurtured it, coaxing and cajoling until it became an indubitable flame and that flame, with gentle but persistent encouragement developed into a fire. Then, almost of its own volition it seemed, the fire grew rapidly into a raging conflagration, one which consumed her utterly, casting the merest fragment of her ash into the heavens where she drifted, dreamlike, before floating ever so slowly back to a form of reality.

That reality found her lying in a rumpled bed, flushed and sweaty certainly but also so gloriously contented and replete that she struggled for a moment to make her mind function. David was propped up on one elbow, gazing at her with something very close to adoration.

"What happened?" It came out as a mumble so she tried again.

"What happened David? ...Did we make love?"

"Yes Kathy, we made love, the most glorious and satisfying love that two people could ever have made!" His words were filled with joy and maybe a tiny amount of amusement.

"Is that how it's meant to be?" I mean, something like that could happen again?"

"I very much hope so!" More amusement this time.

"Oh!" She assessed his answer for faults but could find none.

"Oh," she said again, a smile breaking out on her face. "Does that mean I'm not a 'frigid bitch' any more?

"My dear love, you are certainly not a frigid bitch, you are a beautiful and incredibly sexy woman who could make a marble statue come to life if you wanted." He went on, telling her things which she was sure were exaggerations but were so nice to hear that she kissed him comprehensively as a reward.

"Dear David," she told him eventually. "I think I love you too but it's as though Kathy Pierpoint has always existed as a number of broken pieces; now you've made her into a complete person, she needs a bit of time to get used to it."

"Of course," he agreed immediately. "So long as I can be with her, Kathy Pierpoint can take as long as she likes to decide."

She tossed his answer around in her mind for a while, the serious expression on her face gradually lightening as the implications became clear.

"I suppose that you'll be doing your best to influence me to make the decision you want?"

""You can't expect me not to do that!" His reply was emphatic.

He was lying on his back, hands behind his head, so she raised herself on her elbows to lean over him.

"That means," she ventured, trying somewhat unsuccessfully to look solemn. "That when I need reassuring that I'm not a frigid bitch any more, you'll be willing to do what you can to convince me?"

"I'm glad you said 'when' and not if!" He reached up, his fingers finding and gently stroking the nape of her neck. "Just let me know when 'when' happens!"

"I think any time about now would be just fine," she assured him happily.

"Maybe I should go to my own room and let you get some sleep," she suggested, a considerable length of time later. "You've got an early start in the morning."

"I won't be able to sleep," he assured her hastily. "I'm just too happy."

"I might as well stay here then." she offered hopefully.

"I think you should," he agreed. "You never know, you might want some more convincing before morning!"

CHAPTER TWELVE

The window of David's room faced to the west, so there were no direct rays of early morning sunlight to rouse Kathleen from her slumber. That may have been the reason why she slept late, waking slowly, wondering for a second at the unusual surroundings until memories of the previous night returned, bringing a surge of warmth and contentment. Drowsily, she tried to focus on something lying on the pillow beside her, but had to lift her head to see clearly that it was a single wild flower with sparkles of moisture still adorning the petals.

Not only had he managed to get up without waking her, he must have gone out to pick the flower and returned to put it where she would see it as soon as she opened her eyes. If she had needed any confirmation of his feelings it was right there in front of her.

'I think I do love him' she concluded after a quick survey of her emotions. 'No, make that I know I love him!'

With the decision came a renewed appreciation of the sheer pleasure of being alive. Jumping out of bed and heading for the bathroom, she caught herself singing as she conducted her ablutions and her steps across the yard had an extra spring to them.

Expecting to find no-one in the kitchen, she was surprised to see the whole company assembled in attitudes of relaxation. Even Peter was there, sitting beside a lean, athletic looking girl with a blocky face and determined chin. 'She must be Terisa' Kathleen noted to herself.

"You look very chirpy this morning," Jenny greeted, looking at her closely. "You must have had plenty of sleep!"

Kathleen felt a warmth creeping up her neck. Was it so obvious or was she just reading too much into an innocent remark. Not that it mattered, she resolved, it would take more than a few words to disturb her new serenity.

"Yes, I did, thank you," she answered cheerfully. "I thought you'd all be at work by now, cursing me for being an idle slugabed."

"I don't think anyone wants to be far away from the VidCom at the moment," Jenny replied. "But please feel free to go and plough in some stubble if you really want to."

"Not really. I think I'll just force myself to laze around with the rest of you," Kathleen assured her lightheartedly.

"You must be learning sense at last. Come and meet Terisa, she's decided she wants to join us so Peter's let her out of the handcuffs for a bit."

"I didn't have a lot of choice," Terisa announced as she gave Kathleen a firm handshake. "I wouldn't get far without a persaCom; to start with I thought Bonzo here was being kinky when he wanted to take it off along with every....!"

Peter coughed loudly to drown out the last words. Astonishingly, he seemed a little embarrassed but worse was to come.

"If there's no work to be done," his charge continued remorselessly. "Is it all right for us two to go and play for a while?"

Kathleen could hear amusement bubbling in Jenny's voice as she gave a hasty assent.

"Come on then Bonzo." Terisa pulled a sheepish Peter up out of his chair. "Remember, it's your turn to wear the handcuffs!"

It was too much for Kathleen; before the couple were out of the door she had collapsed in a heap, trying to contain her amusement until they were out of earshot. Everyone then joined in and a wave of laughter swept through the room.

"I would never have believed it," Alex choked as he wiped tears from his eyes. "Peter's finally met his match."

"Matching handcuffs I hope," Sonya interjected, setting them off again.

Eventually, when they had all calmed down, Kathleen asked if David had got away without any difficulty.

"No problems," Alex assured her. "Jason has been keeping an eye on the network, and the shipment is on the main line now, running to schedule."

"When is it due to reach the tunnel." She had a pretty good idea but asked anyway.

"Soon after midday at the marshalling yard," Jason spoke up. "Then it may go straight through or it may be delayed for other traffic. I suggest that we have an early lunch and keep constant watch on all the terminals from then on."

An early lunch sounded a good idea to Kathleen, as she remembered that she hadn't got round to having breakfast. She made tea for herself - and everyone else - and ate a couple of biscuits to pacify her stomach for the time being. The morning dragged by so slowly that she went to the crypt, and sat watching a row of dots change colour as David's cab passed each checkpoint, feeling somehow closer to him by even such passive participation.

Later, though only she, Sonya, Jason and Alex were needed for the four terminals, the others crowded around, moving with restless anticipation from one screen to another.

"Marshalling yard arrival, right on schedule," Kathleen informed them as the last of the chain flicked to red.

"Now we wait," Alex grunted. "Maybe for hours!"

His pessimism was misplaced however; less than five minutes had passed before Jason sang out.

"Tunnel entrance checkpoint one now! It's going straight through."

"Christ!" Alex muttered, almost to himself. "I hope he had enough time.

"It would only take him a minute," Sonya comforted with a quick glance at Kathleen. "He'd rehearsed it, he knew exactly what he had to do."

Kathleen felt her heart pounding as she typed in commands which would give her access to Security Communications, carefully checking the readout; they couldn't afford any errors at this stage. There was no mistaking the tension as they all waited for Jason to speak.

"Checkpoint two," his words dropped calmly into the silent room and a little later he announced, "Checkpoint three."

The reported weakness in the tunnel had been between points five and six and if the timer was set correctly that is where the explosion should occur.

"Checkpoint four." By his tone he might have been counting eggs into a basket but his forehead was covered with beads of perspiration; he used a cloth to give his hands a quick scrub.

"Checkpoint five."

Kathleen wondered why she had never previously noticed the erratic hum of the ventilation fans as they slipped in and out of phase with each other or the slow inexorable tick of the second hand jerking around the face of the big wall clock. Jason's eyes never left the stop watch lying on his desk.

"Overdue at Checkpoint six!" His voice cracked, the pretence of composure collapsing as a sigh of indrawn breath swept through the assembled watchers. Nobody spoke as they waited for confirmation.

"Checkpoint six signal failure!" His shout was accompanied by banging his fist on the desk. "Sections five and seven are down, now four and eight." After a brief pause he jumped out of his chair.

"Complete failure of the tunnel monitoring system," he told them gleefully. "It looks as though we've done it!"

The round of cheers which followed was quickly silenced when Alex waved his hands for quiet. All eyes turned to Kathleen, who was concentrating on the display in front of her.

"Priority One from Region C14 to CenCon," she read the words that appeared as some anonymous person typed frantically. "Major disaster in undersea tunnel, total flooding, loss of raw Ectol transport, casualties unknown. Resources insufficient, request immediate assistance from Urfor."

"Similar messages from our side," Alex announced. "Sonya, I think it's time."

Sonya's hands were already hovering over the keys, so it took only moments to insert the block that would stop all communications from CenCon reaching the security forces. Jason had already changed over to his next task and Kathleen hurried to do likewise; together they waited for the signal to proceed.

"That's okay now, we can still read them but no-one else can," Alex sounded relieved. "Jason, you can go ahead and delete the Implant program."

Kathleen wondered briefly what would be the result of a sudden cessation of all control to the collars worn by the Impys; guessing that there would shortly be a lot of very angry people on the streets to keep the Police busy she looked a question at Alex.

"Okay Kathy," he nodded. "As quick as you can please."

It was a tricky bit of work; what she had to do was to use the central system to instruct all individual persaComs to switch off their location transmissions without affecting any of the other functions. David had left her a written sheet of the process but she had memorised it so well that she only glanced at it occasionally for reassurance.

"I think that's it," she said finally, leaning back and rubbing her eyes, gratefully accepting the fresh coffee that Jenny proffered.

"Well done everyone," Alex congratulated. "I never dared to hope that things would go so smoothly. Whatever happens now we've certainly given the Federation something to think about!"

"They're in a fair old flap, I can tell you." Sonya was still monitoring CenCon's attempts to communicate. "Nobody wants to make a decision so it's a bit like 'pass the parcel' at the moment."

"If old Jack is right, they'll be doing just that for quite some time," Jenny commented with a smile.

"What we have to do now is to check the newscasts before they are broadcast," Alex advised, "but I imagine that it will be a while before CenCon will want to release this story."

"The watch will have to be continuous though," Jason cautioned. "Do you think we should operate in shifts; two of us at a time ought to be able to handle it."

They agreed that this would be a good idea, but not yet, for none of them wanted to leave the crypt while there was so much going on; three of the screens displayed appeals for help from different locations where the local authorities struggled to cope with the newly freed gangs of Impys, while the fourth monitored CenCon's increasingly desperate attempts to respond.

"There's trouble started at one of the Produnits," Alex read from the latest report. "It seems that a few Impys went in, denounced the Federation and sparked a bit of a riot. That's good, if there's a lot of confusion it should make it easier for David to get clear."

Kathleen was glad of the scrap of comfort offered by his comment. David's plan had required him to take off the persaCom which he had 'borrowed' from Terisa, replace it with his own modified one, leave the cab and find a place from where he could send a signal, setting the timer just before the train entered the tunnel. The fact that the explosion had occurred in exactly the right spot obviously meant that he had succeeded, but there had been such a brief pause in the marshalling yard that she was worried about him getting away afterwards.

The afternoon wore on with the screens mutely relaying details of widespread confusion and disruption throughout Federation territory. Some of the watchers wandered off to other tasks, but they were all gathered again as the time approached for the evening Newscast.

"Here it is!" Sonya called out, reading from the recording in front of her. 'Damage to transport links apparently caused by terrorists, no reason for alarm, authorities have everything under control'. "Hurry, we've only got minutes!"

"Explosion in undersea tunnel caused by freedom fighters. Cencon unable to provide assistance, Local Authorities to act independently." Alex dictated and she quickly made the substitution.

They all watched as the amended report duly appeared on the VidCom monitor.

"That'll really get them going," Jenny commented. "I wonder what their reaction will be once they realise that we can interfere to that extent."

"Panic!" Alex suggested. "David said there's not a lot they can do immediately, short of cutting of the main power supply, and that's not likely because all their privileges and their credits would come to a halt."

"That would be too bad," Jenny commented drily. "It might be worth asking David to have a go at doing just that when he gets back."

Once the initial excitement had worn off they settled fairly comfortably into the routine of shift work. It made sense for Jason and Sonya to be off duty together so Kathleen worked with Alex, grateful for his calm assumption of responsibility. She even managed to steal an hour or two to help with preparing the newly harvested ground for the next planting, welcoming the opportunity to escape from the confines of the crypt. As the days passed however, she became increasingly worried that there was no news of David.

"Give him a chance Kathy," Alex tried to re-assure her, hiding the fact that he was more than a little concerned himself. "With the turmoil that's going on now it could take him at least a week to get back here."

"He should have been able to get to a VidCom to send a message to us," she pointed out.

Alex shook his head. "We don't know what it's like down there, he may think it's safer not to take any risks. I'm sure he'll be all right."

When the newscasts eventually carried a full report of the event, the information that the only casualty had been the train operative added to her anxiety.

"They are bound to say that," the others assured her. "You know that Terisa's persaCom was to be left in the cab and it would be transmitting until the last seconds. The Authorities will believe she was blown to Kingdom come in the explosion, so they are actually telling the truth as they know it!."

Kathleen tried to accept the comfort they offered but during the lone nights she could not fight off the growing fear that something had gone horribly wrong. After a week without any news every one of them shared her uneasiness although they tried to hide it whenever she was in the company. Then, one evening, Jenny arrived in her room and without saying anything, embraced her.

"What's happened!" Kathleen asked urgently, her throat tightening at her friend's grave expression.

"There was a communication from the Urfor investigators to CenCon." The words came reluctantly. "I'm so sorry Kathy, it doesn't sound very good."

"Go on!" She was strangely calm now, almost knowing what she was about to hear.

"The reason they are sure it was sabotage is that they have located a second persaCom among the wreckage. Oh God Kathy, I pray it's not true." She could feel Jenny's tears on her face.

'I should be crying too', Kathleen thought stupidly as her so recent hopes and dreams of happiness crashed into ruin. She was too numb to cry, her mind and her body dead; she couldn't allow herself to mourn openly, knowing that there was a risk that she would break completely.

Jenny stayed with her through the night; vaguely, she was aware that another Kathleen talked about David, the kind of man he was, what he had done for the Revolution and indeed what he had done for her. That other Kathleen even admitted that she and David had finally 'become a pair' on their last night together though this information seemed only to intensify Jenny's sympathy. Unbidden, a phrase from some book she had read in the past came to mind.

"Better to have loved and lost than never to have loved at all," she quoted hesitantly, and the words formed a first tenuous link between her two disparate personalities. As the hours passed the bond strengthened, the strong Kathleen taking control, firmly confining her poor heartbroken twin into a secure and secret compartment. Eventually she was strong enough to let a few tears flow from her eyes.

"It's morning," she commented as daylight reduced the overhead bulb to a dim glow. "Jenny, you must be dog-tired."

"Will you be able to sleep?" her friend asked with agonised concern. Kathleen shook her head.

"No, I don't think I could sleep at the moment," she admitted. "If you don't mind, I'd like to go out in the ForTrak and do some physical work, the harder the better."

"Would you like me to come with you?" Jenny asked diffidently.

"I think I really need to be on my own now," Kathleen apologised. "I want you to go and get some rest."

Ploughing in stubble was not the most difficult of tasks but Kathleen set herself a demanding target; imagining herself back at 'The Beeches' she concentrated fiercely on making her passes as accurate as possible, only stopping reluctantly when Mary appeared, waving a flask.

"I don't feel hungry." Kathleen sipped hot tea but waved away the proffered sandwich.

"You may not feel hungry but you are going to eat it." Mary's determination was so absolute that it was easier to comply with her wishes rather than attempt to argue. Obediently, Kathleen chewed and swallowed before getting back into the ForTrak.

Mary stood and watched for a while before leaving; a little later, Andy arrived on another machine and started working in the next field.

'They're keeping an eye on me,' Kathleen thought, not knowing whether to be pleased or affronted.

"It's still daylight," she protested when he came to tell her it was time for supper. "Please Andy, I've got to make myself as tired as I possibly can. You go, I'll be all right here."

"Whatever you say Kathy," he assented. "But I'm not going until you're ready."

She suppressed a pang of guilt at keeping him from his meal, and continued doggedly until the sun disappeared behind the western flank of the hills; by then her body was aching and her eyes felt so gritty that she had to screw them up to negotiate the gateway. Andy dutifully fell in behind her as she drove carefully back to the yard.

Meeting the others wasn't as bad as she had feared, their low-key expressions of sympathy gentle enough not to intrude too deeply. Mary put food in front of her and she did her best to eat, though her eyes were now desperate to close. Jenny insisted on accompanying her to her room, helping her into bed and then sitting in a chair beside it. How long she stayed there Kathleen didn't know for absolute exhaustion rapidly brought the sweet relief of sleep.

It was a full twelve hours before she woke to the reality that David had gone from her life. However her self-administered catharsis meant that she could function again, and if he could no longer play a part in the Revolution it was up to her to make sure that his efforts would bear the fruit he had so earnestly desired. She was even able to express this purpose to Alex when she joined him in the crypt.

"He wouldn't have wanted us to mope," she explained after he had given her a welcoming hug.

"I suppose that's the right attitude," he agreed sadly. "It would be so easy to become disillusioned about everything we have done, but that would be a betrayal."

"Anything new been happening?" She made her voice business-like.

"It could hardly be better. Our group of regions are in ferment, and there is even a lot of trouble nearer the centre. I went over to see James, you know his equipment lets him monitor non-Federation broadcasts?"

Kathleen nodded in reply.

"Well it seems that outside reporters are being approached by people who are not afraid to tell the truth. Their news bulletins are full of stories about the repressive regime here, and other goverments are demanding that free elections be held under international supervision. Best of all, this Region's Assembly has abrogated Federation membership and has appealed for assistance to repel any forceful attempt to re-impose it. With any luck, some of the other Assemblies will follow suit."

"That's marvellous." Kathleen was genuinely delighted. "How is CenCon reacting to all this?"

"Huffing and puffing mostly. 'It's an internal matter, Security Forces have the situation in hand', they say but Urfor seems to be dragging its feet a bit. Communications of a sort are getting through now, but there's not much in the way of action.

"Oh, and Jason suggested that we should put a bug in ITS, the transport program. We weren't sure at first, because it wouldn't affect the officials but then we decided to put out an appeal on the VidCom, asking drivers to commandeer the vehicles and ply for hire. It was only done yesterday, so it's too early to tell what the effect will be."

"It's incredible how quickly the whole system is falling apart," Kathleen ventured cautiously. "Do you think we're being too optimistic?"

"Old Jack always said that a rotten apple falls with the first gust of wind," Alex shrugged expressively. "And there's no denying that CenCon is rotten through and through."

"I remember him telling us that a Government can't hold on to power against the wishes of the majority unless they are prepared to use ultimate force." For a moment Kathleen was back in the old man's room, with David; hastily, she banished the memory.

It soon became clear that, as the Revolution achieved its own momentum, there was less and less to do in the crypt. Kathleen spent more of her time in the fields, especially when Jenny asked her to teach Terisa how to use the various farm implements. The new recruit proved to be a capable driver and quick to learn; she confessed that she was glad of the opportunity to do something useful for a change.

"I thought Peter kept you pretty busy!" Kathleen ventured tentatively.

Terisa laughed heartily at the sally.

"I'm not as bad as you think you know. Peter's got such a strong 'come on' line and the best way to deal with that is to go over the top, give him a red face in front of other people, He's like a little lamb now, not a suggestive word out of him."

Kathleen had to laugh at the uninhibited reply. Anyone who could tame Peter must have hidden depths.

"How did you come to be driving trains," she enquired.

"It's got to be better than a Produnit," Terisa's tone evinced disgust. "I jumped at the chance even though I had to lend a hand to some old lecher in Admin to get it. I quite enjoyed the job actually, going up and down the line, stopping in different places. You've heard the old expression 'a sailor with a girl in every port'? Well, that was me only the other way round." She heaved a sigh and concluded. "Now it looks as if I've dropped anchor for a while anyway!"

Kathleen felt a measure of shock at the matter-of-fact account, but it was mingled with admiration. This girl would take a certain type of man on at his own game and beat him hands down; the bit about the old lecher though, brought a flashback of the Ectol Inspector and she shook her head to dismiss it. 'You don't want to go there Kathy,' she warned herself.

"Do you disapprove of me?" Terisa had misunderstood her reaction.

"Not at all," Kathleen assured her. "I was just thinking about the old lecher bit, that's all."

"A girl has to do what she has to do to get on in this wicked world," Terisa said philosophically and then laughed again. "I must admit he had me worried for a bit, I was afraid he was going to have a heart attack!"

Kathleen, deciding that too much candour was as bad as too little, hastily steered the conversation to safer topics. The manner of Terisa's abduction had obviously not soured her towards the Revolution, quite the reverse in fact. Her only regret seemed to be that she had not been able to play an important part in it.

A few days later, Alex asked Kathleen if she would like to drive Jason to the Unit E/61 on which James was manager.

"We want to take a terminal there and patch it into their system," he explained. "Then they will be able to transmit outside broadcasts directly to us here, and we will also be able to talk with them freely. Jason isn't very confident in a ForTrak and it might be a bit of a break for you."

"I don't mind," she immediately assented. "But someone will have to show me how to get there."

"I've drawn a map for you." Jenny laid a piece of paper on the table. "It's mostly on proper tracks and takes about two hours; that's me driving of course so if you allow three you should be safe enough!"

"That sounds suspiciously like a challenge," Kathleen smiled as she studied the route. "What do you think Jason? Shall we try for an hour and a half!"

"Please, No," he groaned theatrically. "Three hours will be fine by me!"

In fact she was forced to drive cautiously. It may have been all right to bounce a passenger about but the all important terminal, wrapped in as much padding as they could find, had to be treated with the utmost care. Although they left at first light there was plenty of warmth in the sun when they pulled in to the unfamiliar yard.

"It's good to see you again." She remembered James's booming voice from the conference but was surprised that his welcome seemed to be directed solely at her companion. "We were devastated when we heard about your friend David. Such a tragic waste of a life. I'm sure you must miss him terribly."

Kathleen's flash of resentment at being ignored was not alleviated by the insensitive statement; thankfully, Jason came to her rescue.

"We've got the terminal here," he announced briskly. "I'd like to make a start on the link right away if you don't mind."

"It's all go, is it?" I wish I had the energy you young men have." James escorted them to a version of the crypt where, after a disapproving glance at Kathleen, he left them, pleading important business. Jason immediately commenced the tricky job of connecting into the VidCom cables and Kathleen tried, without much success, to help.

They were soon joined by Andrew, an earnest young man who, it transpired, was the 'electronic geek' on this unit.

"Your Boss certainly didn't seem to be pleased to see me here!" Kathleen said caustically. "Have I done something to upset him?"

Andrew flushed before answering.

"He doesn't think women should be involved in the Revolution, that they only distract the men from their work," he told her apologetically. "The prettier they are, the worse he is about them. I daren't tell you what he says is the only thing women are good for!"

She could well imagine what that might be but, after a moment of resentment, she decided that someone like that was better ignored. Andrew's arrival made her attempts at help redundant, but she had anticipated this and had made her own preparations. Back upstairs, she hurried outside and climbed into the ForTrak.

Jenny's map had depicted hills rising directly from the unit's northern boundary and it was in this direction that she headed. Reaching the perimeter fence she drove slowly along until she found a weak spot, parked the ForTrak, hung her lunch bag over her shoulder and wriggled through into the wilderness beyond.

Ever since that first day with Jenny, when she had marvelled at the grandeur of the mountains, they had called to her, though she had always been too busy to respond. Now, on a fine summer day, she at last had free time to indulge her desire to ascend them, and to view the land from above.

Apart from the rough scrub, the going was easy enough to begin with; she climbed steadily, startled occasionally by the harsh cries of birds as they rose from the ground almost at her feet. As the steepness of the slope increased however, she was forced to stop frequently for a rest.

'You're out of condition, Kathy girl," she censured herself, panting with exertion. 'You've spent too long sitting in that crypt, you've let yourself get fat and flabby.'

She knew at once that it was an unfair accusation; in truth her body was as taut and firm as it had been when she left 'The Beeches' and her skin still shone with the glow of youth. Ruefully, she acknowledged that climbing a hill of this size was a lot harder than it looked from below.

Patiently plodding upwards, she noticed that the scrub had given way to wiry clumps of grass interspersed with slabs of grey, lichen-covered stone; the grass was slippery under her feet and she frequently had to use her hands to keep herself upright, but eventually the slope levelled off into an area of smooth turf, surmounted by a rocky outcrop. Filled with a new burst of energy, she almost ran the last hundred yards until she could collapse, gasping, against the sun-warmed stone.

When she regained her breath, she was disappointed to see that what she had regarded as a mountain was merely a foothill which had hidden much higher peaks, their tops composed of sharp cliffs broken by boulder-strewn gullies. Time of day and common-sense forbade the impulse to go any further however, and she made herself content with what she had achieved.

Even from here, the view was magnificent, the land below spread before her like a patterned cloth. Large areas of brown earth where the recent harvest had taken place were broken up with smaller patches of yellow/green depicting the later, still ripening crop; here and there, grey roofs surrounded by trees and inter-connected with threadlike tracks punctuated the vista, until it eventually disappeared into the afternoon heat-haze. Turning round, she saw deep valleys with the occasional glimpse of a busy little stream and, in the far distance, a gleam of sunlight reflected off what must be a larger body of water.

'It can't be the sea,' Kathleen decided. 'It must be one of the big lakes I've heard about.'

There was a noticeable breeze on the hilltop, so she moved to find a sheltered corner before unpacking her lunch. After she had eaten, she lay back on the soft grass and her mood changed to one of gentle melancholy. Since arriving at Jenny's unit she had not thought in any way about her personal future; a comfortable acceptance of David's presence had changed dramatically on their last night together, but her resultant fleeting dreams had been cruelly dissipated by his non-return. 'He must have been trapped in the train,' she thought sadly, 'he would have come back to me if he was still alive. I might as well accept that whatever future I have now will be on my own.'

That her future would be unlike the past was the only certainty. Over the last twelve months of being in the company of young and uninhibited people, she herself had grown and developed into a different person, far removed from the naive and bucolic woman who had beavered away in the enclosed environment of 'The Beeches'. 'Maybe Albert had a point when he said I was a frigid bitch', she allowed with a glimmer of amusement. 'I was certainly a bit of a prude back in those days!'

She wondered, briefly, what had become of Albert. Had the asociation with her and Barney been enough to get him collared, or had he managed to avoid blame sufficiently to have been put in to a Produnit. Either way, she didn't really care, and only hoped that she would never see or hear of him again.

She lay there mulling things over, until the sun's position made her realise that it was time to leave. Starting the descent with insufficient caution, she slipped, and discovered accidentally that it was quicker and safer to slide down on her bottom; she was laughing when she reached the level of the scrub, wondering ruefully as to the state of the seat of her trousers. Jason was sitting outside with Andrew and James when she got back to the Unit.

"Finished already," she enquired, feeling a little guilty.

"Only a few minutes ago," Jason assured her. "We ran a couple of tests and everything seems to be okay. Andrew knows what to do now, so I'm ready to go as soon as you like. Where did you get to?"

"I just went up that hill." Kathleen waved vaguely in the appropriate direction.

"Whatever for?" James glared at her. "There's no way you should have gone up there without someone to help you. You might have fallen and hurt yourself, and caused a lot of trouble for the rest of us!"

Kathleen managed to suppress the angry retort that was her first reaction; muttering some excuse, and making an attempt at polite farewells, she and Jason climbed into the ForTrak. A feeling of gratitude that she had not ended up on this Unit rapidly developed into an urgent desire to return to familiar surroundings.

"Hold on tight Jason," she warned, stamping on the go-pedal. "We'll see if we can beat Jenny's time!"

Ignoring the occasional yelp of pain from behind her, she drove the heavy vehicle as fast as she dared, bouncing on the hummocks so hard that only a firm grip on the steering bar kept her from flying out of the seat, sliding round corners, leaving a plume of dust behind from the dry track. She was keenly disappointed to find that she had missed the target by at least ten minutes.

"You're mad Kathy!" Jason complained, as his trembling legs touched the safety of the ground. "Quite, quite mad!"

"Jenny must be madder then," was her unsympathetic reply.

Later though, when she assured Jenny that her record was still safe, the younger girl was incredulous.

"Have you forgotten that my machine has been tweaked?" she demanded. "Two and a half hours would be a fair time for that old thing you were in, pushing it hard you might make two-twenty. What about poor Jason?"

"I don't think he'll get into a ForTrak with me again," Kathleen told her mournfully, and the two of them laughed together.

Two months after the tunnel explosion Richard arrived and after a quick re-union with his daughter he came looking for Kathleen. He said very little, but the way he embraced her conveyed more than words ever could have done.

"Thank you Richard," she murmured when he released her. "I don't feel so alone now."

"You must never feel alone Kathy," he insisted. "Never so long as we are here."

The reason for his visit was to bring them up to date with the rapidly changing political situation. The Com system could no longer be relied upon for accurate news, and until it could be separated from Federation influence that would remain the case. He told them that most of the local Regions had declared their independence, and that fair and free elections had now been promised.

"Your work here is virtually finished," he went on. "And it is time for you to consider what you want to do next. At present the economy of our Regions is based mainly on grain and energy, so there will have to be rapid diversification. On the plus side, the rest of the Federation will desperately need our produce, at least for the short term so there should be a reasonable prospect of trade.

"One thing we will have to do is to forget the Federation's inefficient ways if we want to become like the free countries you have heard about. There will be great opportunities in the years ahead, but it will mean a lot of hard work and taking a few risks. You all need to consider carefully where you would like your place in that future to be.

"I have been involved in talks with the Interim Councils trying to push them in the right direction, and in effect I am the 'face' of the Revolution. So far as I am aware, you are all virtually unknown and can probably stay that way if you wish. Alternatively you could declare yourselves and become heroes to an awful lot of people."

"I might enjoy being a hero and having groupies clustered round me for a while." Peter's face brightened.

"No you wouldn't," Terisa told him sternly. "One wrong move with a groupie and you'd find out at first hand how your crusher gets the oil out of the pods!"

CHAPTER THIRTEEN

There was more than a hint of sadness as the preparations for leaving came to a close. The group which had sustained Kathleen for over a year was breaking up and, though everyone was full of promises to meet again, the future was as yet too uncertain to know if these plans had any chance of fruition.

Alex and Mary were staying on to manage the Unit along with Peter and Terisa. Sonya and Jason were staying too, but only until such time as the situation clarified enough for them to find something else that suited their particular talents.

Jenny's father and old Jack had been invited to take part in the interim Administration which had been set up to arrange for the first free elections so she and Andy decided to move to 'West Malling' (it had already reverted to its original name) where they would take charge. Kathleen would accompany them and stay for a while but she had plans of her own of which she had spoken to nobody.

As she cleared her room of the last vestiges of her sojourn they came, singly and in pairs to say goodbye; some more emotional than others, all full of adjurations to take care of herself in the future. Peter was the last to arrive.

"I'll really miss you Kathy," he murmured as he gave her a respectful hug. "All my life I'll regret that we never got it together."

"Maybe I'll regret it a little myself," she joked, adding hastily as his eyes lit up! "No, don't take that as a hint!"

Jenny had acquired a Transa from somewhere but their combined luggage topped by a cargo of fresh meat and vegetables meant that there was only just enough room for Kathleen to wriggle into the back seat. However, unlike her journey of arrival they were travelling on metalled roads and she was surprised at how soon they passed through the barrier denoting the southern limit of the Ectol area; she was more surprised when the vehicle turned off the main highway and on to a much smaller road.

"A bit of a detour," Jenny assured her blithely, refusing to give any details.

"Here we are," she announced later as she steered between derelict cottages to stop in an open area where a strong salt smell pervaded the air. "I thought you might like to have another look at the sea."

Kathleen jumped out eagerly but there was no stretch of sand with open water dancing beyond it. Instead she saw crumbling and weed-festooned concrete enclosing a basin where the oily looking water heaved with restless frustration. In the midst of an expanse of black mud uncovered by the tide lay a handful of half-buried rusting hulks; these along with some rotting timbers reaching imploringly towards the sky were all that remained of the harbour's former users. Beyond the walls the water rose and fell uneasily, occasionally crashing in white foam against the concrete; facing the wind she felt a drift of salt spray on her face.

"It's kind of depressing though, not as I saw it before," she remarked, almost to herself.

"I'm sorry," Jenny apologised. "It's the only place I know about here where you can get a Transa to the coast. Dad says he can remember when fishermen lived in these cottages and sailed out every day to bring in fresh fish. Maybe in the future, villages like this will be able to come back to life."

Kathleen tried to visualise bustling activity on the quayside, business in the boarded up shops, boats heading proudly out to sea, but the picture refused to form out of the sad and decaying surroundings. Involuntarily, she shivered.

"It is a cold wind isn't it," Jenny said, noticing her movement. "Shall we get going?"

It was cold certainly, so Kathleen decided not to reveal the reason for her shiver. Her depression persisted for some time though; she wanted to believe that Jenny's hope could be realised, but feared that it would never happen. 'So much of what we were has been destroyed' she thought sadly, 'so much has been lost that can never be regained'.

Her mood was forced to lighten when they arrived to a rapturous welcome from Jenny's parents, even old Jack coming outside to congratulate them. A bright-eyed Hazel quickly directed the men to convey the foodstuffs to the larder, clattering pots and pans and declaring her intention to make 'a feast to surpass all feasts'. Kathleen found herself installed in the same bedroom she had occupied what seemed several lifetimes ago; trying with only partial success to suppress the recollection of David being in the next room, she was grateful when a tap at the door heralded the appearance of Jenny.

"I thought you were a bit down today and I wondered if you'd like some company for a while?"

"I was depressed by the old fishing village for a while," Kathleen admitted. "And I can't stop myself from thinking about David sometimes."

"Of course you can't," Jenny sat beside her on the bed and put an arm round her. "It's only natural, especially when you've been alone so much in the past. But you mustn't keep grief to yourself Kathy, you must share it with us; we are your family now, you've got no choice in the matter. Mum and Dad have adopted you even if it's not official so I'm your younger sister and I know Andy would be proud to be your brother. We are here for you Kathy, you never need be alone again."

The lump in Kathleen's throat threatened to choke her and she hid her face on the younger woman's shoulder. They embraced silently for a while and both their faces were wet when they finally drew apart.

"Better now?" Jenny dabbed at her eyes with a handkerchief.

Kathleen nodded, not trusting herself to speak.

"I'd better go and offer to help Mum then, before she gets in a tizzy."

"I'll come down with you," Kathleen jumped to her feet.

"I think you'd better wash your face first," Jenny advised with a smile as she opened the door. "See you in a minute."

It would have been easy to stay on at Old Malling as they so obviously expected, but Kathleen had her heart set on her own plans. One evening, when they were all sitting around doing nothing in particular, she raised the subject.

"Go! Where!" Jenny demanded immediately.

"To see Nellie and George and Barney first. Then I want to go back to 'The Beeches' to find out what has happened there. If there is to be a new system of land tenure, then I want to establish a claim to my parents place; I am sure that I have more right to it than anyone else."

She looked at them to gauge their reactions. Jenny and Andy looked worried, Hazel non-committal while Richard nodded in approval and perhaps admiration.

"Dad!" Jenny appealed but it was to Kathleen that he spoke.

"I don't want to see you leave Kathy, but I appreciate your reasons. There is far too much in you that would be stifled if you were to stay here permanently, and that would be a tragic waste. If you do decide to go it would be with my blessing, along with an appeal that you will come back to us whenever you want and hopefully that will be quite often."

"If you must, you must," Hazel gave her a searching look. "Are you sure you feel up to it?"

"I'm as fit as a fiddle," Kathleen protested hastily, and turned to Jenny. "Will you two give me your blessing as well?"

"I suppose we have to," her new sister admitted sadly. "But you will promise not to be away for too long?"

"I'd like to come and spend Christmas with you if I may," Kathleen suggested, and was gratified by the unanimous chorus of approval.

A few days later, having manoeuvered her borrowed ForTrak through yet another gap in a crumbling stone wall, Kathleen recognised her surroundings as where she and David had hidden from the searching helicopters. Braking to a halt, she switched off the engine, revelling in the sudden onset of peace and quiet. Gratefully, she climbed down to the ground, for the driver's sprung seat had seen better days and her body ached for a rest from the continual bouncing. A glance at her wrist told her that she had plenty of time and might as well eat her lunch in comfort.

The ridge where they had sheltered under a ledge beckoned, and after reaching it she tested the ground for dampness before sitting down. There had been no rain for a while now, and the unseasonal midday warmth was tempered only by a subtle suggestion of a breeze. Hungrily, she tackled her lunch of home-made bread and meat sandwiches, sighing regretfully when it was finished, wishing that she hadn't refused Hazel's urging to take rather more!

Allowing herself a little longer, she lay back and stretched her arms above her head. 'I'm so lucky to be here,' she thought, wishing for a moment that David could have been with her to enjoy this moment.

Dear David; she could think of him now with gentle regret rather than the savage sense of loss she had managed to suppress. He had tormented himself with guilt but she fervently hoped that, at the last, he had achieved some kind of peace. He had done so much in expiation, giving the Resistance an immeasurable boon which would hopefully bring millions of people out of tyranny. And he had given her everything since that night he had spirited her away from imprisonment, and a future too awful to contemplate.

He had given her hope, companionship, laughter and finally he had given her his love. She wished he could have known that he had given her more even than that. She had told no-one yet, not even Jenny, though it was possible that the ever astute Hazel had guessed her secret! In the absence of a reminder from her replacement persaCom, she had completely forgotten to renew the annual precaution, and now she smiled as she stroked the barely perceptible swelling of her stomach. Her child, hers and David's would grow up to know the wide sea and the high hills as well as the gentle land; insofar as she was capable, he would never be short of love and he would know freedom as a birthright.

They must have been keeping a lookout, for when she drove into the yard the three of them were waiting to greet her. Nellie claimed her first, then George gave her a whiskery embrace before Barney came shyly forward.

"Missa!" he burbled happily, clasping her hand between his two rough palms. "Missa come back! Missa!"

"Missa come back Barney," she agreed, giving him a quick hug, greatly relieved to see that he looked no different to when she had left him behind. Briefly, she recalled a remark of David's when they had been discussing her previous life.

"Could Barney be your brother?" he had suggested, to her complete astonishment.

"Whatever makes you think that?" she had responded.

"Just an idea really. Similar facial structure I suppose, the lack of any other explanation; some folk of your parents generation may well have felt ashamed, have tried to keep a thing like that quiet."

"It's possible I suppose," she had admitted, considering. "And they certainly would have wanted to protect him from the Authorities."

Now, she looked at him carefully, trying to see a likeness to the face she knew from her mirror. Not that it mattered, she loved him whatever the truth of his origins.

"I hope you're hungry Kathy," Nellie welcomed. "You're just in time for supper and it's a bit special tonight."

"I'm starving," Kathleen admitted frankly. "I think I could eat enough for two!"

She flushed as she realised what she had said, but luckily they were all too excited to notice. Barney followed her, dog-like, into the kitchen; now and again she heard him croon 'missa come back' under his breath.

Supper that was 'a bit special' proved to be a rival to one of Hazel's feasts. Kathleen did her best, but had to admit defeat before Nellie would stop pleading with her to take some more. Afterwards, they eagerly plied her with questions and she did her best to satisfy their curiosity;

Nellie, ever tactful, tried to change the subject when David's name was mentioned.

"It's all right, really," Kathleen assured her. "I've come to terms with the fact that he won't be coming back. I suppose that we'll never find out what actually happened, but I know that we could never have achieved our aims without him."

Her listeners nodded in solemn concurrence and they went on to discuss lighter subjects. Kathleen felt tiredness coming on and had to cover a yawn with her hand.

"I'm sorry," she apologised. "It must be the travelling."

"It's about bedtime anyway Lovie," Nellie comforted. "Come on, I'll show you to your room."

She stayed for a few days enjoying Nellie's mothering but, having started her journey, she was anxious to proceed. When she had at last convinced them of her determination, she had to refuse George's proposal that he convey her to 'The Beeches'.

"After the transport system collapsed, a number of the drivers commandeered vehicles and can be hired in exchange for credits," she told them. "It's only just getting started further north, but in the more populated areas it seems to be working quite well. All I have to do is to make the arrangements."

"Are you sure you'll be safe?" Nellie's face wore a worried frown. "By all accounts there's still some nastiness going on."

"I'll be fine," Kathleen assured them. "It's only a few spots in the cities that there is a chance of trouble now, and I won't be anywhere near them."

"Will you take Barney with you then?" they suggested.

"Not yet," she spoke firmly. "I don't know what I will find until I get there; it wouldn't be fair to him if he was stopped from wandering round his old haunts."

Not without misgivings, they eventually accepted her decision and she contacted one of the new agencies to order transport for the following morning. The hardest part was telling Barney that she was leaving again.

"Missa no go," he pleaded unhappily.

"I won't be away long this time," she promised him. "I

want you to stay here because George needs you to help him with the work."

She had obviously said the right thing for he stood back and squared his shoulders.

"Barney work good," he declared with a touch of boastfulness.

Kathleen was impressed when, exactly at the appointed time, a Transa pulled into the yard and a smartly dressed young man jumped out.

"One fare to 'The Beeches' right?" he enquired politely. "I'm Tony, would you rather ride in the front, Miss, or the back?"

She elected to take the front seat and he moved quickly to open the door for her, taking her bags and stowing them in the rear.

'Some things have certainly improved', Kathleen thought, remembering the surly if not downright hostile attitude prevalent under the old system.

"You know where we're going?" she asked, waving her goodbyes as Tony set the vehicle into motion.

"I certainly do Miss," he assured her. "Since I started up on my own I've studied the whole area until I know it inside out."

He drove in silence for a while before asking. "Do you mind if we talk Miss, or would you prefer to be quiet?"

"I'd be happy to talk if you want to Tony," Kathleen replied. "But I think it might be easier for both of us if you call me Kathy."

"Thank you Kathy." He gave her a warm smile. "But do stop me if I rattle on too much."

Without further ado, he went on to tell her how delighted he was to be free of the strait jacket which had controlled him prior to the revolution, and of his admiration for those who had made it possible.

"There is a rumour that a girl from around these parts played a big part in bringing it about," he continued. "I don't suppose that you have any idea if it's true, and who she might be?"

"I'm afraid I haven't," she responded innocently.

"Oh well," Tony sighed. "If it's true, she must have

been incredibly brave and clever. If I ever find out who she is, I swear I'll go down on my knees and worship her."

Kathleen had a momentary vision of herself surrounded by bowing acolytes; she changed the subject hurriedly to mask her amusement.

"What do you plan to do when we really get clear of the Federation and live in a free society?"

"I've been watching the vids from other countries," he told her enthusiastically. "I'm going to work as hard as I can till I've got enough credits to have a place of my own like they do. Then I'll look for a nice girl to pair with, and we'll have lots of wonderful children."

Kathleen was glad to wish him every success with his ambitions, and in return he quizzed her about her own circumstances.

Deciding that the safest story was to stick with her updated file, she told him that she had spent a year learning about different crops and was now returning to her job as manager of 'The Beeches'.

"You'll need to be careful," he warned thoughtfully. "An ex-Federation manager might not receive a rapturous welcome nowadays."

"I'm sure everything will be allright." She hoped she sounded more confident than she felt, for she had indeed felt some concern as to her reception.

They made general conversation until, surprisingly soon, Tony swung into the familiar farmyard, last seen in the dark at the end of her previous life.

"I'd like to give you my private number so that if you want transport again you won't have to go through the agency," he told her seriously as he retrieved her bag. "No, it's not just that I want the business, the truth is that there are rumours that a couple of the drivers have unsavoury reputations; they might even try to take advantage of a beautiful young woman travelling on her own. We'll get rid of them as soon as we can but in the meantime, it would do no harm to be careful."

"Thank you for the warning, I'll certainly call you the next time," Kathleen assured him, as she used her persaCom to transfer the appropriate credits to his account. "And thank you for the compliment too!"

"I'm only stating a fact Kathy," he insisted gallantly and went on. "And I would still like to be sure you are going to be okay here. I'll tell you what, I haven't got another call for an hour and it's not far from here so I'll wait for a while in case you need any help."

He was so adamant that she had no choice but to accept; admitting to herself that the availability of an immediate escape route was of considerable comfort, she knocked on the, no, **her** kitchen door. It opened slowly to reveal two rather frightened looking young women.

"I'm Kathleen Pierpoint, Manager of this Unit," she introduced herself in a no-nonsense tone.

It was the taller of them who replied. Dark haired, swarthy, and angular, she gave an immediate impression of being the one in charge.

"We've been expecting someone," she said with resignation. "I suppose you had better come in."

Kathleen turned and gave a discreet 'thumbs up' to the watching Tony, returning his farewell wave before going inside to where she was awaited with obvious trepidation.

"Right!" she told them briskly, pulling a chair to the table. "Sit down and give an account of yourselves. Start with your names."

Hester, the tall one and Emily, fair and petite huddled together on the opposite side of the table.

"You can't blame us," Hester sounded sullen. "It wasn't our fault that we failed to make the target."

"We did everything by the book," Emily chimed in earnestly. "Exactly like they taught us at Agricol."

Kathleen rapidly appraised the situation; it seemed that these two, having failed the target, thought she had come to banish them to a Produnit; not that there were any Produnits now but they must be anticipating something equally unpleasant. Perhaps it was time for a change of approach.

"I think that you have a lot to tell me," she gave them a brief smile. "Why don't you put the kettle on and see if a cup of tea makes it easier."

Emily hurried to comply with the suggestion, though

Hester's attitude remained one of resentment. It took some time to coax the full story out of them.

Fresh out of Agricol - and still wet behind the ears, Kathleen thought - they had taken on the assignment of 'The Beeches' with naive enthusiasm. Through lack of experience they had sown too early, failed to take remedial measures and finally missed the best weather for the harvest. The shortfall in the yield had been substantial and since then they had waited for eviction, assuming that the turmoil of the Revolution had only delayed the inevitable.

"How soon do you want us to move out?" Emily asked as bravely as she could.

Kathleen considered her options. She had to accept that as her pregnancy advanced she would find the work increasingly difficult, whereas until the spring this pair, suitably guided, could carry out all the essential operations. They had told her that they had hardly any credits left but, thanks to David's gift she had plenty of her own to resolve that difficulty. 'How I wish he were here now', she thought, experiencing a sudden pang of loneliness. 'We would make these decisions together and then we would.......'.

Hester and Emily were gazing at her with worried expressions when she managed to drag herself back to the present.

"I'm sorry," she apologised. "I was somewhere else miles away."

"It can't have been a nice place," Emily ventured cautiously. "You looked terribly sad."

Kathleen deliberately forced a note of cheerfulness into her voice.

"I don't intend to throw you out at the moment. If I offered you the chance to work here under my supervision for a year, would you be interested?"

"Interested!" Emily burst out, sounding both startled and hopeful. "I'd say we would!"

"We're nearly out of credits," Hester reminded her partner sourly.

"I could make a transfer into the farm account," Kathleen informed them. "And arrange for you to draw enough for your personal needs for the moment."

"That would be marvellous, wouldn't it Hester?" Emily appealed. "Miss Pierpoint must have lots of experience and we could learn so much from her."

The dark girl awarded her partner a sharp glance before giving the proposal a rather grudging assent.

"Now that's settled we'd better get organised, hadn't we," Kathleen declared firmly. "Incidentally, you might as well call me Kathy."

As her new helpers were ensconsed in her old bedroom, she decided to use the spare one which had not been occupied by Albert. Then, leaving them in the house, she boarded the ForTrak to inspect her re-aquired territory, checking the state of the hedges and ditches as well as the ground itself. Finding nothing seriously amiss, she returned to find Hester busy cleaning while Emily prepared a meal.

"You've been doing fairly well on the whole," she congratulated them. "The place is in pretty good shape."

"I'm so glad you think so," Emily beamed. "We really have worked as hard as we could."

Her attitude to Kathleen seemed to carry a genuine welcome, a sharp contrast to Hester's reluctant acceptance of her presence. That was the way it continued as, for the next few weeks, the three of them filled the decreasing hours of daylight making sure that nothing that should be done was left unattended to. Kathleen sent occasional messages to Jenny, and to George and Nellie to let them know that she was all right, but apart from that, the mental and physical effort combined to make her end each day in a state of near exhaustion. She felt an increasing heaviness too, as the gentle swell of her stomach developed into an unmistakeable bulge, and though she wore loose tops to disguise it, she realised that her condition couldn't be hidden for ever.

She had decreed that her helpers have a day off each week, but of course she didn't apply this rule to herself. She was surprised when, after boarding the ForTrak on one of these mornings, Hester came running out, waving her arms for attention. Sighing, she switched off the engine and climbed carefully to the ground.

"Please Kathy," Hester pleaded urgently. "If there's something that has to be done, let me do it for you."

"But it's your rest day," Kathleen said with surprise.

"I know, but...I don't know how to say this but.... you are pregnant aren't you?"

"I suppose it couldn't stay a secret much longer," Kathleen admitted ruefully.

"You should have told us." Hester's normally sullen look was full of concern. "You've been working so hard and I've been so nasty to you without reason. I feel terribly guilty!"

"It's quite understandable that you should resent me coming here and taking charge," Kathleen consoled her.

"No! It's not like that at all," Hester cried. "I'm grateful to you for letting us stay and teaching us what to do. I've been nasty because.." She hesitated as a flush spread over her face then rushed on.

"The truth is that I was jealous. When you were so nice, and offered to let us stay here I thought that it might be because you fancied Emily, and that you'd take her away from me because you're so much prettier than I am. I said something bitchy about you last night, and that was when she told me to go easy, you were having a baby and I realised how foolish I was being."

Kathleen let herself sag back against the bulk of the ForTrak. So that was the reason for Hester's resentment; a measure of sympathy made her consider her response carefully.

"Your relationship with Emily is your own private business," she assured. "And I have absolutely no intention of coming between you."

"Oh, I've been so silly," Hester was full of remorse. "Please, please let me make amends by taking over some of your tasks. What were you meaning to do today?"

"It wasn't anything important," Kathleen decided. "Let's all have a rest day instead."

The change of atmosphere resulting from Hester's confession made life at 'The Beeches' far more pleasant. No longer constrained by her fears, the dark girl proved to be quite garrulous, and on occasion extremely witty. Left to herself, she wouldn't have allowed Kathleen to do any work at all and had to be assured more than once that her employer was not exactly an invalid.

The short days of early December were darkened by a spell of miserable weather that all but brought outside work to a halt. The three of them were sitting in the kitchen, discussing the timetable for next year when they were surprised to hear a knock on the door. Hester hurried to answer it and a moment later Jenny burst into the room, closely followed by Andy. Startled, Kathleen rose to her feet.

Jenny face registered stark amazement as she noticed Kathleen's altered contours.

"Kathy!" she squealed. "Oh my God Kathy, you're pregnant!"

"Why didn't you tell me?" she sounded almost angry as she released her embrace long enough for Andy to give Kathleen a cautious hug.

"I wanted to keep it to myself for as long as I could," Kathleen apologised. "Anyway, would you have let me come here if you had known?"

"Certainly not!" her friend declared. "We would have tied you up if there was no other way."

"So what has brought you here?" Kathleen asked, after introductions all round saw them sitting down while Emily bustled with the kettle.

"Mum insisted we come. She said we were to bring you back to Malling and not to take no for an answer; we would know why when we got here!"

"I thought she might have guessed," Kathleen smiled as she recalled Hazel's piercing gaze.

"You can't keep a secret from my Mum," Jenny averred. "But she never breathed a word to anyone. Oh Kathy, I'm so glad for you, for us all. How soon can you be ready to leave?"

Kathleen raised her eyebrows at her two helpers.

"We'll look after the farm for you," Hester promised with alacrity. "Please trust us. We've been so worried that you might overdo things and hurt yourself."

"We can send you messages now," Emily added her concurrence. "You can go as soon as you like; do you want me to pack your things?"

"I'm not incapable yet," Kathleen demurred, amused by their eagerness. "It sounds as if you can't wait to get rid of me!"

"Not at all," Hester protested. "But you will insist on bouncing about on the ForTrak all day and we're sure it's not good for you, or your baby!"

Kathleen knew herself that she had found controlling the heavy vehicle an increasing strain. Without further argument, she made her preparations and shortly afterwards waved goodbye as Jenny steered her Transa out of the yard.

"Could we call in to see George and Nellie?" Kathleen asked. "I promised Barney that I wouldn't stay away too long this time."

"That's a great idea," Jenny agreed instantly. "It'll break the journey, make it easier for you."

Kathleen had to laugh at her friend's solicitude.

"For goodness sake," she chided. "I don't need to be treated like a china doll, I've got months to go yet."

"Not that many." Jenny made a play of counting on her fingers. "I'll be a lot happier when I get you home to Mum."

Kathleen resigned herself to being molly-coddled, and it was as well that she did; the fuss made by George, and to an even greater extent by Nellie, could well have been appropriate for the first woman in the world to give birth. Barney however, showed little emotion.

"Baby come," he acknowledged calmly. To him it was a perfectly natural event, occurring seasonally among the inhabitants of the fields and hedges which were his true domain. He had no reason to consider his 'missa' to be any different, and Kathleen was glad of the breath of sanity his attitude brought to the otherwise frenetic excitement.

Hazel was reassuringly down to earth however, when they eventually arrived at Malling farm. After a quick examination, and a few cogent questions, she pronounced the putative mother to be 'as healthy as a heifer' and that reasonable exercise would be beneficial. Later though, when Kathleen mentioned returning to 'The Beeches' to get ready for the spring sowing she vetoed the suggestion.

"No!" she declared, in a tone that would accept no denial. "You are staying right here where I can keep an eye on you. It's already arranged that George will take Barney to your place when the time comes, and you say yourself that your two girls are quite capable."

"I can't sit around and do nothing," Kathleen protested.

"Nobody said that you were to do nothing," her mentor retorted. "There's plenty of light work here that Jenny will organise for you. Just accept it Kathy, you're going to be at Malling until that baby is born or my name's not Hazel Greene!"

If it was indeed captivity it was of a very pleasant kind. Christmas went by in a welter of merriment; by the time the gradually lengthening days signalled a burst of activity in the fields, Kathleen had acknowledged the fact that she was too heavy and clumsy to play any other than a minor part.

The sowing had just been completed when, while resting comfortably after the evening meal, she felt her first contraction. She thought for a moment that she had successfully concealed it until she noticed Hazel glance at the clock before raising her eyebrows in a question. Kathleen gave a barely perceptible nod in response; she tensed again about ten minutes later and Hazel raised her voice slightly to interrupt the conversation.

"Andy," she said calmly. "I'd like you to go and collect Martha now."

A stunned silence greeted her words. Jenny was the first to react, dashing to put her arm round Kathleen's shoulders.

"Oh my God!" she declared on the verge of panic. "Has it started."

"Of course it's started you silly girl." Hazel said in her most matter-of-fact voice. "I've been expecting this for a couple of days now. And the last thing she needs is people making a fuss so quieten yourself."

Jenny obeyed immediately, dropping to her knees and

clasping both of Kathleen's hands in mute encouragement.

Hazel had recommended that the birth should take place at Malling farm with the assistance of an experienced midwife. Kathleen had been happy to agree, and had already undergone an examination by Martha, who had confirmed that the pregnancy was proceeding normally and that there was nothing to worry about. Now, as the pains followed each other with text book regularity, she gratefully gripped Jenny's hands for comfort.

"Right!" Hazel announced briskly as soon as she saw Kathleen relax again. "We'd better get you up the stairs before the next one."

The following few hours remained a blur in Kathleen's memory; vaguely she recalled Martha's cool professional voice insisting 'push' and also Jenny begging her to 'share the pain with me Kathy darling'. Soon after the sun appeared over the horizon her torment ended, rapidly replaced by euphoria when she heard a healthy cry.

"He's a boy Kathy." It was Jenny, her face showing a mixture of wonder and delight, who laid the infant in his mother's arms.

"Little David!" Kathleen cradled her baby, not knowing if her tears stemmed from joy, sorrow or relief.

Malling farm took on a different aura with the arrival of little David, almost as if he were a living symbol of the new era ushered in by the Revolution. Nellie and George came to admire him of course; Kathleen was surprised however, to see Hester and Emily appear for a quick visit during which, as well as doting over the baby, they managed to assure her that everything at 'The Beeches' was in good order. For the first few weeks, there were so many eager hands wanting to nurse her son that he ran a fair risk of being spoilt; again, it was Hazel however, who eventually objected when Jenny came in from work and made straight for the cot.

"Let the wee mite lie," she ordered. "If you lift him at every squeak he'll get used to it and poor Kathy will never get a minute of peace."

"Mum!" her daughter grumbled. "That's not fair; it's all

right for you, you're here with him all day."

"I know it's not fair." Hazel was unrepentant. "But that's a grandmother's privilege. God willing you'll have your own to fuss over in the future."

Kathleen smiled inwardly as Jenny flushed and shot a quick glance at Andy; she had already confided to Kathleen that having little David in her arms made her feel 'rather broody'!

He turned out to be a happy and undemanding child, only shouting when feeding time approached. She fed him herself for as long as she could, but as he grew she had to supplement her own milk with the bottle, grateful at least that she could at last get a decent sleep. It also meant that she was able to leave him with Hazel for a few hours each day while she helped out in the fields for, after months of feeling heavy and bloated she was determined to regain her fitness as soon as possible.

She was having the 'quiet time' that Hazel had insisted she allow herself each day. In the late afternoon, she would go to her room where she would feed the baby, play with him for a while, do her appointed exercises and then put her feet up and maybe doze off for an hour. This day had been no different, little David had gone to sleep and she had just lain back on the pillows when she heard hurried steps on the stairs followed by an urgent knock on the door.

"Come in," she called, sitting up and swinging her feet onto the floor. It hadn't sounded like Jenny, it must be Richard or maybe Andy.

Totally unprepared, she could only gape as the door opened to reveal David; scruffy beyond belief, gaunt and haggard with a wild look in his eyes but her own dear David nonetheless.

"David?" she uttered wonderingly, rising to her feet.

"Kathy!" was all he said, but his voice told her everything she wanted to know.

"David!" she said again, feeling her face crumple as she tried to go to him. Blindly, she held out her arms, clasping him to her as he caught her in his own firm embrace.

"Kathy my darling," he whispered, but the secure compartment containing all her stored sorrows had suddenly burst open making her incapable of reply. While racking sobs heaved in her chest, he held her tenderly, rocking her gently, stroking her hair, his kisses melding with the tears flooding down her face. The first storm of weeping served to lessen her pent-up grief at losing David; after that, more gentle tears washed away the stain and humiliation from her abuse by Albert, her beating at the hands of Stephen Lock, her subjection to the lusts of the Tank Inspector. She wept over her parent's fate, wept away her hatred of those responsible, and finally wept away any lingering fears of the Federation Authorities. The resultant emptiness, she came to understand, would be comfortably filled by the man she clung to now with all the strength she could command. Later, when she had quietened sufficiently, he led her to sit beside him on the bed.

"What happened to you?" she managed to ask, though there was still a catch in her voice. "They said that the divers found your persaCom on the train; David, I thought you were d..dead!"

The words set her off again and she wept quietly until the long months of suppressed grief had been diluted into something bearable.

"I'm so sorry Kathy," he assured her. "I wanted to get a message to you but it was impossible.

"It all happened too fast," he continued. "I'd only just taken off Terisa's persaCom when the damn train started moving. I used my own to set the timer, but I was in such a hurry to get out I must have dropped it. I wrenched my ankle when I hit the ground and though I tried to hobble away I wasn't able to move fast enough; after the tunnel flooded the whole area was crawling with Police and I was soon discovered.

"They were in such a panic to start with that they assumed I'd been injured in the aftermath so I was carted off to hospital; once they spotted that I didn't have a persaCom though, they were all set to send me for an Implant but luckily you had disabled the control by then. It wasn't long afterwards that the Urfor advance party arrived and took charge, shoved me into a helicopter and took me to a military base for interrogation. They were pretty sure that I was involved, but with CenCon in such a flap they kept me in their own cells under wraps until they could see what was going to happen.

"Apart from the third degree stuff they treated me fairly well. Once the level of support for the uprising became clear, they were reluctant to use the amount of force that would have been necessary to suppress it. I became quite friendly with the local commander eventually, in fact we played chess two or three times a week, and though I never admitted to anything he treated me with a kind of grudging respect.

"I wasn't allowed anywhere near a terminal though, so I had no news of what was happening except what they told me, and of course no hope of getting a message to you. Even after it became obvious that there would be a huge political shake-up, they kept me locked up until they were sure that I had been officially forgotten. A week ago they chucked me in a Transport and dropped me off on a deserted road in the middle of the night; when I got to the coast I waited for three days until I found a boat that would bring me across, and since then I've been scrounging lifts wherever I could to get back to you."

"How did you know where to find me?" She was calmer now after hearing his story.

"I didn't." he admitted. "I called in here on my way north; until Hazel told me you were upstairs I was ready to go on to where I left you."

He paused, startled, as a combination betwen a cry and a gurgle announced that the baby was awake. Wonderingly, he watched as Kathleen crossed to the cot on the other side of the room.

"Don't you want to come and meet your son?" she enquired, with just a hint of pride.

"My son!" Total astonishment sounded in his voice, and she nodded in confirmation.

"My son!" he repeated, kneeling down beside the cot, holding out a trembling finger to touch the baby's tiny fist.

"But Kathy, how..?"

"I hope you haven't forgotten our last night together David," she teased. "It's not unknown for something like this to happen after what we did!"

"Forgotten! It's the only thing that kept me going through the interrogation procedure, the only thing that kept me determined to stay alive!" He looked up at her, and this time it was his cheeks which were wet.

"What do you call him," he asked, gazing adoringly as the baby decided that this strange face was funny enough to merit a chuckle.

"I had to call him David because of you." She gulped but managed to continue. "I think he'd better be Davie now to avoid confusion."

He rose and took her in his arms again.

"Are you going to let me be a proper father to him?" he murmured softly, and she had no need of words to convey her agreement.

Later, she was able to ask him. "Have you given any thought to what you want to do now that there's so much change going on? I would think that the whole Com program will need a lot of changes before people will trust it again."

He held her away from him, studying her face intently.

"I'd be happy if I never see another terminal in my life." He spoke slowly, as if after deep reflection. "What I would like is to learn to appreciate the simple things that are really the most important; I want to know about the land and the things that grow on it, like you do; I want to know the sea and the mountains too; I want to learn to laugh and love and I think that you could teach me. Will you teach me Kathy?"

Her heart full as she saw the humble appeal in his expression, she made a token pause for reflection.

"I'll teach you David," she consented at last. "But there would have to be conditions."

"What conditions?" he sounded surprised.

Kathleen glanced over at the cot.

"I don't want little Davie to grow up as an only child," she told him seriously. "So you'll have to agree to provide him with a couple of sisters or brothers!"

David's face lit up as he took in the implications of her stipulation. Pressing her to him, there was unmistakeable hunger in his voice as he whispered. "When do you want to start?"

She held him for a moment of acceptance before pushing him away.

"I do love you David, but I'll love you even more when you've had a bath. And if I know Hazel, she'll have a 'feast to end all feasts' prepared so we'd better be ready when she calls. You look as if you could do with feeding up anyway.!"

"I suppose I don't smell very nice," David admitted apologetically. "And I can't remember eating anything these last few days."

"You do remember where the bathroom is?" Kathleen pushed him towards the door. "Just don't go any further than that away from me! Ever!"

"You could come and scrub my back if you like!" he suggested hopefully.

"I'd love to David darling, but I think that it might take rather a long time! No, I'll see if I can borrow some clean clothes for you, and get changed myself." Moving over to the mirror, she examinined her reflection critically.

"Not bad Kathy," she complimented herself. "Not bad at all. I think it will still fit me."

"What will," he queried from the doorway.

"If it's going to be a celebration, I think I should really wear that green dress again. But this time...." she let the words trail off.

"This time what?" There was a note of anticipation in his question.

"This time," the words and her smile carried all the love and promise that she could put into them. "This time, in case you're worried about tearing it off me, I'll make sure you know where the fastenings are!"

www.ingramcontent.com/pod-product-compliance
Lightning Source LLC
Chambersburg PA
CBHW020835260626

47169CB00003B/989